THE QUIET WIFE

DIANE SAXON

B
Boldwood

First published in Great Britain in 2025 by Boldwood Books Ltd.

Copyright © Diane Saxon, 2025

Cover Design by Head Design Ltd

Cover Images: iStock

The moral right of Diane Saxon to be identified as the author of this work has been asserted in accordance with the Copyright, Designs and Patents Act 1988.

All rights reserved. No part of this book may be reproduced in any form or by any electronic or mechanical means, including information storage and retrieval systems, without written permission from the author, except for the use of brief quotations in a book review. This book is a work of fiction and, except in the case of historical fact, any resemblance to actual persons, living or dead, is purely coincidental.

Every effort has been made to obtain the necessary permissions with reference to copyright material, both illustrative and quoted. We apologise for any omissions in this respect and will be pleased to make the appropriate acknowledgements in any future edition.

A CIP catalogue record for this book is available from the British Library.

Paperback ISBN 978-1-83518-070-9

Large Print ISBN 978-1-83518-071-6

Hardback ISBN 978-1-83518-069-3

Ebook ISBN 978-1-83518-072-3

Kindle ISBN 978-1-83518-073-0

Audio CD ISBN 978-1-83518-064-8

MP3 CD ISBN 978-1-83518-065-5

Digital audio download ISBN 978-1-83518-068-6

This book is printed on certified sustainable paper. Boldwood Books is dedicated to putting sustainability at the heart of our business. For more information please visit https://www.boldwoodbooks.com/about-us/sustainability/

Boldwood Books Ltd, 23 Bowerdean Street, London, SW6 3TN

www.boldwoodbooks.com

In loving memory of Betty Diana Parkes
19 August 1930–29 November 2024

1

PRESENT DAY – FRIDAY, 28 FEBRUARY 2025, 3.30 A.M. – SORIAH

Dense black velvet presses down, closing the curtain of evil so tight I sob, dragging air in small, panicked snatches as claustrophobia engulfs me.

'I can't breathe. I can't breathe!'

I kick out, my heels drumming on the cold, hard surface I'm trapped against.

My hands turn to claws as I tear at the heavy weight lying on me, crushing me, gasping in desperation.

I rip it away, roll.

I smash onto the floor, my hands and knees vibrating in pure agony as my nose crunches into the fine silk Chinese rug we have on our bedroom floor.

The terrified thump of my heart still drums

against my ribcage as I draw in long, purifying lungfuls of air. A whimper escapes my lips.

I'm not there.

I'm here.

I'm safe.

I raise my head from the rug, the wet rush of tears drenches my cheeks while I pant, waiting for my heart rate to steady. My hands and knees to stop burning.

The soft release of something warm gushes from my throbbing nose and I wrench the hem of my shorty pyjama top up to cover my face and catch the fluid before it falls. Blood on that silk rug would never come out. It would be ruined.

Just as I am ruined.

Silently, I push up from my hands and knees and stagger to my feet. Although silence is probably no longer an issue as I imagine I'd screamed the house down in the midst of my dream. My nightmare. My terror.

I spare a quick glance, but there is no movement from the bed. No acknowledgement of the fear screaming from me.

I stumble through to the bathroom, turning on the light we use solely at night-time. The glow is soft and golden, designed not to bring you to full wakefulness while it illuminates enough so you can see what you're doing.

I stare into the large mirror above the sink, the light almost haloing me and casting my face into deep shadows.

My eyes are dark hollows, terror seeping out of them.

My nose is swollen and bloodied.

I turn on the cold tap, hold my hands under it and swoosh water over a face so hot it heats the liquid cupped in my hands instantly.

Drips of blood smear down the inside of the white porcelain sink, water diluting the colour, so it turns pale pink before washing away. I reach blindly for a flannel from the top of the small bathroom dresser, soaking it before I press it against my face.

I tip my head back, unable to pinch the bridge of my nose as it's so painful.

I'm pretty sure it's broken.

I let out a quiet sigh as blood trickles down my throat to pool in a thick glut that makes me splutter it out and spit it in the sink. The running water swooshes it away, cleansing the sink in the way I wish it would cleanse my mind.

It wouldn't be the first time my nose has been broken. Does that make it more delicate, more likely to break again?

I swallow yet more blood and it triggers a long-ago memory of choking on the thick texture, the metallic tang. Unable to get my breath. Dying in the dark.

Panic squeezes my throat, choking me.

The running water has turned colder and I splash more on my face. A kind of shock therapy to bring me back to the present.

I don't want to think about that time. My past.

I straighten my head and study my face in the mirror again.

My nose throbs with every beat of my heart.

I lean in.

Watery tears still fill bloodshot eyes as I reach up and tenderly touch either side of my nose with shaky fingertips, investigating the damage. It's sore, but actually I don't think it's broken. Not this time. Although there is a thin, dark purple line running horizontally across the bridge.

The blood flow stops, almost as quickly as it started, and I lower myself to the edge of the bath. Boneless. Exhausted.

A sigh shudders out of me, and I close my eyes.

Nightmares come from time to time, but it's been

a while since I had one so explosive, so vivid. As though someone really was pressing down on me, on my covers, trapping me inside, suffocating me.

I haul in another breath and reach for the small glass I leave on the side of the sink for when I wake in the night, mouth dry, unable to swallow. I don't leave it on the bedside table as I've knocked it off too many times to count. I'd rather get up in any case. Turn on a light. Chase the shadows away.

Cool water slides down my throat, dispelling the image of those hands around it, square fingers tightening, air constricting.

I place the empty glass back on the side of the sink, fingers still trembling so it rattles against the porcelain, as I push to my feet.

I fill the sink, strip off the blood-spattered PJ top and press it down into the now icy water. I sprinkle grains of salt over the scarlet splashes of blood. Salt I always keep in the bathroom for just such an occasion.

Things happen.

I am clumsy.

I'll let it soak until morning and then wash it through.

The tap gives a judder as I turn it off, a reflection of my own inner turmoil.

My legs are still wobbly and weak, but I turn the door handle with one hand and reach out with the other, hesitating before I pull the light cord and plunge myself into darkness once more.

There's a soft mewl and Luna, my beautiful British Blue Shorthair kitty, winds herself between my ankles and lets out a little 'brrrrddd, brrrddd' of pleasure. She wants me to feed her but I'm not sure I have the energy or inclination to trot down the stairs in the dark.

Sweat has evaporated to leave my flesh cold and peppered with goosebumps.

Luna lets out another plea. God, I'm half-naked but I don't want to risk going back into the bedroom, and my dressing gown is still in the utility room downstairs after I washed it yesterday – but it's got to be done. There's no way Luna will leave me in peace now she knows I'm awake.

I glance at the bedroom door that I must have automatically pulled partially closed when I dashed out.

There's no sound from within.

No one else is going to do this. It's my job.

On swift feet, I dash down the stairs, one arm across my bosom, Luna charging ahead of me in anticipation of food she probably doesn't need, but she wants. Now.

I can't bear the thought of getting into bed and her sitting on my chest tonight, slowly unsheathing her claws to investigate if my eyelids are open or closed. It's a favourite pastime of hers. She never does it to Marcus. In fact, she's always been quite cool with him. She doesn't need his cuddles, but she spends many an hour on my lap. On my chest. Wrapped around my head. Marcus doesn't tolerate it. He'll lift her off, or push her away. He doesn't like her smothering him.

Maybe that's what induced my full panic attack. Perhaps that weight pressing on my chest was simply my own cat. Suffocating me because I've not fed her. I almost snort out a cynical laugh.

Without turning the utility light on in case anyone can see me sneaking around half-naked, I dump a small sachet of food into her bowl and smile as she gives a desperate leap on it as though I've starved her for a week. I run my hand over a pelt that's so thick I can barely get my fingers through to her skin, taking comfort in the way she manages to purr at the same time as she's feeding. I'd spend longer with her, but I check my dressing gown which is hanging over a dryer in the utility and it's still damp on the thicker areas of the wrists and neck.

An icy draught is forcing its way under the closed utility door from the outside. We need to fit a draught excluder, just another of the many little jobs that seem to have been ignored.

I shiver, all the heat radiating from me before evaporating with a swiftness that makes my teeth chatter.

It's black out there. I don't want to look.

I'm not frightened of the dark. I'm frightened of the monsters that dwell in it.

When I was a little girl, my mother used to say, *it's not the dead who can hurt you, it's the living*. I never believed her at the time. Until I knew better. The living can hurt you, and *they* are the monsters.

My toes curling against the cold floor tiles, I risk a fleeting look outside and then race upstairs away from unseen eyes that could be watching. To safety.

I went from furnace to freezer in a matter of minutes.

I sneak through the bedroom, feeling my way with chilled hands and icy feet, touching the dressing table on my right, the side of the wardrobe on my left, the soft cover of the bed in front of me. I inch along and slip inside, unwilling to search for a clean top or nightie. I don't want to make a noise pulling out a drawer, especially the one with my nightwear in as it jams, and then I need to slam the heel of my hand against it to get it to close again. Only a small job to fix, but one we've not got around to.

The covers are cool against my naked skin, the window wide, letting in a wintery breeze. I'd pull it shut, but I'll soon heat up again, I'm sure. It's preferable to closing the window and letting the claustrophobia close in around me.

With a quiet sigh, I turn on my side and curl into the foetal position. My teeth chatter not just from the cold, but with dread hovering on the periphery of my mind.

Tiredness washes over me, but I fear closing my eyes again. Fear the dark. Fear those monsters that reside there.

Despite my resolution not to sleep, my eyelids slide closed.

A warm arm encircles my body, and my eyes fly open again. My breath jams in my throat and I stiffen. Waiting.

'Christ, you're noisy. I thought you were never coming back to bed. Everything okay?'

The gruff voice whispers in my ear as Marcus pulls my body close into his and we spoon, his body heat pulsing through until I suffocate once more. My lips part and my breathing speeds up again.

'I'm fine. Just—' I sigh, needing his sympathy, his comfort. 'I had a nosebleed.'

I wait for his answer in the darkness but all I hear is the deep, even breathing of someone who has fallen asleep. Maybe he wasn't even fully awake when he spoke. When I disturbed him.

I slip his arm from my body and edge away, keeping only my frozen feet on him.

Claustrophobia tightens my throat once more as that dream snakes through my consciousness. I need space. I need to move away.

From this man.

My husband.

2
TWENTY-ONE YEARS EARLIER – JUNE 2004 – CRAIG

She's stunning! My lovely Soriah.

The most beautiful woman I've ever known.

And she's going to be mine.

I can't take my eyes off her as she flicks long raven-black ropes of hair, that her short, blonde friend, Gilly, told me are called box braids, over one shoulder with a fine, slim-fingered hand. Her unpolished nails are short, neat and unbitten, unlike so many students'. Mine included. I bite the delicate flesh around my nails until little slivers of skin peel back, allowing tiny beads of blood to seep out.

Soriah doesn't do that.

Everything about her is perfect. Exotic. Entrancing.

From smooth skin the colour of polished conkers to strangely striking eyes like soft moss on a dewy morning, so unusual they make people take a second glance. They're the product of a black dad from Barbados and a white mum from Liverpool, so Gilly tells me. It's a flawless combination. She doesn't have a blemish or imperfection.

Soriah's sweet high breasts barely jiggle like some of the other girls who we all know stuff their bras with what they call chicken fillet things, lifting their tits high so you can almost see their nipples out of the top of their bras. It's not flattering. Not attractive. It looks slutty. I don't like sluts.

My Soriah isn't a slut. She doesn't employ those tactics. She runs with the athletics team. You can't have big boobs if you want to run fast, not unless you want to end up knocking yourself out. All the lads think it's hilarious to watch the big-boobed girls run. It kind of throws them off balance. Unlike Soriah.

She is quite simply delicious. We all know what her body looks like slicked into Lycra activewear. There's no one who has studied it quite as closely as I have.

Not curvy nor plump, but an almost boyish form, slender, svelte, with whiplash muscles which I find eminently more attractive than voluptuousness. And she's not stupidly conscious of it like the rest of the girls. She has nothing to prove. I watch her on the track, her slender legs striding out, ever since I found out her hobby, her passion.

She's a distance runner, rather than sprinter, but her long legs eat up the ground. I love to watch her run. Better still, when she stops. Her face flushes as she pulls to a halt, high ponytail of braids swinging while she bends, hands on knees to take in long pulls of air.

I'm never sure whether I'm better placed in front of her to see that beautiful darkening of her smooth cheeks in a flush, or behind her to catch a glimpse of her other cheeks giving a teasing peek from beneath the hem of her shorts.

It makes me happy to have discovered her. Every moment I'm near her I feel alive. Invigorated.

Now, her laughter carries from where she sits across the packed refectory of Shrewsbury Sixth Form College. Always the end seat so she can stretch her long legs out. The glitter of those strange green eyes brightens as she meets my stare across the room.

The smile drops from her face.

I find it so difficult to read what's on her mind.

That first day when we stood together in the queue to get our photo IDs for college, she was so friendly, smiley.

I touch my pocket now. I still have the pen she lent to me so I could sign the security agreement. Still feel her cool touch as our fingers fumbled together. I know there was a connection. I felt it buzz between us like a faltering electric circuit just getting ready to fire up.

We laughed at how crap the photographs were, our faces distorted so I looked like a hamster. Worse than a passport. Although I had to admit I've never been abroad. Never wanted to go when my parents went but stayed instead with my grammy at home, and now I'm older and grammy is gone, I can stay there alone. It suits me.

My parents trust me. I never have mates coming around to party. On the whole, I don't have mates.

I want Soriah to be my friend. More than a friend if I tell the truth. We're soulmates. I'm sure of it.

Now, I can't take my gaze from her. I can't quite read her expression, but I may have unnerved her.

She lowers her head, shaking it as Gilly stage-whispers, her hand cupped over Soriah's ear. Giggling, she shoots me quick, nervy glances as her jaw juts out. A kind of challenge. I think Gilly is jealous, but I'm not quite sure of whom. Soriah, or me.

Gilly is short with immense tits. She definitely doesn't need chicken fillet stuffing and I know from witnessing it, she certainly can't run. She doesn't need to. She has it all. Including a six-foot-four boyfriend who she looks ridiculous with as she's probably only five-foot-one. He's one of the rugby boys. Broad in the chest, thick in the head. A prick of the finest order. He may be thick, but Kev's not to be messed with.

He's dangerous. Someone I'd rather avoid at all costs. I've seen what he can do with his sledge-hammer fists. On the rugby field. In the changing room.

It's not *his* girlfriend I'm interested in, but Soriah. Although he often hangs around with them both, a bit possessively, sort of as though they both belong to him. I suspect if Soriah had bigger tits, he'd have made a play for her instead of Gilly. Who wouldn't? Soriah is elegant and elite, whereas Gilly is – common.

There's no competition. Soriah would win hands down if there was.

There's a roaring rush of white noise in my ears as I stare at her. She's beautiful. My heart squeezes in my chest. I love her, with every ounce of my being. I'd do anything for her. I know if she'd agree to go out with me, she's going to feel the same way too.

I just want a chance.

Soriah doesn't have a boyfriend and Kev's not around at the moment. We all have to take our chances where we find them.

I know she's coy, but I think she secretly likes me.

Perhaps I just need to make my move, be a bit more proactive. That's what Gilly told me in any case. She's a bit of a busybody. Likes to get involved.

Soriah casts me a quick glance from underneath those thick black eyelashes of hers and I know she's as attracted to me as I am to her. I can feel it in the vibration of air between us. Shimmering.

I stand just as the bell sounds for lessons.

The crowd surges towards the exit doors, but as usual, Soriah takes her time, preferring, it appears, to avoid the rush. It's all elbows and bustle as they funnel through the two sets of double doors leading out into the hallways.

I make my way towards the exit doors, knowing she won't have moved yet. I've watched her do this often enough, and I make it unavoidable to pass her en route. Not that I would avoid getting close to her.

She's dazzling.

My heart is thudding against my ribcage, desperate to be heard.

I need to play it cool, even though sweat has broken out across my upper lip and my underarms are sticky with it.

This is my chance.

As I reach her, she's rising from her seat, and slinging her backpack over one shoulder.

Gilly is already standing on the other side of her, although you wouldn't necessarily know it, she's so short.

There's no one between us as I reach Soriah. I've managed this loads of times. I normally slip into the queue behind her, bump her, lean in to absorb her scent, that freshly showered smell that reminds me of lightly perfumed flowers.

This time is different though. She's not yet turned to go.

My heart surges with lust. With love.

I step in as close as I can, and pause, just long enough for her to become aware of my presence.

She looks up at me, her eyes widening in surprise. She may be tall, but I'm taller still at six foot one.

I look into her captivating eyes.

And I lose my mind.

Before she reacts, I reach out, cup her face in my hands and snog her.

I mean really snog her.

Made all the easier by the fact that her mouth has dropped open in surprise, I slip my tongue inside for that first taste of her. I knew this was the way it would be, dreamed of her in my arms.

My knees melt as I wrap an arm around her waist, jerking her closer to slide my hand over her tight little arse. Jesus Christ, who knew her flavour would be so exotic, so entrancing? Every muscle relaxes into that kiss, and I groan, pulling her into my body. I grind my hips against hers so she can feel my hard-on, which I hope like hell I don't lose control of.

I want her to understand what I want to do to her. What a perfect fit we are.

If I could fuck her right here and now, I would.

She shoves me away, recoiling as if I disgust her, but I know I don't. She's doing that for effect. To keep her reputation pristine in the eyes of any onlookers. But we both know better.

She swipes the back of her wrist across her mouth and almost spits.

I grin.

Delighted with myself, I stride towards the exit doors. Cocky and loose-limbed.

I fucking kissed Soriah Howell. How about that?

That was good! Great, in fact.

I can't believe I did it.

She'll be all over me by the end of the day.

Gilly will make sure of it. She's a great co-conspirator.

I'm a fucking god!

I fist pump the air.

A heavy hand on my shoulder stops me and I turn in confusion, my fingers still curled into my palm, a snarl forming on my face.

Mr Sharma is a short, stocky man but his grip is that of a steel vice. He's my main tutor on my engineering apprenticeship and there's not one of us who doesn't respect him. Or fear him.

I almost shit myself when I meet the outrage in his eyes.

I haven't done anything. What does he want?

'What do you think you were doing?' He sweeps his arm to encompass the room.

I glance past him into the almost deserted refectory. There are a few stragglers who have stopped to watch.

Gilly has her arm around Soriah's waist, pulling her into a hug and when she looks over at me it's with a kind of stunned amusement, and possibly a small stream of admiration.

Soriah's face is covered by both hands and she's shaking her head, those beautiful braids moving like snakes.

Mr Sharma wraps a sturdy hand around my upper arm. 'Come with me, boy.'

I stutter, but no words come from my mouth. I'm stunned. What does he think I've done? Moreover, can't he remember my name? I see him at least three times a week. Where is the respect?

He marches me through long, now empty hallways until we reach a door, almost at the end.

It bounces back at me with the ferocity of his shove as he leans past me, to fling it open.

He manhandles me inside his office, which is barely larger than a box. I'm not sure he's allowed to touch me like this, but there are no witnesses here.

'Sit.'

I do as I'm told. I'm used to being obedient. To be honest, I am not the type of person who gets into trouble. I don't drink – much – and I never do drugs. Well, I can't stand the smell of weed, makes me want to puke. I've had the occasional uppers, but you can't class those as drugs. Can you?

If that's what I'm here for, he's going to get a surprise. I have nothing on me.

Mr Sharma's face has flushed with annoyance.

Really, I have no idea what his issue is. I've done nothing wrong.

He rounds the small desk and sits opposite me, square-fingered hands flat on the dark walnut top, his eyes gleaming at me with barely suppressed fury.

'What did you think you were doing?'

It's a repetition of what he's already said, but I bite my tongue. Probably not the best time to pull him up on that.

'I—'

'I saw it.' He stabs a blunt finger at me. 'That is considered assault, Craig. I could call the police, right now.' His hand reaches for the phone on his desk.

My breath sticks in my throat.

What the hell? Now the penny drops. He's talking about Soriah and me kissing. I didn't do anything wrong. She wanted it. Anyone could see, if they looked close enough. He doesn't understand.

'Sir—'

'No, Craig.' But his hand drops from the phone, making it an idle threat. 'Now you listen to me. What you did was sexual assault. We have zero tolerance for that here.' His lips tighten and he pauses for a long moment as though trying to come to a decision. 'You will collect your belongings and go home.'

My mouth falls open. He's got to be kidding me. What the fuck is wrong with him? I'm getting kicked out of college all because he saw Soriah kiss me. Who the fuck does he think he is?

I no longer care that he's not about to call the police. I'm in deep shit.

My dad is going to kill me. He's completely invested in me becoming a mechanic. His dream job. The one he should have had instead of becoming a painter-decorator.

'I did nothing wrong.' My voice is weak and squeaky, hitting all the high notes like when it was just beginning to break.

Mr Sharma stabs that finger at me again. 'And that, precisely, is your issue. You cannot see the error of your ways.'

'She wanted it—'

Air hisses in through his teeth as he grimaces. 'Dear God, this is exactly what we're trying to instil into your generation. It's not okay to do that!'

'But—'

He comes to his feet, chair scraping like nails down a blackboard.

'There is no *but*. Get your stuff. Get out. We'll contact you in the next few days by letter. You'll be informed of the process and whether or not you will be required to attend a hearing so you can put your side forward once we have discussed the matter with the young lady concerned. Got her viewpoint.'

His anger is unwarranted, but I have no words. How do I explain that Soriah wants me as much as I want her?

Humiliation washes over me in waves as I trudge towards my locker in the silence of the empty hallways, Mr Sharma at my shoulder. He's going to send a fucking letter home. When my dad sees it, he's going to explode. He'll probably chuck me out, and through no fault of my own.

Tears fill my eyes while I collect my belongings.

'Mr Sharma.' I turn to face him.

I desperately want to plead my case, but he is immovable.

I sniff at the runny snot filling my nose as his dark eyes burrow into mine.

'I never meant—' My voice stutters. 'I didn't mean any harm, sir. I love her.' It's a pathetic whisper that slides from between my lips. 'I just love her so much.'

There's a softening in his eyes and his broad chest seems to deflate a little.

My bottom lip is trembling, my mouth turned

down, but I sense a small crack in his demeanour and press my advantage, letting out a soft sob as I place a hand against my heart. It's not exactly contrived, but I don't hold anything back. 'I'm sorry. I never meant to upset anyone.'

He sighs. 'Shut your locker, lad. Come back to my office.'

I keep my head lowered as this time, I follow him along the corridor.

I don't want him to glimpse my triumph.

3

TWENTY-ONE YEARS EARLIER – JUNE 2004 – SORIAH

My mouth falls open as I stare at the head of year. 'He loves me?'

I shudder at the thought of it, wrapping my arms around myself as if to ward off the horror.

Mr Sharma gives a slow nod, his soft brown eyes meeting mine. 'That's what he said. Of course, it is entirely up to you. I can suspend Craig for his wholly unacceptable behaviour and we can formalise everything...' He draws in a long breath, and I already know before he says anything further that there is a 'but' coming.

'But he's a very intelligent young man with a bright future ahead of him.'

I quiver with rage at this impunity. What about

my future? What about *my* intelligence? 'He grabbed me. His hand touched my breast. He shoved his tongue into my mouth.' I hesitate at telling him that I felt Craig's hard dick grinding into my pubic bone. That would be too embarrassing to confess to this old man, this teacher. 'How is he intelligent? That was a stupid and—' I can't think of the word I want to use. I stammer to a halt and Mr Sharma takes a little bit of advantage to guilt me into seeing things his way.

'Look, Soriah. I understand you're upset.'

'Upset' doesn't really cut it. I'm all kinds of furious and insulted and devastated. I feel dirty. Cheapened. How do I lay that out for Mr Sharma when somewhere underneath it all lurks a horrible guilt that somehow I encouraged this behaviour from Craig? Gilly's been telling me for a couple of weeks that he fancies me, that I should do something about it because although he's quiet, he's dead hot.

I never found him hot and nor do I want a boyfriend. But maybe I did do something. Put out a signal. He's always staring at me. Perhaps I stared back for too long. Let my eyes linger on him. By some means, could I be responsible? Did I wear the wrong clothes, walk enticingly past him, cast him flirtatious glances?

I didn't. I know I didn't. I have no idea why I let

these thoughts slip through my mind. I have a vague recollection of lending him a pen on our first day so he could sign his security agreement. I only remember that because he never gave it back and it was a good pen. I've never had a conversation with him since. How can it be my fault? I know it can't. That knowledge doesn't dissipate my own internal doubt, so how can I convince Mr Sharma?

I dab at my eyes with a tissue I've managed to shred to pieces, so it drops like snowflakes to the floor. 'He scared me.'

There's an understatement, but I find myself subdued by this man's authority. His quiet conviction that I've overreacted.

Mr Sharma leans back in his chair almost as though my words cause him concern. 'I'm so sorry about that. He's not a bad lad, he just needs to control his emotions... We don't wish for you to be scared, but at the same time, I am concerned that this boy's future could be ruined by—' He flicks a casual hand in the air as though sweeping aside the whole event. 'An indiscretion. You are, after all a very attractive young lady and—'

My mouth drops open. Please don't let him say something about my short skirt and slim-fitting T-shirt. He surely can't be such a bigot.

'You are dressed a little provocatively.'

As my respect for Mr Sharma drops away, I gasp and leap out of the chair I'd been seated in.

'What? What do you mean?' My voice rises to a pure shriek as I stare at Mr Sharma and catch the quick flicker of judgement in his eyes. 'Are you blaming me?' I thump a hand against my chest. 'I'm not the one who caused this. If Craig gets suspended or preferably expelled, then it's not my fault. It's his actions that caused this. Not mine. The way I dress should not be the issue, Mr Sharma.'

It's the middle of summer, the weather is scorching. What does he expect me to wear? All the girls dress like this. Just because my legs are longer than most.

The teacher lumbers to his feet, his complexion taking on a ruddy tone. 'Soriah, calm down. I spoke with Craig, and he was very reasonable.'

My breath shortens. What the hell is going on? How have I suddenly ended up with the blame for this? Am I being *un*reasonable? Is that what Mr Sharma is implying? Hell, not implying. Saying. He has just told me I'm being unreasonable!

I stumble towards the door, my hand grasping for the handle as I turn to face him.

'You've got to be f-f-fucking kidding me.' I don't

swear much, and that word was difficult to force from my stiff lips, but it was the only word I could think had sufficient power to express my disgust.

Horror streaks over Mr Sharma's face and I realise my mistake. I have exposed myself in his eyes. I'm not the quiet, demure young lady he expects. But I am furious.

'Soriah! I will not tolerate such language! Get out of my office and get back to your lesson.' He points a finger at me. 'Just be grateful I'm taking no action on this matter, but I will be keeping an eye on *you*, young lady. This kind of behaviour is unseemly.'

'Unseemly? What about the boy who shoved his cock against me?'

Well, I think that may have had an impact, but not necessarily the one I would wish for, as I turn my back on Mr Sharma's slack-jawed expression.

I resist the temptation to slam the door behind me and then storm along the corridor, the soles of my trainers slapping on the hard wooden floor. Fury sends my heart spiking, and I want to hit something. Hard. I really want to punch someone.

Craig, if he was here.

How did this get to be my fault?

I really don't understand.

I fling open the door to the toilets and only when

I stare at myself in the mirror do I realise tears are streaking down my face.

The violation of Mr Sharma's words and opinion feels almost as bad as Craig grabbing me.

That was a short, sharp, physical incident. A moment in time and shocking as it was, I'm positive I would get over it once Craig was removed from college. I can't have him stalking me, and I certainly don't need him to do *that* to me again.

Only that's not going to happen. Mr Sharma evidently values Craig and *his* future, *his* intelligence more than he does the insult to me, to my safety.

My fingers tremble as I scrub at my wet cheeks.

I can't believe this.

Breath shudders out of me as I lean over and splash cold water over my face, washing off the evidence, but it does nothing for my swollen eyes. I snatch at several sheets of stiff green paper towel and dab at my face, check my mouth where Craig crushed my mouth beneath his, a tooth catching on my lower lip which is puffy and split.

I straighten and blow out a breath.

I need to pull myself together. I can't go back to class until I do. There's nothing anyone is going to say or do to help me. The teachers are not on my side. My parents won't be either. The shame of the incident wells up inside me and I know I won't tell them. Because if I tell them, I'll have to admit to speaking to Mr Sharma the way I did, and disappointment will lurk in my mum and dad's eyes. They won't shout or even punish me, although the punishment can be non-physical, non-verbal. The punishment will be silence. So I will keep my own counsel on the matter. No need to upset anyone.

My big sister is away at university, and my little sister is way too young to have that conversation with.

The hallways are empty, echoing with silence as I trek my way up three flights of stairs to my classroom. I'd forgotten where I was supposed to be by the time I'd cleaned my face and gathered together the tatters of my emotions. So I'm even later than I would have been if I hadn't had to rummage around in my bag and haul out my timetable. Honestly, I'm a mess. Or I was a mess.

I'm okay now.

I straighten my shoulders, knock and enter my classroom.

Mrs Duprees turns from her audience of pupils, a flicker of irritation creasing her forehead as she gives me a swift perusal. 'Miss Howell. This is not like you. Take a seat, quickly.' She indicates the single empty seat right in front of her as I make to move towards the back of the classroom. 'Without disturbing anyone more than necessary,' she insists.

Without disturbing anyone more than I already have, she means.

I slink into the seat, peeling my books and pens from my bag and resist the urge to turn around and catch Nola Jacobs' eye.

Gilly isn't in this class with me, and I'd normally sit next to Nola. The two of them don't really get along and as Gilly is my best friend, or has been since we started college back in September last year, I tend only to sit with Nola when Gilly isn't there.

I like Nola. She's quiet and controlled without all the hysteria that builds up around Gilly. She's easier to be with.

Gilly gets the bus home in the opposite direction to us. I've passed my driving test and have a little car, but it's too expensive to use every day as I don't currently have a job. But I don't live far, and I prefer to keep fit and walk, especially in this weather.

Nola and I often walk home together, if I'm not staying late for athletics, which I'm not tonight. Even if I was supposed to, I wouldn't. I couldn't. I'm just too shaken. Even now tremors run up my thighs, turning my muscles to warm jelly, like I've just finished a full marathon, and I acknowledge how upset I am. By Craig. By Mr Sharma.

It'll be good to walk home with Nola. It's an opportunity for me to speak with her about the incident without Gilly getting bitchy. Because she is bitchy. There's a kind of possessiveness to her. Although she has lots of friends, she only has one best friend, and her expectation is that she is my only best friend too.

Maybe it's because she's an only child and she's spoilt rotten.

We'll be breaking up for the summer soon, and perhaps when we come back in September, I'm going to back off from her a little. I don't feel comfortable being someone's possession, which is what Gilly treats me like.

I want to have more friends like Nola. Someone who doesn't cling as much, someone I can tell my worries to without them getting spread around or dissed.

I'm sure there will be time enough when we walk home later to tell Nola what happened today. I feel by telling her, there will be a lack of judgement.

I'm sure she will be on my side when I explain how suddenly, I've become the guilty one.

4

PRESENT DAY – MONDAY, 3 MARCH 2025, 9.30 A.M. – SORIAH

My whole head throbs as I reach for the mug of coffee Nola has placed on my desk. I turn to face her and send her a weak smile. 'Thanks, babe.'

Her expression changes. Shock freezes her features. 'What the fuck?'

My hand flies to my nose, I don't know why. Automatic defence. Maybe, somehow to hide it.

She grabs my wrist, but she's gentle as she peels my hand away from my face. Her eyes fill with concern and her voice lowers to an angry whisper as she leans in so no one else in the office can hear. 'Jesus Christ, Soriah, what the hell did he do to you?'

My mouth drops open. 'No...' Oh no. I can't have her thinking that.

I twist my wrist from her and turn it so my fingers clutch hers. 'No. No. I slipped. I fell.' My voice almost peters out as I realise how poor it sounds. Weak, like I'm defending Marcus, when actually I don't need to. He's not done anything. I'm not sure he ever would. He's too apathetic. Isn't that one of the reasons I'm comfortable with him?

I take in a slow, calming breath and start again. 'I had a nightmare last night. I rolled out of bed and clunked my nose on the floor.'

I stare at her all the time I'm explaining myself and just there, under the surface of pity, is the disbelief.

She thinks my husband hit me. I know she does. She's never been overly fond of him. There's a certain stiffness between them when they're in each other's company. Probably because since he came along, she sees so little of me.

If that makes me a bad friend, then I am sorry, but everyone knows you can't dedicate your whole life to everyone. Not all at once. It's not like I've dropped her. I still see her at work. We have lunch together a couple of times a week, if we're not pounding away at our keyboards trying to keep up with the ever-evolving world of athletics marketing.

It's tough though. I no longer go to aerobics

and swimming with her because I want to get home to my husband and make his dinner for him. He loves when I do that. It makes him happy. What makes him happy makes me happy. Right?

Does that make me a bad friend, or a good wife?

Nola slides a quick assessing look over the rest of my face, to the dark bruising that's turned my skin a deep mulberry beneath my eyes despite the concealer I dabbed as thick as I dared.

I don't wear much make-up, so maybe that was as much a giveaway as my swollen nose.

She narrows her own eyes and hisses, 'Are you sure?'

It's exactly this that makes my heart race and fear pulse at the base of my throat.

I look down because I can't bear to look at her. It hurts. Not my face, my heart.

My eyes are so full with tears that when I shake my head with vehemence, a couple of drops flick out onto the back of my hand.

Nola's long scarlet nail swipes over it. 'Really?'

She hunkers down next to my chair, her head now lower than mine, her face tipped up. 'Soriah, if he's touched you, so much as bullied you...'

'He hasn't.' This time my voice is filled with conviction which it should have been before. He'd have to show more interest to bully me.

I shake my head. 'It's not him.'

Her hand gives mine a gentle squeeze. 'Do you want to talk about it?'

I shake my head again, lips compressing into a straight line. How can I tell her? Drag up the past instead of leaving it dead and buried?

Apart from Gilly and my family, she's the only one who knows. The only one alive in any case. The only one who cares.

Not even my husband knows the grim details. How could I tell him everything? He'd never look at me the same. As it is, I keep getting sideways looks from him whenever my past is brought up. Grey and murky is how I keep it. Mostly, he doesn't show that much interest anyhow and yet I know everything there is to know about Marcus, his upbringing, his ex-girlfriends, his two brothers who compete for their parents' affection. Maybe it's a man thing.

I glance around the office. Everyone else is studiously thrashing their keyboards, not daring to look up in case management notice and another disciplinary is invoked. Honestly, I think that's all we get since we were taken over by that huge conglomerate who are only in it for the money and are slashing department budgets in half and clamping down on coffee breaks, everything that brings morale down.

Luckily for Nola and me, we're working on a project together so it's accepted that we will confer to a certain degree, and we're way ahead of target this month. Which probably means they'll increase our target for next month and make it almost impossible to reach. It seems no matter what business you're in, targets are the be all and end all.

Nola glances sideways to make sure no one is looking before she leans in. 'Are you sure there's nothing? I can feel your stress, hun.'

I let my head drop and then sigh. Reaching inside the handbag I keep beside my feet, neatly tucked under the desk, I pull out the letter I'd balled up and bundled in there three days earlier so Marcus didn't see it.

Now, I unscrew the envelope and ease the letter out, handing it to Nola who flattens it against her knee to straighten out the creases.

I don't need to read it again. It's emblazoned on my mind. It's hardly surprising it triggered my nightmares. I've lived through worse than that, but the reminders come thick and fast on occasion.

The letter is from Victim Communication and Liaison, informing me of Craig Lane's early release.

That despite my best efforts when I responded to the Victim's Right to Review, putting forward my reasons why he should be further retained, the Board found he was repentant and apologetic, and considered him a rehabilitated individual.

I'd heard that before.

Just prior to him committing his crime.

Isn't that what Mr Sharma told me?

He's not a bad lad, he just needs to control his emotions... but at the same time, I am concerned that this boy's future could be ruined by— I shake off the incessant chant of voices whirring in my head. Memories which have surfaced lately and don't seem to want to leave. I gingerly touch my nose with the tips of my fingers. This is my fault. No one else's.

Nola raises her head after reading it. 'Oh, Jesus.' She covers her mouth with her hand, meeting my eyes with sympathy-filled ones of her own. Her voice is a desperate whisper as she leans right in, her nose almost touching mine. 'How long have you known, Soriah?' She stabs one of her pointy fingernails into the letter, almost piercing it. 'This is dated three weeks ago.'

My nod is ferocious. 'I know. It only arrived the day before yesterday.'

'Surely that's not right. Why weren't you allowed to appeal?'

At my silence, Nola narrows her eyes. 'Are you telling me you didn't appeal?'

I shake my head. 'I appealed. It was months ago. The Board overruled it.'

'Shit.'

'Ladies! Is there something we should know about?'

My heart leaps into my throat as I whip my head around to see our team leader approaching us from across the room.

Nola scrabbles with the letter, shoving it into the top of my handbag as she bobs her head up above my desk like a meerkat.

'No, thanks, Fenella.' Nola sends her a tight smile as she slides her backside into her own chair. 'Just sorting out the timeline for this marketing campaign.'

It's just as well she says something because as usual, I find I can't even open my mouth.

Fenella's face darkens. She's such a tyrant. Despite sitting two desks over, facing her 'team', she normally communicates via email. We must have sounded too interesting for her to resist. She dips her head, and her fingers tap out a dance across her keyboard and I know we're about to get it in the neck. Prize bitch would be too kind for this woman. She has the unrivalled ability to reduce anyone under the age of twenty-five to tears within the first week of working for the company. Added to that, her track record for keeping staff is terrible. I don't know how she gets away with it, but she's very close to the HR director. *Very* close, if you get my meaning.

Unless the HR director goes, I think Fenella's job is safe. Until she's no longer as close to him. Just like the last team leader.

My laptop pings, signalling an email. I give Nola a sideways glance before reading it.

> To all staff,
>
> Please note that there are several meeting rooms available which can be booked in advance for both arranged and ad-hoc meetings. It would be much appreciated if you all note that these should be utilised in order to avoid any disturbance to other members of staff in the central office who need to concentrate on their workloads.
>
> For ease, I have copied and pasted the link for meeting room booking forms below.
>
> Kind regards
>
> Fenella Goodrum

Office Manager

'Jesus Christ, when did she become the office manager? I thought she was only our fucking team leader,' Nola hisses under her breath and then raises her hand, waving it in the air. 'Thanks for that, Fenella. I'm sure everyone here is aware that I'm the guilty party, seeing as you just flagged that up two seconds before your—' she hangs air quotes above her head '—helpful email.' Nola scrapes her chair back. The one that doesn't meet health and safety requirements. 'I'll just bugger off to my own desk and hammer out a few more jobs, earn us another packet.' She slides her feet across the floor in an exaggerated drag, eliciting sniggers from the surrounding staff. She knows Fenella won't challenge her head on. She also knows that with the amount she turns over for the company, no one else will be willing to challenge her either.

I'm not sure why Nola stays. She is consistently the highest earner in the business.

It could simply be for my sake. This work has always been within my comfort zone. Predominantly a female workforce, I feel safe here. Although the dynamics are changing, I wonder if for both our sakes we should look for something else. Neither of us would have much difficulty. Not with our track records. In fact, it was only last month I had an approach from one of the mainstream marketing companies who wanted me on board. I'd been distracted by the whole Victim's Right to Review at the time. That and hiding from Marcus anything that arrived in the post.

It's not that I'm being deliberately deceptive. He does know that something bad happened to me. He just doesn't know the specifics. He's never asked, and I've never said.

Marcus and I have been married seven years now. It was thirteen years before then that the 'thing' happened. Why would he need to know the details? Why would I want to dig up that whole coffin of rotting emotions?

Nola reaches the door to one of the meeting rooms and with her hand on the door handle turns to look at me, eyes hard, jaw flexed. 'Are you coming, or what? Someone has to keep this company on their feet.'

With that she turns, opens the door and walks in, not even bothering to check if I'm scuttling after her. She knows I will be.

Determined not to meet anyone's eye, least of all Fenella's, I pick up my laptop and race after Nola.

'Make sure that meeting room isn't booked out by someone else,' Fenella calls out after me, brave in the absence of Nola.

I'm not as fast witted as my friend. Instead of replying, I simply give a backward wave and step inside the room, closing the door behind me so I can be engulfed by the silence.

5

TWENTY-ONE YEARS EARLIER – JULY 2004
– SORIAH

It's a steamy hot day. The rain from last night's storm is evaporating under intense sunlight, leaving everything wet and humid. The air is so heavy I can barely breathe it in.

Still, I wrap my arms around myself as I wait on the sidelines under the shade of the trees, ready to take my turn. This is the one hundred metre sprint, not my favourite. I prefer the fifteen hundred metres. Longer distance where I get my pace right, stretch my legs and run for the joy of it. The one hundred metres always feels forced. I barely hit my stride by the time it's all over.

I'm still the fastest in the college though. Most of the girls are pants at running. Gilly included. I mean,

I love her to bits, but she can't run for shit. Her knees seem to direct the bottom half of her legs to splay outwards, her elbows held away from her body while her hands flap on loose wrists. Too self-conscious of her boobs bouncing around. Although she is very proud of them in her own way. She likes the attention she gets from boys.

I'm not interested. I prefer sports. I guess I'm lucky I don't have much of a chest in that case. What I have is a damned good sports bra. Thanks greatly to Brandi Chastain, the famous US female soccer star who in 1999 stripped off her top in victorious salute, revealing a bra every nation wanted. You wouldn't necessarily know that unless you were a female athlete, but it's important. I feel proud of my sports bra. Given the right circumstance, I'd probably strip my top off too and do a victory lap.

I love football, and they want me on the team – I'm what they call an 'all-rounder' – but my preference is still track and field events.

I step from the shade into bright sunlight, getting ready to line up on the track.

With one hand, I gather the top half of my box braids together and loop a thick elastic around them. It saves them whipping around my face as I run.

As I look up at the kids sitting on their coats or jumpers on the hillside, all thought vanishes.

He's there.

Watching.

I certainly wouldn't strip my top off here and now. Not when there are freaks and perverts around.

With the sun in my eyes, I squint, sure that Gilly was sitting where he is now only two minutes ago.

I use my hand to shade my eyes. A quick jolt of surprise zings through my body.

She's sitting right next to him.

His large body almost obscures her from my view until he leans back on his elbows, evidently quite relaxed in her company, taking in the sun.

Are they talking? Did she just laugh with him?

I hold my breath, and her head turns so she looks directly at me. She scrambles to her feet and stomps away down the hill, making for deeper shade in the trees by the river.

What the hell did he say to her?

Her face is set in furious lines.

I hope he's not harassing *her* now.

The whistle blows to grab my attention, and I step up to my mark. Ready, but distracted.

He's not allowed to come anywhere near me, that was the one concession the teachers made. Not that any of them seem to care, or even notice. No one has checked with me to see if I'm okay. Not since the day after the incident when my form teacher took me aside and said Mr Sharma had spoken with her and certain buffers had been put in place for both our sakes. *Buffers.* What the hell does that even mean? But I didn't put up any kind of argument. What was the point? Not once I looked into her eyes and saw the disillusion with me hovering.

I just have to get on with it.

He's not in the same class as me for anything, but he's lurked in the library, and I often pass him in the hallways. I've been told to go to early lunch and he gets late lunch, which to my mind is unfair as everyone knows late lunch is always the best time. It means you get to hang out for longer with your friends in the refectory. They never asked my preference.

Seems to me he got the better end of the deal.

Now, as well as harassing me, he's approaching my friends too.

Is he telling Gilly that he didn't mean anything by it? Like he told Mr Sharma. That he loves me so much he just couldn't help himself?

That's a load of bullshit.

I am not flattered. If that's love, he can keep it.

The second whistle blares and I bobble the fast start I'm known for. Despite powering along, I come third.

Fury whips through me and I want to storm off as Dawn and Carol celebrate their win over me. They know I wasn't at my best, but that doesn't take away their joy. I'm not exactly showing sportsmanship here and I know it.

This isn't their fault. It's not my place to blame them.

The irony of that strikes me as funny and I grin as I stride over to congratulate them, actually feeling good as both girls flush up with pride and we have a quick girl huddle before I turn to go while they make for their group of friends waiting on the sidelines.

I chance a quick glance up at the hillside and he's standing now. Watching.

I whip my hoodie up from the ground and sling it over my shoulders as I make for the changing rooms. I need a shower. There's something about the way Craig stares with such intensity that makes me want to wash away the dirt.

He makes my skin crawl.

It's not just that he grabbed me and kissed me, it's the underlying look in his eyes. It's dark and assessing. Almost like he wants to devour me.

That can't be right, can it?

As I step out the shower and wrap my towel around me, Gilly waits for me, a half-smile on her face. I want to ask her about Craig, but she already seems to think I'm being coy. I am not. I don't like him. The mere thought of him sends an uncomfortable shiver down my spine.

She thought the whole incident in the refectory was funny. I did not. I don't think she understands my annoyance at Mr Sharma's remarks either. She's happy to show her body off and grab attention, but how would she feel if someone grabbed her? The truth is, she'd probably laugh it off, think it was flattery.

Whenever he's in the vicinity, she nudges my elbow and does that horrible pinching thing. She squeezes a tiny bit of my flesh between her fingers and twists. She knows it's wrong, because she does it sneakily, normally under the table where no one can see – on my inner thigh when she's sitting next to me, or the back of my arm. I've bloody well told her to stop, but she can't help herself. She does it when she's overexcited. All I can think is, God help her boyfriend. Let's hope she's not got hold of his dick when she does it. That's gotta hurt.

I whip my towel off, unperturbed by my nakedness as I scrub my body, but I see Gilly giving me an assessing look. I haven't washed my hair; that would take hours for it to dry and it becomes really heavy as the added synthetic hair used for the weave absorbs more water than natural hair.

I had the thick swathes of it braided at the beginning of the summer. They are far more practical than my Afro when I'm running so much. Convenient. Although it took virtually a whole day at the hairdressers and I was exhausted by the time they were finished with me. Mum paid for it in exchange for me doing household chores. I got the better end of the bargain as she's quite easy on me. There wasn't exactly a lot of ironing, and the bathroom took twenty minutes tops, once a week for six weeks. I don't mind. She's busy too, working full time, so it's okay if we all pitch in. My younger sister Leonie was a bit put out. She wants braids. And a tattoo.

I never asked for my braids, but Mum's proud of my athletic achievements. She knows I wanted them from the hints I dropped, but unlike Leonie, I would never directly ask. We don't have enough money for that.

Not that money is really tight. Dad has a good job and so does Mum, but we don't have enough to fritter away.

I open my locker and let out a shocked gasp, attracting Gilly's attention.

'What is it?' She leans in, elbowing me out of her way.

My jaw is clenched.

Gilly reaches into the locker and pulls out a small bunch of bright flowers, colours vibrant and almost garish. My stomach lurches at the sight of them.

'Oh, how gorgeous.' She pulls them towards her and sniffs, but I know there is no scent. Pretty flowers with no soul.

Ignoring them, I reach into my locker and grab my clothes out.

'You have them. I don't like gerberas.'

Surprise lights her eyes and she hugs them to her chest in an over-exaggerated Disney princess pose.

'Do you know who they're from?'

From my own shudder of revulsion, I can guess.

I give her one long stare before her face registers.

Her smile spreads wider. 'Oh! My! God! He really does love you. That's so sweet.'

I slip two fingers into my mouth and make a gagging noise and she laughs.

I tug on my fresh clothing, a pair of shorts and a loose-fitting cotton top. It's too hot for anything else and despite the cool shower, adrenaline is still boiling because that race wasn't enough for me and these bloody flowers have riled me.

How the hell did Craig get into the girls' changing rooms?

I never lock my locker, none of us do, but I will from now on. If I can just find the key.

'Aww, come on. Don't be miserable.' Gilly elbows me and I sigh. Some days I could just do without her. I don't understand why she can't see my point of view, side with me instead of forever pushing Craig at me.

'He's so romantic.'

She's cradling the gerberas, and I want to rip them from her arms and pluck every petal from them, scattering them on the floor where I can grind my heel into them until the lifeblood squelches out of them.

That's how much I hate Craig.

That's how much Gilly bugs me.

I turn away and will myself to forget about it. Move on. Concentrate on myself.

I look in the mirror and decide I don't need to take my heavy ponytail out. I like it. It looks good.

Although I don't care about looking good for the boys, there is a small sense of my own satisfaction that this style makes my eyes look larger and my cheekbones higher. Even some of the other girls have commented. Not Gilly, though. She's a bit strange that way. If the attention isn't on her, or about her, she gets a teeny bit jealous, I think.

She tucks her fine blonde curly hair behind one ear as though she can hear my thoughts and smiles up at me.

'So, I was talking to some of the girls in class, you know Becky and Sue, and like, they're up for a barbecue tonight.' Her gaze searches mine. 'You up for it?'

I shrug as I push my running gear into my backpack. 'Where is it?'

She imitates my shrug. 'I have an address. Like, one of the girls on beauty and hairdressing invited us.'

I'm not that bothered, but from the light in Gilly's eyes, she's desperate to go. I don't know why, but it's easier to agree.

'Is Kev going?'

'Nah, he's, like, working again.' She does an overexaggerated eyeroll and I smile. Kevin is not long for her world. She'll soon move him along, especially if he has more important things to think about than her. I guess his one asset is also his downfall. That he works. Therefore, he has money and a motorbike. She likes bikers. But he works, so that money and bike don't necessarily avail themselves to Gilly whenever she wants.

I can see her ditching him for someone more available.

She did the same for me. I know we're friends now, but I have become uncomfortably aware that Gilly is a user. Her last best friend was soon shuffled along when she met me. As though she can only give her full attention and enthusiasm to one person at a time. It made me uneasy at first, but she's such an effusive friend. She sort of bowls everyone over with her zeal.

It might be nice to have Gilly to myself. Well, not exactly to myself at a party, but without a boyfriend around, she's fun. A typical bubbly blonde. And at least without Kev, she won't be sitting in the corner snogging, yet still insisting I stay with her until I feel like a voyeur.

'Yeah, okay. Sure. I'll let my mum know just in case she's got anything planned.'

I pull my phone from my locker and send Mum a quick message.

> Home late. Off to a party with Gilly. Don't wait up. Love you.

Not that Mum will take notice of that. She always waits up. Even if she's in bed, a mouse could sneeze, and she'd want to know if it was me home.

With Carly, my older sister, at university and Leonie only twelve and too young to stay out yet, Mum has all the time in the world to concentrate on me.

I close my locker door and slip my phone into my bag, realising I only have 3 per cent battery left. How does it go flat so quickly? I've barely used it today.

'Have you got your charger on you? My phone is almost dead.' I look at Gilly.

She nods. 'I have it in here.' She pats the huge bag with the designer tag swinging from the zipper. Possibly a practical choice for college, however hers isn't stuffed with books, but make-up. She's offered me some of her make-up before, I'm not sure if she's kidding because her skin is snow white and I'm black. I'm not bothered about make-up, but she still seems to want to shove her black mascara and thick black eyeliner at me. I don't need it, not when I'm running, otherwise I end up with it streaked down my cheeks.

I borrow it now though as Gilly holds out the wand for me and I apply it, leaning into the mirror and opening my eyes wide. My lashes are long and lush, and this just emphasises their thickness. I smile at myself, pleased with the effect.

'C'mon. You can plug your phone in at the party.' Gilly is bouncing on her toes, impatient to get off.

Has another guy taken her fancy? Is that why she's so keen to get to the party quickly? Is Kev already yesterday's news?

She's so fickle.

I don't know why she's my friend, but she seems determined to hang on to me.

6

PRESENT DAY – MONDAY, 3 MARCH 2025, 5.45 P.M. – SORIAH

Dear Soriah,

I hope you are keeping well. Since the last time we spoke, I need to inform you that despite your letter to the Board appealing their decision, it has been agreed that Craig Lane should be released from HM Prison, Leyhill in Gloucestershire on Monday, 3 March 2025.

We understand that this news may cause you some concern and perhaps even distress.

Please let me assure you that your safety and well-being is of utmost importance to us. On release, Craig will be subject to specific conditions including but not limited to:

Being noted on the sex offenders' register.

> Being under strict reporting conditions to a probation officer.
>
> Being required to attend a rehabilitation programme.
>
> He will also be required not to attempt to contact you in any way.
>
> We want to assure you that we will monitor Craig's compliance with these conditions very closely.
>
> Our Victim Support Services team is here to provide support and reassurance to you as you go through this phase and we would encourage you to reach out to us during this time. Our contact numbers and opening hours are at the top of this page, should you need us. Please feel free to contact us at any time.
>
> We understand that this may be a very difficult time for you. Please be assured that we are here to support you should you need it.

I've been sitting outside my house for the past ten minutes and I'm pretty sure Marcus will be home shortly. I need to get the dinner on or he'll wonder what the hell is wrong with me. I've hardly been the perfect wife, attentive and adoring, that he's come to expect.

He works longer hours than me, so I tend to get dinner started as soon as I arrive home. He's often tired these days, so I clean the kitchen afterwards too. It gives me the chance to listen to music while he watches some mindless drivel on the television.

To be honest, I don't even know what we're having for dinner tonight. It might be omelette. Although according to Marcus, real men don't eat omelette.

He will if he's hungry.

I ball the letter up again and ram it into the bottom of my handbag. A cold sweat breaks out on my upper lip.

He could be out now. Craig, that is. Right now.

I wonder what time they released him. If it was early morning, or mid-afternoon.

Then where would he go?

They never gave me that much detail. I may be his victim, but often victims want their own revenge. Personally, I'm not interested. I never want anything to do with him again. If I never see him, it will make me a happy person. Living with the notion that he may appear in my life does not.

Will he even come back here? After all, his parents no longer live locally. They moved away as soon as he was convicted. In opposite directions, I heard. I don't think his mum could bear to face him or his dad. Or me.

Who could, after what he did?

The remembered caress of icy fingers strokes my spine, sending goosebumps pebbling across my skin.

I slip out of my car, pressing the fob to lock it. I step up close to test the door. Just in case. You never know. I always check the back seat as well. Always.

It's been a dull day, turning dark earlier than normal. I dash up the short path to the front door, breath backing up in my lungs as I expect an invisible hand to fall on my shoulder.

My keys rattle in nervous fingers as I choose one, push it in the lock and turn it, letting the door swing wide, I contemplate walking into a dark, empty house. Fear tightens my throat.

Music is playing from the kitchen and my brows twitch into a puzzled frown as I hesitate on the threshold of my home. The place I should always feel safe, yet strangely never do.

Funny how life gives you these little twists of the knife, to keep you on your toes. Just as you think the fear has gone, there's a sharp little reminder never to become complacent. Never to relax long enough or deep enough that you'll be caught unaware.

I'm not unaware. If anything, I am hypersensitive. Particularly recently.

I freeze. It can't be Marcus. His car's not on the drive and he always takes the single space in front of our house, leaving me to park on the road.

My hand grips the door handle as saliva pools in my mouth and I consider whether to run. Run now while there's still a chance.

There's a soft golden glow lighting up the far end of the hall, casting shadows from the staircase.

I was the last one out this morning. I never leave music on. It's not possible as it's connected to my phone app. When I leave the house, the music is silenced.

'Hello.'

I despise myself for the wobble in my voice and inject a little more authority the next time.

'Hello?'

'Hey, Soriah, in here,' Marcus's voice rumbles from the kitchen.

A physical rush of relief floods my system, giving me that sensation you feel when you're about to wet yourself after hanging on for far too long, and suddenly you're on the toilet with your knickers around your ankles breathing like you've run a marathon.

Only every endorphin in your body is doing a hula and you're laughing to yourself, knowing you dodged that bullet.

My legs have gone to overcooked spaghetti, and I wilt against the door I've just shut behind me.

'Jesus,' I whisper in the darkness of the hallway as a silver shadow slinks down the stairs and Luna lets out a soft meow of greeting that sounds remarkably like 'hello, hello'.

'I'm in the kitchen!' he yells, louder this time. I'm assuming he thinks I've not heard above the bass notes of whatever crap he's playing. I really hate his music. It's that repetitive thud of dance music, which is fine when you're pissed on the dance floor, but any other time, totally inappropriate. Not only does it send my heart crashing into my ribcage, but anxiety notches up several stages.

It's nothing to do with Marcus, or the rhythm of the beat. It's me. I'm not in a good place. I really need to pull it together. I'm not the sweary type. Really, not even in my own head, but the profanity is running wild and it's all because of him.

I'm not thinking about my husband, but the other him. Craig Lane. I don't want to think about him. I don't want him to take up any of my head space.

I push away from the door and strip off my coat, dumping it over the newel post at the bottom of the stairs. Marcus hates when I do that, but I don't care. I haven't the energy or emotional strength to pull open the understairs cupboard, lean in and hang it up. It just seems all too much. Apart from anything else, I know the moment I open up that cubby hole, Luna will be straight in, and I'll have to crawl into the void to tempt her out.

Trapped.

Just the thought of it has my breath hitching in my throat.

I can't think about it now.

Nor can I ignore it. Claustrophobia doesn't wait for an invitation to close in on you. It's there, hovering on the periphery, waiting for your weakness to let it in.

I turn my back on my coat and the understairs cupboard and with Luna running ahead, I concentrate on the flick of her tail and the tilt of her head which tells me she's hungry, but I bet she wouldn't take food from Marcus, even if he did remember to feed her. She's my cat, not his.

There's the vibrant aroma of Marcus's favourite curry filling the house. Normally I would be ravenous, but somehow my appetite has failed me in the last few days.

As I step into the brightness of the kitchen, Marcus turns and holds up a glass of ice-cold beer, the condensation running down the sides. It's a Monday and we don't normally drink during the week, but I accept it from him in any case and take a grateful sip. My eyes cruise the chaos Marcus always creates when he deigns to cook for us and I bite my tongue, willing myself not to complain.

He's made dinner.

I should be grateful.

I force a smile on my lips. 'Where's your car?'

He runs a distracted hand through hair that's started to thin at the temples. 'It went in for a service, and it wasn't ready to collect. The morons never valeted it, so they're keeping it until the morning, and they'll drop it off at work, so you'll have to give me a lift in tomorrow.'

I can, but it's in totally the opposite direction to my office which means we'll have to set off forty-five minutes earlier than normal because by the time I drop him off, I will hit rush-hour traffic right through the centre of Shrewsbury and that means gridlock. It's not worth making an issue about. I whisper the mantra in my head, *it's not him, it's me.*

Instead, I keep the smile on my face. 'What's all this in aid of?'

Marcus turns his back and, removing the lid from the pan, he stirs the curry, kicking up the warm fragrance of spices.

If I didn't know Marcus better, I would say he's avoiding direct contact with my gaze. But I do know him.

'Marcus?'

He lifts the kettle and pours boiling water into another pan, which I assume contains rice, and then turns to face me, resting his backside against the kitchen counter next to the hob. His smile doesn't quite cancel out the anxiety in his eyes.

'I've won Salesman of the Year.'

Shocked, my mind spins. Why is he so wary?

'Oh, Marcus, that's fabulous news.' Thrilled for him, as he's worked so hard for this, putting in all those extra hours, I head straight towards him, my arms wide to take him into my embrace. But there's a miniscule hesitation. Just a fraction of a second before he opens his arms to allow me in.

I press my cheek against his chest, hearing his heart hammering wildly. What's wrong with him? There's something ever so slightly out of kilter.

I lean away and look up into features that have darkened with something akin to annoyance.

'What's up? Aren't you pleased?'

His nod is short and abrupt. 'Yes.'

'But...?'

'But they want me to go to the awards ceremony this weekend.'

I can't see the problem, except it's pretty short notice, I'm going to have to dash out and grab an appropriate outfit, or I could do some online shopping, but it'll have to be tonight so I can get something in plenty of time. 'Brilliant!'

'It's down in Brighton. Two nights.'

Again, I'm thrilled. More online shopping. 'Wow, they're really pushing the boat out.' I step back out of his arms, allowing my fingers to make a leisurely trail down his forearm before I pick my glass of beer up again. I prefer wine, but Marcus is insistent that beer should be the drink of choice when eating Indian food.

Personally, I feel the drink of choice should be the person's choice, but it's his night, and I'm not going to spoil it for him.

'That'll be wonderful, we could do with a weekend away. And Brighton. I've never been.'

It's the company's head office so he has to go from

time to time, but always a weekday with maybe one overnight stay. Never a weekend. A quiver of excitement trembles through me. Brilliant, we can get away together and I can leave all thoughts of everything else behind. This could do me the world of good.

But the look in Marcus's eyes halts me. 'There's a bit of an issue.'

'Issue?'

He nods, his expression grave. 'It's employees only.'

'You're kidding me?'

He shakes his head. 'No. You know we've had cutbacks since Covid. They're still struggling to keep their heads above water.'

'Then why bother doing Salesman of the Year at all if you can't take partners?'

'Because they still want to keep morale high.'

'Keep morale high? By making you all go on your own and leave your other halves behind? Christ almighty, it's not like it costs much more to have a second person in your bedroom. What kind of morale boost is that?'

'Soriah... I knew you'd be like this.' He sounds defeated and it makes me feel like a prize bitch. I know I should be delighted for him, but—

'I'd understand if the ceremony was midweek, but how inconsiderate of them making it the weekend.'

His face falls, his whole expression darkening into a sulk. 'I won't go.'

Guilt swarms over me. He's worked so hard for this. I know he has and it's not fair of me to dampen the whole atmosphere. He's made dinner, hasn't he? Even if I have to spend an hour or more cleaning it off the wall tiles and surfaces where he allows the curry to bubble too hard and splash up. I can guarantee he'll let the rice boil over until the thick stickiness of it burns on the shiny, flat surface of the electric hob.

I sigh. 'It's fine. You go. I have plenty to do here and it'll be nice to have some me time.'

His face brightens instantly, his warm smile spreading wide like he's a different person. 'Brilliant! You can always have a go at decluttering the garage.'

I turn, placing my beer on the kitchen counter and walk towards the utility room, grinding my teeth to stop me from saying something. I won't spoil the moment. I don't need a sulky little boy this evening. It's not him, it's me, I keep reminding myself. I just want peace.

One thing I will not be doing while he's away, though, is clearing his clutter from the garage, nor any of those other jobs he's promised to do and just not got around to. No way. But I don't need that to escalate into an argument now. We've had too many of those lately and the stress is not helping our situation. They're not really arguments, more of a bicker, because I don't stand up for myself. I always back down. In the beginning, we never argued, but he seems to have got a foothold, knowing I won't retaliate.

I make a slow perusal of the utility, with dirty crockery and pans piled high ready to stack in the dishwasher. I guess we should consider ourselves lucky we have one next to the washer-dryer but it is a bit of pain having to bring everything through to the utility. It was the builders who installed it, and I suppose that is the whole point of a utility. When Marcus's friends come around, at least we can shove all the dirty dishes in here and shut the door to dull that rhythmic thudding sound dishwashers make.

I look around now. God, how does he manage to use so much? It's only a damned curry. One frying pan to fry the onions and add the spices, one pan for the curry, one for the rice. That's it, that's all he should need. He's got two of those items on the stove right now, so where did all of these come from, and why?

I blow out a long, weary sigh and open the dishwasher ready to load it.

'Shit.' I close my eyes, weariness stealing over me. It's still full from the night before.

His job, you'd think, as I had cooked last night.

I snatch items out, then look around for somewhere to place them for a moment before I take them through to the kitchen to store them away. There is nowhere. Our utility is tiny and there really isn't much room at all.

It doesn't help that there's a long, narrow cardboard box filling the counter, with dirty dishes on top.

I scoop the dishes up, hoping I don't chip any of them but almost beyond care. I balance them on top of the two frying pans in the small sink and then turn to pick up the box, tempted to sling it across the room. But I pause. It's addressed to me.

'Hmm.'

I've not ordered anything from Amazon, as far as I recall, but we each of us order so much from there these days, it's rare not to have a parcel.

But this is a specific shape. I edge it towards me, balance it on my hip while I place the remaining crockery down on a small empty patch of the bench.

The box is very light.

I snatch a clean, sharp knife from the cutlery rack and slit the sticky tape attaching the box lid to its base.

Sticky brown tape that I try desperately to ignore even as a chill slides down my spine.

I prise off the lid and my heart gives a little hitch.

An abundance of vibrant pink, orange and yellow gerberas and stocks are tied with a natural jute bow. My stomach gives a fast lurch like a fist gripping it inside. But I ignore it, pushing aside those dark memories that nudge at the periphery of my conscience.

They're stunning. Not something Marcus has ever bought me before as he prefers more subtle colours. Normally, he would send blush pink roses, or white lilies. He's a neutral kind of guy.

Nonetheless, he's bought me flowers, and it's been a few years since he's done that without prompting.

I scoop up the bouquet and walk through to the kitchen, a huge grin on my face. He's obviously bought them as an anticipatory apology for the upcoming weekend. Guilt slides in as I think of the hard time I just gave him.

'Marcus, they're beautiful. Thank you so much.'

He turns from the cooker, lowering a spoon from his mouth, his eyes wide with surprise for a moment before they narrow.

A frown knits his brow. 'They're not from me.'

I laugh. 'Yeah, right.'

And then the smile drops from my face while his expression doesn't change.

'Soriah. They're not from me. I never sent them.'

I blow out a breath and glance down at the beautiful bouquet cradled in my arms.

'If it wasn't you, who would send me flowers?' But something inside of me knows and my throat tightens so I can barely swallow past the constriction.

'I don't know. Have you got a secret admirer?' He smirks as though the mere thought of someone having the hots for me would be out of the question.

But I know better. I don't want that kind of attention. I've been admired before and look how that turned out. Admittedly, less admiration than obsession, but it all starts somewhere.

I swallow as I stare at them, the heavy scent of the stocks turning my stomach until I want to retch.

Marcus turns back to the dinner, not even noticing my reaction. 'Are they from your mum?'

'No.' I answer quickly because I know for a certainty she would never send me flowers. Not these flowers, in any case.

'Didn't they come with a note?'

I can barely speak because I never checked, so

sure they were from Marcus. Now I'm too scared to look, so I shake my head, knowing he's no longer interested. I let out a negative grunt which he's obviously satisfied enough with to respond.

'I wouldn't worry about it.' He shrugs. 'I'm sure someone will let you know who they are from.'

He's totally oblivious to my concerns. There's a curling disappointment that he doesn't even seem to care enough that someone might be sending flowers to his wife. I know I don't want him to be jealous, but a little curiosity or even interest would go a long way.

I stare at the flowers and a burst of revulsion skitters over my skin, sending my veins to ice as I make my way back into the utility.

Marcus switches off the extractor fan and the noises of him draining the rice and getting clean dishes out of the kitchen cupboards fade into insignificance as I stare at the empty flower box.

There's no card inside. Nothing to identify who sent them to me.

But there is one person who would send flowers uninvited.

One man, to be precise.

I lay the flowers back in the box and cover them with the lid. My knees have turned to water, and I have to lean against the utility sink and breathe in through my mouth to rid myself of the smell.

I don't want this. Not again.

I don't want that kind of obsession.

That man, these flowers have the ability to transport me back to the time of my youth.

And I don't want that.

I'm not simply worried.

I am terrified.

7
TWENTY-ONE YEARS EARLIER – JULY 2004
– CRAIG

My heart hammers in rhythm with the beat of the music as I walk into the small end-of-terrace house.

I've not personally been invited by the girl whose party it is, but Gilly said it would be okay. Everyone is going. No one takes any notice as I walk into the kitchen and snag myself a stubby little bottle of German lager I don't recognise. I'm pretty sure I should have brought some kind of contribution, but hey, who would notice?

Most of the kids are half-cut already.

I'm not so keen on the smell of weed, so I avoid the spliffs that are being smoked by the parents of the girl whose house it is, parents who are supposed to be supervising the whole party. I forget the girl's name in the fog of drugs and wander into the living room as I try not to breathe in any more of it.

That small blast of cannabis is already reeling around in my mind. If it wasn't for the nausea it invokes, I might give it a go.

I take a slug of my beer and cruise my gaze around the place, taking in the roomful of predominantly females dancing with each other, the cheeks of their arses on display as they raise their arms above their heads, gyrating in sexual fantasy, oblivious to their short dresses riding up. Or maybe it's a deliberate invitation.

There are some guys glued to the wall, beers in hand not dissimilar to me, but unlike me, they're not looking for a certain someone. I assume not, in any case. I am. I'm only here for one person. No one else matters.

I scan the room for twenty minutes or so, and then move on. It's not exactly a big house, but the party seems to have spilled over into the garden under a canopy of clear skies and vibrant stars.

I glug down the rest of my beer and grab another one out of a cool box on the patio, narrowing my eyes so I can see the shadows milling around between fucking stupid garden lights which seem to form a pathway through untended grass and straggly weeds to the far end where battered old panel fencing stops anyone from going further.

The neighbours must fucking hate these people.

Parents who think they're cool enough to join in their kids' parties are fucking weird.

These ones certainly are.

My mum and dad wouldn't dream of allowing me this kind of party, where there are no boundaries, and they join in. I find this freaky. I don't want my parents to be my best friend. My dad never would be anyhow because he thinks I'm a loser, but Mum is better than that. She's pretty chilled and I love her. But I wouldn't want to see her smoking weed, drinking cheap wine, and chilling with my friends.

That's just too weird for fucking words.

But these parents are doing exactly that.

Like they haven't moved on from their youths. Or they're trying to recapture them.

There must have been a door through to the garden from the kitchen too because those oldies are out here swaying to the music like a couple of nutjobs. Does no one else notice how stupid they look? This is not cool.

I dip my hand into the cooler for a third little bottle of beer and the world sways a little. Maybe it's a bit stronger than I anticipated. Perhaps I've slugged it down too fast. I never had anything to eat before I came. The last thing I had was a scoop of fries in the canteen at lunchtime. I couldn't afford a burger as I wanted enough money for bus fare tonight.

I scan all the faces.

Shit!

She's not here.

What a fucking waste of time.

Gilly lied. She's such a fucking little bitch. She thinks she's so fucking funny all the time as she bounces around like some kind of bunny on speed, tits wobbling and hair springing all over. She's not funny. She said they'd be here. She swore she'd fix it if I made it worth her while. And I did make it worth her while.

I swig down the rest of the bottle and pluck another one from the box. Who the fuck knows how many I'm drinking? Not a fucking soul has taken notice. Nobody cares.

I stumble through into the house so I can take a quick piss.

I dip my hand into my jeans pocket and pull out a small plastic bag with four tiny blue tablets inside that Greg swapped for the piece of homework I did for him. Well, two pieces of homework. He drives a hard bargain. Not the same ones as the couple I gave

Gilly earlier. I've tried one of those before and didn't like the way it made me feel so I was happy to hand them over. For a favour. One she's reneged on.

Bitch.

I fish a tablet out and pop it on the end of my tongue before washing it down with a mouthful of beer.

Fuck it. I'm going to get off my head. No one will notice.

Mum's working nights, and Dad will be fast asleep, snoring when I arrive home. He doesn't give a shit as long as I don't get any girls pregnant. He's made that clear by the amount of condoms he makes available in my bathroom. Like he'd be proud if I use every one of them as long as I don't bring a girl home. Yet.

He wants me to sow my wild oats, as long as they're trapped in latex.

I flush the loo, zip up my jeans and wash my hands before snatching up my beer from the small ledge in the downstairs loo.

As I open the door, there's a girl waiting. I smile, but she ignores me, almost barging me aside in her haste to get into the loo. The bolt slides across with a sharp snap.

I wander back out into the fresh air and stand on

cracked uneven slabs at the edge of the lawn while I watch, unnoticed.

I've been here an hour or more and not a single person has spoken to me. I don't really recognise any of them apart from some of the girls from the hair and beauty courses who I don't tend to mix with. None of the guys from the mechanics course are here. What a wash-out.

My head is no longer a gentle sway, but a violent swirl by the time I turn to leave.

I stop dead.

My heart hammers.

There she is!

Right in front of me.

My tongue thickens in my mouth and even though she's face-to-face with me there's no way I can form anything intelligible.

I stagger. I may be drunk and high, but I'm aware that I have no control. I watch myself as if from above, holding out wavering arms as I stagger towards her. The love of my life.

'Shhhoriiiah.'

I stumble.

Lurch into her.

I've lost control of my limbs, but I manage to loop my arms around her and catch her scent. It's dark and earthy with a touch of innocence which escapes me as I cling to her to stop myself from falling.

She is too beautiful. Too stunning to be a mere human.

I bury my face in her neck and inhale. God, I love her. She's not like any other girl here. She's beautiful. So beautiful, I could cry for the want of her.

She stiffens in my arms and somewhere over my head I'm aware of a voice, high pitched and hysterical.

'Get off. Get off me. You stupid fuck! You're drunk!'

She smacks at my shoulders, my face, my head. My arms slacken and Soriah gives a hard shove with arms that are whiplash muscle.

I fall back, my arse smacking on the grass, my head following with a sickening crunch. White foam spews from the neck of the bottle as it rolls from my slack fingers, across my chest and onto the grass beside me.

Doused in embarrassment and beer, I scramble to my feet, hoping no one has seen.

Laughter surrounds me from faces I don't recognise, except for the parents who hold their stomachs while they belly laugh, their faces seeming to contort and enlarge in my vision, yellowed teeth bared.

Stumbling around in uncontrolled circles, I snatch up a fresh bottle of beer and pop the lid, leaving the garden behind, humiliation consuming me as I stagger through the patio doors and back into the living room a few steps so I can lean against the back of their settee.

I lift the bottle to my lips. Maybe I shouldn't drink any more, but I don't care.

I love Soriah but she's being a complete bitch. Gilly said Soriah fancied me, and she should know, she's her best friend. Soriah's made a complete dick of me. She's humiliated me in front of everyone.

Why? Why would she do that? I love her. I just want her to love me back.

I drag in a tortured breath.

Rage vibrates through me and my jaw aches as I turn. Without even a glance, Gilly has looped her arm in a protective manner through Soriah's and they've moved into the shadows of the garden. I thought Gilly was going to help me become friends with Soriah. She said she would. She took payment and she's done nothing to help.

I'm glaring out at the garden. Everyone is having fun. Everyone but me.

Those two fucking aged hippies are still laughing. At me. Like I'm some sort of freak show.

My eyes glaze over. I'm not sure if its tears or rage but there's a red haze closing in from the outside.

Fuck them. Fuck them all.

I lob my full bottle at those laughing faces. Just to shut them the fuck up.

It spins in a wild circle, beer spraying like a Catherine wheel, white froth shooting out from the mouth splattering bystanders, so they squeal in delighted horror.

Until it smashes into the glass pane of the patio door and explodes like a shotgun.

People leap back or duck, shock streaking their faces, but I don't wait long enough to gauge Soriah's reaction. I turn on my heel and stride through the living room, down the hall and slam the front door behind me, making that glass shudder too.

I leave behind the pounding music and raised voices. The confusion and shock.

I don't run. I think most people were too stoned to realise what happened. Voices are raised, following me. The music stops with a suddenness that plunges my whole world into silence.

Ducking my head, I make my way through the back lanes for what seems like miles before I recognise my surroundings. It's not like I can jump on a passing bus out in the middle of nowhere, nor would they probably allow me in the state I'm in, so I keep walking.

Frustration and indignation combine, lending me the energy I need to make my way home, sobering with each step I take.

Gilly promised me it would be easy. She said Soriah liked me really. That she had the hots for me.

Had she lied?

I fucking love Soriah.

Why can't she feel the same way about me?

How can I persuade her to love me in return?

All I need is a chance.

Just one chance!

8

PRESENT DAY – FRIDAY, 7 MARCH 2025, 6.45 A.M. – SORIAH

The week has flown past. Guilt and frustration wrestle with each other as I take my annoyance out on Marcus by offering up my silence.

He's oblivious to the reason. In fairness, there are so many. Not least of all the fact that he's not once mentioned my swollen, bruised nose apart from his initial 'God, I hope no one thinks I did that', when he noticed it that first morning.

I'm irritated. Irritable.

I'll put that down to the fact that I'm due to start my period. In fact, I'm overdue, but that's not unusual for me. I've given up getting excited, thinking I might be pregnant. I think that ship has sailed. We've been trying for the past five years and despite my suggestion that we should maybe take the next step and look into getting checked out, Marcus has been resisting. He wants things to happen naturally.

Well, there are only so many years of natural in me.

I need medical intervention if anything is going to happen, because quite frankly I'm on the edge right now. My hormones are raging inside, telling me it's the right time. It's been the right time for five years, but while it was a quiet whisper at the beginning, it's now a raging howl.

The other point is, I'm hardly likely to get pregnant without having sex and lately there hasn't been much of that. Marcus is under so much pressure at work to keep his head above water. Not only has he strived and achieved Salesman of the Year, but because of that, they've increased his target even before he's been given his award. Why do companies do that? Isn't it enough or even fabulous that their salesman has smashed his target for this year? Instead of giving them a pat on the back and saying, 'Great, son, now do it again,' their attitude is 'Well, that wasn't bad. Can you put some more effort in?'

He's exhausted.

He comes home late, eats his dinner in front of the TV, if he can get away with it, and then slouches off to bed. Normally by the time I've fed Luna and turned off all the lights, cleansed my face and smoothed on moisturiser, he's already snoring, his back to my side of the bed so it's me who has to make the move to snuggle up.

'I'm off. I'll see you Sunday night. It'll be late, I imagine.' His words drag me back to the present.

'Have you left the spare door key?' This is the umpteenth time I've asked this week since Marcus didn't bother putting it back into the key cupboard on the side of the house after he used it on Monday when he left his whole bunch of keys at the garage. From his expression, he thinks I'm a nag.

He rolls his eyes and makes a show of digging in all his pockets before he smacks it down on the kitchen counter. 'Happy?'

Now is perhaps not the time to remind him that I bought a new key safe ages ago as water got in, making our old one rusty around the edges. Another job Marcus has been promising to see to for the past year.

Instead, I keep the peace and give him a benign smile.

Marcus leans in to drop a quick kiss on the top of my head like I'm a friend instead of his wife, before he makes his way to the front door, leaving me in the kitchen, cup of strong coffee in one hand and slice of buttered toast in the other.

'Okay,' I call out after him. 'Have fun.'

There's no reply as the door closes behind him.

His career is the be all and end all.

I consider my job important, but I see him looking down his nose at it sometimes, as though it's not as worthy as his.

Admittedly, he's paid considerably more than me and there will be a huge bonus for achieving Salesman of the Year. That shouldn't diminish the importance of my career though.

It does. In his eyes.

If Marcus works overtime, it's because he's doing the best for us. If I do, it's a damned nuisance that our family time has been disrupted all for nothing. I'm sure he never means it to sound that way, but the longer we've been together, the more it's built. The slow, insidious undermining of me, of my self-worth.

Or is that purely how I see myself and it's nothing to do with his opinion? It's my own self-doubt. My own imposter syndrome. Perhaps I should not have contented myself with a man who loves himself more than he loves me, but I was comfortable with that. In the beginning. I never wanted obsession. That way can only hold danger. The sand has shifted though.

I'm a convenience. Almost invisible. Did I really want that?

I understand his need to compete. I too was once a competitor. I lost all of that. Now I'm the one who is happy to lurk in the shadows of someone else's success. It's not him. It's me.

I finish my toast, dusting off my fingers over the sink and then swallow down the rest of my coffee while I think of things that will help to pick me up.

I know what will help. I may no longer compete, but a strong, long run will do me the world of good. I have a way of switching off my mind as my feet pound the pavements.

Checking the time, I give myself a little nod. Yes, I can do it. I got up an hour early to see Marcus off, otherwise he might have just slipped out without even saying goodbye.

I have time. A forty-minute run will energise body and soul.

My trainers are under the stairs. I open the door, snatch them out, dump them by the front door and race upstairs. Stripping, I fling my dressing gown and pyjamas on the bed as I enter our bedroom.

Luna is stretched out on my pillow. Her golden eyes give me a cursory glance before she closes them and dismisses me.

Adrenaline and endorphins already race at the thought of my body being pushed to run.

Navy Lycra slides up my body like a second skin and I dash back downstairs to slip my feet into my trainers before bending to fasten them.

I snatch up the single door key that Marcus left and leave the house, turning the corner to our side wall where I slip the key into the safe. I click the little door closed firmly. You have to give it an extra push to make sure it's shut.

It takes around ten minutes to warm up before I set off on a light jog.

Clean air fills my lungs and my endorphins kick in. I pick up speed and power along the footpath. Few people are around at this time of the day, except for the occasional dog walker.

My limbs relax into a steady gait, and I circle the block, around the perimeter of a small park where pathways interlink, going nowhere. The only other person about is a young woman who stands with a baggy in hand waiting for her dog to finish having a poop.

I'd love a dog, but Marcus isn't keen. He's not terribly bothered about Luna, but at least he's not required to walk her. If we didn't both work full time, I'd get something like a spaniel that could run with me every morning. Perhaps it would inspire me to do it more frequently.

Forty minutes later, as I head for home, ponytail swinging, I am smiling. This is what my life has been missing lately. For the past few months, I've forgotten the joy of running and here it is. This is the magic I crave, the freedom I love. I vow to myself I'm going to make the time to do this every day. An hour I will allow myself. My indulgence. After all, spring is coming, which is the best time of the year.

I shake out my limbs as I stand in our small front garden, cooling down before I step around the side of the house and up to the key safe and raise my hand to tap in the code.

For a moment, I think I'm imagining it, but the key safe isn't fully locked and I don't need the code. I touch my finger to it. The front cover drops down and swings on its rusty hinges. I'm absolutely positive I clicked it shut. Didn't I?

I scoop the key out and, slightly puzzled, I unlock the front door and step into the house.

I pause, door still open, and stand for a moment.

All joy from my run evaporates, leaving behind just a cold sweat.

There's something not right.

I swivel and look at the key in my hand, think of the key safe I've left wide open.

I walk back outside and deliberately place the key back inside, instinctively pushing the front cover closed, but the code is in the right place on the wheels and the door doesn't lock properly. I always spin the little wheels when I shut the key safe. You have to, otherwise it won't lock.

A trickle of alarm skitters over my nerve endings as I step back inside the house, trying to convince myself, but my instinct doesn't want to listen to my brain.

I know I locked the key safe. I know I spun the wheels. I know I gave it that extra push to click it in place. It's automatic. Just like it was automatic now.

Heat creeps over my skin like fire ants racing over fresh kill, injecting their toxic venom.

Breath traps in my lungs and I consider if I should step back outside while I decide whether to ring the police.

They're going to think I'm mad.

'Hello, police, please. Yes. I have a funny feeling in my stomach. Yes, I do suffer from anxiety. No, the key was in the key safe, but the key safe wasn't quite shut. Yes, I'm sure I locked it. I'm positive. Yes, the key is still there. No one actually took it. No.'

I don't think they'll take me seriously. They have so much more to deal with.

Besides, my phone is on its charging stand in the kitchen where I left it when I went out. Perhaps I should have taken it with me, but there are not many places you can keep a phone when wearing Lycra. I need to get one of those phone pouches you attach to your arm. Running armbands, I think they're called. That's another Amazon order I'll have to put in tonight, but I can't think about that now.

There's a heavy, strained silence and I catch my breath, hold it so I can listen for any sound.

Sweat pools in the dip at the base of my neck.

I step inside and close the door. I need to chill. This is not real. It's not happening. I employ every tactic I know to stop myself from racing back out again. My imagination is just on a run. Like my body has been. There is nothing here to fear.

My counsellor's voice whispers in my ear until my breath steadies, my muscles unclench.

Craig has not caught up with me. He has not been in the house.

He won't even know where I live and besides, he's under supervision. He can't come after me. Not now. Not yet.

I am safe.

Aren't I?

I must not have properly locked that key safe in my haste and excitement to get going.

Satisfied that I've placated myself, I push away from the door.

Walking through my house, one room at a time, I'm further mollified. I pick up my phone on the way through the kitchen and set my cup under the espresso machine. Press the button and continue my task.

By the time I reach the bedroom, I'm feeling pretty stupid.

This letter set me on edge and now I'm struggling to keep my own rampant imagination in its box.

My breath halts in my throat at the connection. A box. A box of flowers with no name, no card.

It's a coincidence. Surely? There's been nothing since Monday. Then again, Marcus has been here every evening.

There's nobody home but me. And Luna, of course.

I lean over and scratch the top of her head, taking comfort in the quick, reactive purr she starts, as though I exist only for her benefit. Which I acknowledge, I do.

'Alexa, play Soriah's music mix.'

Music pours through my smart speaker as I move to the bathroom, stripping off my running gear and leaning into the shower to start the jets of water in our very modern shower.

I step inside while the water is still icy and suck in my breath at the shock. It's like hitting reset. Every molecule quivers, and as the sweat sluices away, my mind stops its manic search through its own conspiracy theory.

By the time I emerge, my body dripping as I reach for a towel, I am once more fully in this world. I sigh as I scrub a rough towel over my body. I hate soft towels. It must be left over from my youth when my mum insisted on hanging them out in the sunshine to dry until they resembled a stiff board.

I love the roughness of them.

Marcus prefers me to tumble dry his. Marcus is a pussy.

I grin to myself, gyrating just a little to the music blaring away as I slip into my underwear. I'm fine. I'm back in the zone.

Reaching into the wardrobe for a white blouse, my stomach gives a sudden unexpected lurch like it's about to leap out of my body. I pause mid-stretch.

Saliva gushes into my mouth and I swallow rapidly to stop the onslaught.

I dash to the bathroom, fling up the toilet seat and vomit my coffee and toast into the loo.

I gasp, trying not to taste the vile bitterness clawing at the back of my throat, burning the inside of my nose. Jesus, why is there carrot in there? There's always carrot no matter what you've eaten.

What had I eaten?

Dinner last night was—? I made dinner last night, a chicken casserole with dumplings. No carrots involved. We both ate it. We were both fine.

I flush away the vomit and sink back onto my heels, just in case. I don't want to move away too fast and find I need to be sick again.

Saliva pools in my mouth once more and I spit it out.

From feeling absolutely fantastic, I'm now weak and helpless, like a newborn kitten.

After several minutes when my stomach no longer feels as though it's about to revolt, I push up from the floor, pad across the bathroom, hang my head over the sink and turn on the tap so I can splash water over my once again overheated face. What is going on?

It has to be all the stress of late. All the upset. Even little things, like Marcus going away for the weekend for work, add up. I'm going to be in the house all weekend on my own. Anxiety doesn't choose a convenient moment. It piles on the moment it senses a crack in your defences. And my defences currently have a yawning chasm.

I brush my teeth and straighten up. There's a fine tremble to my fingers as I push my hair back from my face. I wear it au naturel these days and it's getting a little out of control. Perhaps I should go back to wearing it in box braids, like I used to. The memory of that sends another gush of acid to burn the back of my throat, but this time I hold it down. I control my breathing as I stare at myself in the mirror.

Nothing I did caused that situation.

Nothing was my fault.

I am not to blame.

The responsibility lies with Craig Lane and him alone.

His name burns into my mind, but I grit my teeth, determined to keep control of this.

I'm going to make an appointment with the hairdresser. It takes hours – literally a whole day – but it's not like it's going to interfere with Marcus's arrangements. He's not here. He's doing his own thing. He'll barely know I've been. Apart from when he sees the credit card bill, because this is not a cheap hairdo.

Mind made up, I'm once more in control.

I'll see if they can fit me in this weekend.

I open the bathroom door and step into my bedroom, reaching for my phone.

I blink.

It's not there. Not where I left it.

Breathe.

I cast my gaze around and there it is on the bed.

I must have dumped it there when I dashed for the bathroom. I sniff. Strange, because I never had it in my hand when I shot to the loo to throw up. Did I? I'd placed it on my dresser when I first walked into the room and I can't recall picking it up again.

I have an image in my mind of reaching for my blouse with both hands, ready to slide it off the hanger.

I give a mental shrug.

I must be going mad.

My phone can't have sprouted legs and walked.

I pick it up and glance at the time.

For crying out loud, I'm going to be late for work if I don't get a move on.

While I throw on my clothes, I scout around for a pair of sensible shoes I can wear into the office. I feel the need for flatties today. I don't want glamour, I just want to melt into the background. Like I always have.

I snatch up my phone and hurtle down the stairs.

My coffee is cold but the aroma of it gives my stomach a little heave in any case. I really don't want coffee. I pour it down the sink and give the mug a quick rinse. It'll have to do. I'm running really late now.

I snatch my keys from the key hook we have in the kitchen and grab my little handbag, all the time scoping the room out, checking for anything out of place, even though I don't really have the time.

As I dash along the hall, a noise stops me mid-stride.

'Luna?'

I turn in a tight circle, tilting my head as I try to pin the noise down.

There's a light scuffle and a muffled cry. I stare at the closed door to the cupboard under the stairs.

My veins turn to ice.

I hear it again.

'Miaow, miaow.'

Luna doesn't have a strong voice, it's babyish and pitiful, full of woe that makes my heart contract when I hear her so that I'm instantly inspired to pick her up, cuddle her, feed her.

'Miaow.'

The soft, tragic cry comes again, and I step forward, slowly turn the knob on the understairs cupboard door and—

Luna stalks out, bright yellow eyes accusatory, tail flicking as though I have committed some unforgiveable sin.

I put one hand out and steady myself as I close the cupboard door behind her and watch her walk away, stiff-legged and affronted, heading for the stairs and back to my bed where she'd been lying just moments before I stepped into the shower.

My heart knocks against my ribcage as I glance between cat and cupboard door. She's clever, but not that clever.

How the hell did Luna get locked in the cupboard under the stairs?

9

TWENTY-ONE YEARS EARLIER – JULY 2004 – SORIAH

'Oh my God!' I cup my face in my hands.

I can't believe what Craig has done.

The music cuts and we're all staring at each other in horror.

The girl whose party it is, Lissie, stands frozen, both hands still covering most of her face with only her huge kohl-rimmed eyes showing. Impeccable eyebrows, probably tattooed on, are raised almost comically as her gaze slides around the garden.

Her parents, five minutes ago loose-limbed and drugged-up, are now stone-cold sober. Lissie's father is raging.

Panic-stricken, we make our way towards the open garden gate, following the kids who are leaving in droves. There's no way we want to get involved in this.

Gilly grabs my hand and squeezes until my bones are grinding against one another. I look down at her and she's not horrified like I am. She's not upset. She's giggling. Disgust rolls around in my stomach.

These poor people. They didn't deserve this. They might have been smoking pot and partying wildly, but no one deserves to have their property trashed. Nor does it warrant being laughed about.

I try to shake my hand loose from Gilly's, but she's now digging her nails into my forearm with her other hand.

'Gilly, you're hurting me, stop squeezing.'

I yank my hand out of hers and she sort of crumples against me, her laughter too obvious and loud. She's an embarrassment and I don't want this. I don't need to attract unwarranted attention. What if they call the police?

The parents might think we had something to do with it, and that is the furthest possible thing I want.

'What the hell have you been drinking?' I snarl under my breath, anger getting the better of me as I drag her down the dark alley running alongside the house, keeping close to the others as we all elbow each other in our haste to escape.

She laughs some more, and I know she's taken something other than alcohol. Her pupils have dilated so much, I can barely see the pale blue of her irises. She knows I don't approve. My body is too precious for me to pop pills. I never even saw her do it, but from the look of it, Craig might have been on the same stuff.

Maybe that's what she was doing with him earlier today.

I rack my mind, trying to visualise what I saw at the time.

Is he a drug pusher?

As we reach the front of the house, everyone spreads out, their whispers loud and shocked.

Lissie's dad roars out of the front door and bellows down the street.

'Who was that kid? Someone invited him. I'm going to rip his head off if I get hold of him before the police do. If you know him, come forward and let me know. The police are on their way.'

Gilly snorts out another laugh and I yank her away as quick as I can. We can do without her getting us involved. If the police see her like this, we're both going to be in trouble and I don't even want to think about what my parents will say.

I seriously doubt Lissie's dad will call the police.

He'd have a lot of explaining to do about the drugs and alcohol, especially as there appeared to be a number of underaged drinkers there. Lissie's sister for one. I assume that was her, hanging around with her big sister, looking remarkably like her and made up to look like a twenty-year-old. Only it was obvious she wasn't. Sixteen, if that.

'Oh my God, that was, like, fucking awesome.'

Gilly's face is slack with drink and drugs and I'm not entirely sure this makes me happy that she's about to get into my car which I've parked at the far end of the street. I was irritated when we couldn't get parked any closer earlier, but I'm happy now that I couldn't so Lissie's bonkers dad can't take down my registration number and report it to the police – if he decides to do something about his smashed patio door.

'Shut up, Gilly,' I grind out. 'It's not funny.'

'Oh, loosen up,' she slurs up at me. 'You're such a tightass.'

And she's been watching too much trashy American TV.

I'm glad now I brought my car as I open the passenger door and shove her in while she cackles like a hyena, her short legs pinwheeling in the air so I can see the whole of her bare arse where her short skirt has ridden up, revealing what I hope is a thong and not lack of undies as she wallows back and forth on the seat trying to get purchase. Her hair is wild and I'm not even sure how that happened, except she was leaning on me a lot and the hairdo she had when we came out seems to have derailed, especially now her head is thrashing from side to side.

I slide into the driver's seat, and she giggles while I wrench the seatbelt around her and click it into place before I tend to mine.

Truth be told, she's really getting on my nerves. Her lack of responsibility seems to have escalated in the last few weeks.

I start the car and pull out slowly to avoid some of the stragglers still walking in the middle of the road. As they step back onto the pavement, some of them weaving, I gently accelerate away, leaving them behind.

Slightly shaky, I glance in the mirror, keen to get away. I don't want to get involved. I've not been drinking, and I never would. My mum would whip my car away from me and sell it to a junkyard if ever I so much as had a sip of someone's drink when I have car keys on me. That's the deal, and I feel privileged that my parents trust me to adhere to that rule.

It means I never get to drink though because I'm

virtually the only one who has a driver's licence and my own car. It's not much, but I love it.

I glance at Gilly, who seems to have managed to sit vaguely upright, although she's leaning against the passenger-side window. She's stopped laughing now and has gone silent. She'd better not hurl in my car.

'Who invited Craig?' I ask.

She closes her eyes, saying nothing.

'Gilly. Did you invite him? Is that what you were talking about with him today?'

She shrugs one shoulder.

'Is that a *yes*?'

Her sigh is heavy. 'He said he wanted to speak to you. Just apologise. He really likes you and feels so bad for what he did. He really loves you. You should be kinder. Sometimes you're such a bitch, Soriah.'

Her voice slurs and I'm done with her. I don't even want to argue about the matter.

She's drunk and I *know* now she's taken something else too.

I pull my car up outside her house.

'Is that where you got the drugs?'

There's a sly shift of her eyes towards me and then away. 'Can I sleep at your house tonight? I don't want to get grounded.'

What am I supposed to say to that?

With a huff, I pull away from the kerb again and head in the opposite direction for a couple of miles or so to my house. As we pull into the drive behind my mum's car, Gilly sits up. The lights are still on in the sitting room, which means Mum is awake.

'Shit!' Gilly fidgets as she unclips her seatbelt with a clumsy hand. 'Don't let her see me like this. I don't want her telling my mum.'

I don't know what to do about Gilly. One minute she's my best friend, the next she's an irresponsible pain in the arse and I am so conflicted.

Pity stirs in me at the mess she looks. You'd think she'd been rolling around in bed with her boyfriend for a couple of days. Her hair is like straw, straggling around a gamine face, thick kohl smudged around already small eyes to narrow them further. And those pupils! Jesus, Mum is going to know. Apart from the smell of weed clinging to us, which admittedly neither of us are guilty of smoking. It was the overall smell of that party.

She wallows in her seat as she reaches for her small clutch bag.

I don't know what it is boys see in her. She's not beautiful. She's got a lovely heart-shaped face and pouty, but mean lips. Her nose is cute, but those eyes can turn spiteful in a split second.

Her breasts are huge though. Maybe that's the sum total of what boys our age want.

Which is why I don't have a boyfriend.

Craig may have a thing for me, but I really am not interested. There are other boys too who look. I am aware, but they're all so juvenile. Maybe I just have high expectations.

I get out of the car and Gilly stumbles as I make my way around to her. She bumps against the front wing of my car and slithers with remarkable elegance onto her backside, managing somehow to end propped up against the front tyre.

The grin she sends me is sloppy and woeful.

'Did you take anything else?' I know she has. I run my gaze over her, assessing her condition. I hope she's not going to throw up.

She shakes her head. 'Only the one. I've never tried them before.'

She's smoked weed, I know that much. She also knows I can't stand the smell of it and won't be around her if she lights one up. I don't want the stench of it clinging to my clothes. I'm pretty sure it does in any case as that place was filled with it which was why I wanted to go straight out into the garden.

'What was it?' I bend down, looping my hands under her armpits, and yank her up. She's really not very heavy, and I am used to throwing the javelin and swimming. My upper body muscles are pretty good, but I don't like the strain on my back as she wriggles, trying to get her feet under her and tug her skirt down at the same time, like she's suddenly become aware of the fact that it's almost around her waist.

'I dunno.'

It looks like she can barely keep her eyes open.

'When did you take it?' I can't recall seeing her do anything sneaky, but then I was quite distracted.

She wriggles her fingers dismissively in the air. 'Before you picked me up.'

Sighing, I haul her to the front door and drag her inside.

'Hi, Mum.' I keep my voice bright and airy.

'I'm in the kitchen.' Her reply comes almost immediately. She's heard my car draw up.

A tingle of relief runs through me as Gilly sags, even heavier against me now. I might be fit, but by Christ she's starting to feel like a sack of potatoes.

'I'll be with you in a minute. Gilly's with me and we're both desperate for the loo.'

'Okay, love. Hi, Gilly.'

There's not even a hint of suspicion in Mum's voice. Why would there be? I've never done anything bad before.

I manhandle Gilly into the bathroom and hold her upright on the loo, watching her while she pees. She manages to do the wipe with folded toilet paper I hand to her before she slumps back onto the toilet seat. A faint giggle comes from her as I haul her minute thong up and she tries to bat my hands off.

I'm desperate for a pee myself, but I can hold on until I've sorted her out, helping her to wash and dry her hands.

Shoving her back through the bathroom door into the bedroom opposite with its two single beds I share with my big sister, and which Gilly sometimes uses while Carly is away at university, I watch as she collapses on the bed. I drag her legs around so she's lying the right way, yank off her stupid heels that are high enough to break her ankles, and flip the light cover over her. With one last look to make sure she's okay, I switch off the light and close the door behind me. Just relieved to get rid of her.

My nerves are rattled.

It's not just about Craig. Gilly has betrayed me. She's acted irresponsibly. Not just taking drugs but taking on the obligation of assuming I want anything to do with Craig, let alone become his girlfriend, or whatever crazy idea she has swimming around in her head. Why is it she just doesn't seem to get it? Just because she thinks it's right, doesn't mean it is.

Once I've paid my own visit to the loo, I dash downstairs.

Mum turns as I enter the kitchen, and her astute eyes do a quick scan of me. She's in her dressing gown, holding a mug in her hand and from the smell of it, it's hot chocolate. I reach for it and her mouth stretches into a smile as I take a sip and then hold it out to give it back to her.

'Mmmm. Nice.'

She doesn't take it. 'Keep it. I can make another. Do you think Gilly wants one?'

She turns her back while she opens the fridge and takes out a carton of milk, so she misses the shake of my head as I take another taste and settle myself at the kitchen table.

'No. She's asleep.'

Mum turns, one eyebrow shoots up to her hairline. 'Has she overdone it?'

She means booze.

'Yes.' I can't keep the weariness from my voice. This isn't the first time Gilly's drunk too much, but to my knowledge it's the first time she's taken drugs, apart from smoking a sneaky few puffs of someone's spliff since she doesn't seem to think I'll notice provided it's not her own. This, though, makes me uncomfortable as a wave of worry surges in my stomach.

As the milk heats up, Mum adds a sachet of hot chocolate and then joins me at the table.

Her gaze is full of concern. For me. For Gilly, I guess.

'That girl is heading for a crash.'

I nod my agreement and dip my head so she can't see what's on my face.

I've not known Gilly for long, as we went to different schools and it's only since last September when we started going to college together that we've become close. It's not a closeness I'm enjoying, but guilt rides hard when I think of dumping her. College breaks up for the summer shortly and I'm hoping to distance myself from her. I've got a job lined up working in the strawberry fields for the summer months so it shouldn't be too hard to give her a bit of a wide berth, in the hope that we drift rather than tear apart.

Mum knows this. I can tell by the way she watches me.

She knows Gilly's mum, who works as the housekeeper at one of the local hotels. Quite a good job by all accounts. They're not friends though. Just acquaintances.

She crosses her arms under her bosom. 'Am I to assume that's Gilly's weed I can smell on you, or have you had a go, too?' She angles her head to one side, but I can see the flint in her eye.

I puff out a breath and then blurt out what's on my mind. 'We went to a party. It was horrible, Mum. Even the parents were smoking weed and then there was an incident, glass got broken and we all got thrown out. Gilly thought it was funny, but honestly Mum, it was really serious. Horrible. She was so... embarrassing, so inappropriate. I think she might have taken something earlier. She can be a bit... odd. But this was different.'

Surprise flickers across Mum's face, but I know she's holding on to her emotions. She doesn't want to fly off the handle, so I'm forced to defend my 'friend'. No, she's going to let me dig my own hole. Then she might help me bury the body. She's supportive that way. As long as her children are all honest with her. Lying is the biggest sin in her eyes.

'What do you think she took?'

I shrug. 'I don't know. I never saw her do it, she just went all... limp. She'd not been drinking that much, we barely had a chance to, so it had to be drugs.'

'Did you ask her?' Mum is staying really chilled

about this. Maybe because it's not her daughter taking drugs.

Panic settles in and my voice gives a soft warble as I reply. 'I couldn't really get much out of her once I noticed. She was already floppy. She didn't want me to take her home in case she got into trouble.'

'Jesus.'

Mum gets to her feet, her chair scraping on the tiled kitchen floor. 'We'd better go and check on her.'

'Really? Won't it be better if we just leave her to sleep it off?' I don't want her waking and being embarrassing in front of my mum and I know she's going to be fine. Isn't she?

'No good letting her go to sleep if she isn't going to wake up.'

A chill rushes through me as I follow Mum upstairs, light-footed. Dad and Leonie are fast asleep and there's a silent agreement we won't wake them.

Unless we need to.

We slip inside mine and Carly's bedroom. My heart is hammering inside my ribs. I should have said something sooner, told Mum as soon as we walked in the door so she could see the state of my friend. I never thought beyond letting Gilly sleep it off. Have I left it too late?

Mum sits on the edge of the bed and pulls the

covers down, exposing Gilly's head, neck and shoulders.

'Gilly.' Mum gives her a gentle shake.

'Gilly.' A bit louder, and certainly quite rough this time.

My fingers are shaking as I raise them to cover my mouth. Oh God!

'Gilly.' There's an edge to Mum's voice as she gently touches her index and middle fingers to Gilly's neck as though she knows exactly what she's doing. She picks up Carly's bedside spotlight, stretching the cable across then she moves pincered fingers to Gilly's closed eyelids and prises them open, shining the light into them. I'm guessing she's been watching *ER* again.

She makes a strange humming noise in the back of her throat.

Without a word to me, Mum lowers the spotlight from Gilly's face, delves in her dressing gown pocket and taps 999 into her Nokia phone.

10

TWENTY-ONE YEARS EARLIER – JULY 2004 – CRAIG

The guy standing at the front door is the one from last night. The hippy dad from the house party. He's bigger than I remember.

My dad is by my side. His jaw is clenched, his body stiff. He can barely look at me.

Mum isn't here. She's a nurse and she's currently working the night shift at the Royal Shrewsbury Hospital.

She's going to kill me when she gets home. Of the two of them, she's actually scarier.

I tuck my hands into my jeans pocket. This guy's glare is fiercer than last night.

'So what are you going to do about it?'

My dad gives a slow turn of his head. One eyebrow quirks up. 'Son?'

He's a man of few words, my dad.

'I—' I shrug, my shoulders folding inwards as I shrink against the hallway wall to make myself smaller somehow so I won't be noticed.

But I am.

'It was an accident.'

'An accident?' The words come out as a roar from the guy on the doorstep as he moves closer.

I sense rather than see my dad puff his chest out as he steps just slightly ahead of me. I turn to look at him and realise his ire is directed at the man on the doorstep.

Buoyed by his unspoken support, I nod. 'I'm sorry, sir. The bottle slipped from my hand.'

'It didn't fucking slip, you hurled it.'

'No, I—'

'I want to know what the fuck you're going to do about it.' He stabs a finger towards my dad.

In response, my dad folds his arms across his chest. 'Calm down, mate. We don't need this.'

The other guy goes to speak, and Dad shoots a hand up in a stopping motion. 'I said, calm down.' He cranes his head to look at me. 'Craig, tell me what happened.'

'I was invited to a party. I was just about to leave when the door swung free in the wind and caught my beer bottle.' Shit. Did he notice my slip up?

'Beer bottle?'

'Yes.' My legs quake. I'm going to be grounded forever for this. Not so much that I had beer, I'm allowed one or two at home if we have a barbecue, but I'm not supposed to drink when I'm out. It's a hard and fast rule of Mum's. She says she sees far too many accidents caused by youngsters drinking. I hardly class myself as a youngster, but still…

Dad turns to the other man. 'You invited my underage son to your house, let him drink alcohol and then turn up on my doorstep to complain when something bad happens? Did you check if he'd been injured?'

Shock flashes over the other man's face, making his jowls wobble.

A little stab of pride in my dad makes me straighten up. He may secretly think I'm a loser, but he's just stepped up to defend me in front of this guy. I can't help the little grin that slips out behind his back. Perhaps a little more information might help speed this along.

'He was smoking weed. I think he was too smashed to know what happened, Dad.'

I want to laugh. Really, this big guy thinking he'd face off to my dad is about to get his arse handed to him on a plate.

Dad looks at me. His eyes narrow as he looks back at the other guy.

'So you want me to pay for damage my son caused accidentally because you not only plied him with alcohol, but you were under the influence of drugs—'

'—and drink,' I supply helpfully.

'—and drink.' My dad nods and I edge closer to the door, my confidence rising. 'So instead of contacting the police and risk getting arrested, you decide to come and shake me down for the cost of your broken windowpane.'

'It's a whole patio door glass.'

Dad's lips twist in a wry smile. The one he uses just before he's about to wipe the floor with me. Only this time, it's in defence of me. Pride surges and I stand tall, my shoulders back, chest expanding. For the first time ever, my dad is on my side.

He steps forward and I have to stand on tiptoe to see the other guy, who chooses that moment to take a retreating step.

'Claim it on your house insurance, mate, and chalk it down to experience. Don't let underage kids on your premises unless you're prepared to take grown-up responsibility for their actions, and that means remaining sober and clean yourself.' My dad's hand gives a disdainful wave in the other guy's direction. 'If you want to be a hippy, be one with your own kids in your own time, but don't put yourself in the position of being an irresponsible adult with other people's kids, specifically mine. Now, fuck off before I call the police on you for pushing drugs and alcohol on teenagers.'

He slams the door closed before the other guy can even formulate a reply.

He takes my arm and marches me down the hallway into our small kitchen.

I'm brimming with pride.

My dad stood up for me. He never even questioned whether I was telling the truth. He trusted me.

I've a broad grin on my face when he turns to look at me.

He raises one square finger and points it right at the end of my nose.

'I never want to hear another word about this. Got me?'

Wordlessly, I nod.

'Do not let your mum know. Do you hear me?' His eyes are like frozen crystals.

This time I give an enthusiastic nod. Christ, I

don't want her knowing. She'd murder me, after she gave me the Spanish Inquisition during which I definitely would fold, and the truth would come out. The whole truth. That's the way it's always been with her.

'Good. Now fuck off out of my sight for a while, before I'm tempted to thrash you.'

He wouldn't. He never has. But I don't want to tempt fate, so I turn and dash up the stairs, not even stopping to collect any food, in case he changes his mind. About any of that.

I'm grinning as I meet my own eyes in my wardrobe mirror.

My dad really likes me. He believed every word I said. He's on my side. Pride rushes through, buoying me up.

I've done nothing wrong. The accident was all that guy's fault.

I knew I was in the right.

Again.

11

PRESENT DAY – FRIDAY, 14 MARCH 2025, 5.45 P.M. – SORIAH

Luna is already at the door waiting for me when I swing it wide, actually terrified to step inside.

She circles my ankles.

I hold still and search for the threat, unable to find any before I bend to stroke my hand over her thick, cool fur.

I drop my bag to the floor, kick the door closed behind me and toss my coat over the stair newel. There's no way I'm going to open that understairs cupboard. Not while Marcus is away.

I don't want to know what monsters are lurking there.

Scooping Luna into my arms, I walk into the kitchen. I bury my face in her thick pelt for a moment, taking comfort from her before I pop her back down and grab a small sachet of the most expensive food for her. She's fussy, and only eats a few mouthfuls at a time. The rest tends to go to waste. But I love her, and she's worth it. My princess.

The girls at work had asked if I wanted to go for a drink with them tonight, with Marcus being away. Much as I would have loved to, I didn't want to come back to a dark, empty house late at night. So I made Luna my excuse, saying that I'd neglected to feed her this morning because of my run. Not that she's ever neglected. There's always dry food for her, but I wanted to get away, get home.

I never told anyone about my concerns this morning. Not even Nola. I was going to ask if she wanted to come home with me, have a girly night on the sofa, maybe stay overnight, but she took a phone call about her mum, and I could see she was distracted. She was finishing work early to visit her. I hope it's not bad news.

With it being a Friday, we barely had a moment to speak. We had too many loose ends to tie up before our presentation on Monday to our new client. It was frantic. Neither of us had the wiggle room to be distracted. Both of us were.

It's quiet in the house, but surprisingly, not oppressive as my imagination had led me to believe it was going to be.

I open the fridge door, reach in and pull out a bottle of white wine. The good one Marcus bought for a special occasion. It's the only white we have, but I don't fancy red. Not tonight. That would be too heavy.

I hesitate for a long moment, placing it on the kitchen counter while I check my messages. I sent one to Marcus at lunchtime and I've not heard anything back. Wouldn't you think he'd have just let me know he'd arrived safely?

Sod it! It's Friday night. I'm all alone and I'm going to damn well have a nice glass of wine and order in a takeaway. We rarely have one as Marcus is more of a fitness freak than I am. He's forever in the gym doing weights when he's not working overtime. He certainly hasn't been home much. No wonder he's tired.

I look after my body. I treat it well. It's got to last me a long time. But Marcus can go overboard with his fitness training. Just lately, he's dropped a few kilos and is looking as good as he did when I first met him nine years ago, apart from the fine lines around his eyes and the weariness lurking there. Sleek and toned with every muscle carved from iron. Not a great, bulging physique, but broad shoulders with defined muscles. I've always loved his shoulders. So wide. He's one of the few people who makes me feel small. Delicate even. He's not that much taller than me, but he's powerful.

His strength is in his upper body. I could outrun him in a long-distance race. Maybe not a sprint.

I order an Indian takeaway and while I'm waiting for it to arrive, I remove the cork on the wine and pour myself a glass. Condensation runs down the outside of the crystal. I take a photo of it, my long fingers positioned elegantly around the stem, and shoot it off to Marcus.

> Lonely without you babe, so I'm having a little consolation.

I wait, staring at the screen for a long while. There are two white ticks verifying it's been delivered, but they don't turn to blue to confirm he's read the message or seen the photo.

The doorbell chimes and I realise just how long I've sat staring at my screen. My glass is empty, and I blink in surprise. I don't usually drink much. I like to stay in control. Be aware. But it's okay. I'm safe here. Aren't I?

I open the door and the guy on the doorstep is

wearing a black motorbike helmet, visor down. A tremor runs through me as I snatch my meal from him, mumbling a quick thank you, desperate to shut the door.

I can still see his shadow through the glazed windowpane and I freeze, my hand pressed against the white UPVC.

My breath is stuck somewhere between my throat and my lungs. I can't breathe.

I throw the top bolt over and slip the safety chain as silently as possible, praying he doesn't ring the bell again.

He's still there.

What's he doing? Why won't he move away?

I take a step back, conscious I've left my phone in the kitchen, although goodness knows who I'm supposed to call. The mere presence of it though would be a comfort.

I wait in the dark for another long moment, terrified to move, to breathe.

He moves away and the dark shadow is gone.

Without switching on the lights, I dash into the lounge which overlooks the front of the house and watch while he mounts his motorbike and roars off.

Why did he take so long to move away?

Was he waiting for a tip? Was that it? I cover my

mouth with my hand and close my eyes. What an idiot. I never tipped the poor man, never thought about it. They earn so very little he probably depends on his tip money to keep him going.

Guilt sneaks its way through my mind, and I bat it off. Because I have to, because guilt is what got me where I am now, and I've re-trained my mind not to allow it. To block it out. Although that doesn't seem to be doing such a good job lately.

I make my way back into the kitchen and put the paper carrier bag on the small kitchen table while I pour another glass of wine and sip at it. Waiting for my heart rate to slow down. Bringing myself back under control. I wouldn't normally have more than a small glass, but a little more won't harm. Not this time.

I have no reason to feel guilty. The guy in the black helmet should have raised his visor, engaged in conversation. It's not my fault he frightened the crap out of me because he stood on my front doorstep like a sentinel and never spoke a word. That's scary shit on a good day.

I'm not having a good day.

When I pick up my phone, there's still no reply from Marcus. Irritation stirs in my chest.

Jeez. I know he's busy, but doesn't he take a moment out of his fun day to look at his messages? Doesn't he think about his wife? It may be a work function, but I'd have liked to have known that he misses me. Even for a moment.

Normally you can't pry his phone from his hand. Because his job is so important. Lately, it feels like I'm not. Maybe circumstances have brought out my own self-pity and I should push that to one side. Am I the one who has caused this? Is it me who has made him the important one in the relationship, so it takes the pressure off me? I can hardly blame him in that case.

I serve up my takeaway and rid myself of all the negative thoughts invading my mind as I take the first few mouthfuls. The food is incredible from The Taj Mahal, and I'm determined to enjoy it.

I have another sip of wine and just as I swallow, the warm contents of my stomach lurches up to meet the cold liquid.

Puke sprays out all over the small kitchen table and I leap to my feet, overturning the wooden chair as I cup my hand over my face, trying to get to the kitchen sink before I spew anything more out of my mouth.

I've hardly eaten much at all, but I don't seem to be able to stop from being sick. I retch. Gagging while my stomach heaves in painful contractions and tears stream down my face, until I'm done. Wrung out.

As I hover, lifeless, over the sink, my mind races.

What the hell have I eaten to cause this? Have I picked up a stomach bug? Because other than throwing up, I really feel fine in between bouts of sickness. In any case, it was days ago I was first sick and I've felt fine in between. Except for occasional nausea if I move suddenly.

I splash my face with cold water, gasping with shock.

I've eaten nothing virtually all day. I've been absolutely fine. A little tired, but that was probably due to stress and that long run this morning. This morning when I ate one slice of toast and threw up. Again.

I straighten.

I gaze at the mess surrounding me and gag. Oh God. How awful.

As I clean up, I put the cork back in the bottle which I slide into the fridge. The mere thought of it makes my throat spasm.

By the time I've finished, the place smells of bleach and lemon disinfectant.

I check my phone. Nothing. Why hasn't he called, or messaged?

Misery washes over me.

By this time, Marcus is probably at the dinner and awards presentations, so I can't expect him to respond. But why hasn't he replied before now? When he dashed to the loo, when he got changed into his tux, which I watched him pack?

I slip my phone into my back pocket and inspect my spotless kitchen.

My mind is numb, pushing back on the possibilities I've not considered until now.

I make my way upstairs, to our en suite bathroom, because that's the only place I keep what I need right now.

A few minutes later, I'm staring at the stick that I've peed on, which has developed two bright blue lines.

Tears roll down my cheeks and I cover my face with my hands.

Unbelieving.

This is the most incredible news in the world. I'm pregnant. I'm laughing and crying at the same time. How is it possible when, at the point we'd just about given up, I'm pregnant?

I want to laugh and cry and dance and hug Marcus tight to me. Because we're going to have a baby!

My phone buzzes and I jump, excitement

screaming through me as I reach for where I left it next to the pregnancy testing box which had been in the cupboard for months, until I placed it carefully, thoughtfully, on the little shelf above the sink.

My heart is singing. It's Marcus. Oh my God. What am I going to say? Should I tell him now?

I turn my phone over and pause. There's a message from a number I don't recognise with no name identifying them. I frown as I see there's a photograph attached.

When I click on the photo, the blood in my veins turns to ice.

The caption underneath reads:

Recognise anyone here?

12

TWENTY-ONE YEARS EARLIER – AUGUST 2004 – SORIAH

'Oh, come on!'

I shake my head. 'I don't want to go on a blind date.'

Gilly refuses to listen to me. 'I don't understand why.'

'Because last time you set me up on a blind date, he was a snot-nosed, pimple-ridden twat.'

'I don't think he can be a twat, technically.'

'Stop nitpicking. You know what I mean.'

'But I've already agreed,' she whines.

'Since when have you become my pimp?'

She ignores my words.

I'm surprised her parents have even allowed her out. My mum told me if I'd pulled a stunt like that and ended up in hospital having my stomach pumped, she'd have grounded me until my twenty-first birthday. I believe her. Then again, I'd never dream of doing something so irresponsible. I simply can't understand Gilly taking something from a lad who is, let's face it, odd.

Somehow, though, Gilly managed to convince her parents that none of it was her responsibility and that her drink had been spiked, or someone had slipped something into her food. None of which made sense. She had a bottle of beer in her hand at the party, the lid had just been popped by me. I didn't drug her. Nor did anyone else. She did it all by herself. By her own admission – to me. But she wasn't going to tell her parents that and it would make me a snitch to go behind her back and let them know the truth.

Mum is on my side, of course, but she thinks Gilly might have learnt her lesson and just needs a second chance.

I'm not so sure. Call me judgemental, but there seems to be no remorse. She's carrying on as though nothing happened.

It's been two weeks since she was hospitalised, and the event seems to have been hushed up. No one talks about it. No one wants to acknowledge it. Least of all Gilly's parents, who, apart from when we all met up at the hospital that night, have never discussed it with me again. Like if they don't talk about it, it didn't happen.

It did.

I'd hoped to distance myself from her during the summer holidays, but she's managed to get a job working alongside me in the strawberry fields. I don't know how she managed to swing that because I thought they told me I was the last one on their payroll. Anyway, this means I don't stand a chance of escaping her.

Not only that, but she's become super clingy.

I saved her life. That's her mantra. It doesn't make me proud, or happy. I didn't save her life, my mum did, because I probably would have left her sorry arse to sleep it off and she could have died in her sleep. Or not. Who knows, because I certainly hadn't realised the danger she was in. Gilly, though, isn't the kind of girl to die in her sleep. When Gilly dies, everyone will know about it. She's going to be one of those types of people who has a memorable death, one people will speak about for years.

Since the incident, I've made it clear I'm not going out on a weeknight, which has restricted me to staying at home now just in case she catches me out. Weekend nights are all hers. And I do mean all hers. She's so damned demanding. Clingy. She wants to go to every party going. Apparently, her near-death experience has inspired her to live life to its fullest.

She's found herself a new boyfriend, too. Poor Kev.

Neil is another biker.

She's convinced she's a biker chick now and wants me to join the in-crowd. I'm reluctant. In fact, I'm darn right protesting against it, digging my heels in as deep as I can.

'Come on, Soriah, you know you want to.'

Her voice turns whiny again. Maybe it's meant to be cajoling but to me it's irritating. She does this to me every time, it's a little guilt trip she has perfected. Because I do feel guilty. She almost died because of something stupid she did, but something I could have stopped her from doing if I'd been on my toes, more aware.

'I hate blind dates, Gilly, I really do. I don't want to go.' Just because she's hooked up with someone doesn't mean we all want to be. I'm quite happy single. I can do what I want, when I want. She's shackled to Neil.

The irony of it strikes me. I'm shackled to her. I do her every bidding and Gilly is demanding.

'You do!' she insists and reaches across to pinch the inside of my thigh.

I jerk back, my teeth snapping closed. She bloody well annoys me.

'Don't do that!' Honestly, I don't know what compels her to do that, but it's really getting to me.

I glance at her and her narrow blue eyes have filled with tears.

'Jesus. Stop that.'

If my mum tells me to stop with the tears, I stop. Gilly does not.

I'm not exactly sure if I can continue this friendship, but really I don't have any other close friends right now.

Is that because she's chased them all off?

Perhaps it will be different when we return to college. I've not seen anything of Nola as she refuses to go out with Gilly. They really don't get along.

I sigh as I stare up at the bright blue cloudless sky above. We're sitting on top of a stack of hay bales waiting to be collected by the strawberry farmer to take us all back up to the farm so we can get off home. Our twelve-hour day is almost over, and apart from Gilly's incessant chatter, this could have been such a peaceful half hour. It's been a blazing day and all I want is to rest, put my head down, smell the hay and drift off under the pink-streaked sky. But Gilly just won't shut up.

'What's he going to think of me? They're going to think I'm stupid. They won't talk to me any more.'

I know already that I'm not going to win this, but I try one more argument.

'You can still go with Neil.'

'I can't.' Her voice turns to a pitiful wail. 'Neil's already at the pub. He's gone on his bike and you know I'm not allowed on the back until he gets a spare helmet. They're so expensive and he won't buy one for me.' She sounds like a spoilt brat and honestly, why should he buy her a helmet? She'll dump him in a few weeks. He probably knows that. Gilly's not into long-term relationships. She's not a slut, she simply has such a short attention span and if they can't keep her entertained, she looks for someone who can. They're all very enthusiastic to start with until they realise quite how energetic she is.

'I need you to drive me there. It's outside of town.' She shoulder-bumps me and I groan. 'Go on. It's in Little Wenlock.'

I push my tongue against the inside of my cheek to stop me from snapping her head off.

Of course she needs me. I'm about the only one who's passed their driving test and actually has a car at my disposal. It's a really old Renault Clio that my dad managed to pick up cheap for me from someone at work, but I love it. It's more than most kids have. Fuel isn't cheap though so my use of it is limited.

'I'll give you some money towards petrol.'

Last time she promised that, it never materialised. I don't want to cause an argument, so I keep quiet about it and use another tack instead.

'I can't get four of us in my car.' I know Neil has gone on his bike, but if he's drinking, I bet he'll want to leave it there and cadge a ride home with us. I've known Gilly's boyfriends say this kind of thing before and then my poor car has to limp its way home with the weight of two grown men in the back. And I know they will be big men, because that's what Gilly likes. She loves to feel petite and doll-like. That's one of the reasons she likes me. I'm her foil.

'You don't need to. There's only us two. Well, we'll meet Neil there, but we need to pick up your date on the way.'

'What's the name of my date?'

Her laughter tinkles out as she flicks her fine blonde hair back. It's grown quite a bit in the last few weeks, and it bobs wildly around her head in loose coils.

'That would spoil the whole idea of a blind date.

You'll find out later. First though, I need to see if I can grab Eddie, I think he's the one who can forge ID.'

You'd think she'd have learnt her lesson. She may not take drugs again, who knows, but nothing has curtailed her drinking.

And she will be drinking, and I won't because that is the strictest rule of all time. If I so much as have a sip of alcohol and my dad finds out, he'll take the car away from me and sell it. It's in his name, not mine, so he can do it.

Not that I would in any case.

It means I'll be on the ginger beer and lime and Gilly will be sneaking vodka, because she's not eighteen yet. She's the youngest in our class, and I'm the eldest.

I let out a slow breath and she knows she has me.

'We can't be late back.' I have a curfew of 10.30 p.m. if I'm driving. As my dad says, it's not my driving ability he's concerned about, but I only passed my driving test four months ago and I'm not that experienced. Especially at night. Particularly with passengers who might distract me. And we all know how distracting Gilly can be.

She reaches over and does that quick, mean pinch and I jump. My inner thighs have nasty little bruises and truth be told, I'm fed up with it.

I should say something, but I'm biding my time. I feel that if I open my mouth, everything will just spill out, all my anger and animosity will rage and she'll be left devastated. That isn't me. I don't like to upset people. I'd hoped it wouldn't come to that. Instead, I hold my tongue. I'm trying to do this in the most delicate way I can. It's just really hard.

Resigned, I ask, 'What time are we going?'

'I said we'd be there at eight.'

I sigh again. 'I'll pick you up. You know where we're going?' I don't have one of those new Tom Tom navigators, they cost almost as much as my old car, so I can't afford one. Dad says what's the point when you have a perfectly good map book in the glove compartment? One I can't read, because who reads maps these days?

She leaps to her feet, a bright grin on her face and her blonde ringlets bounce along with her boobs. 'Yep. See you later.'

She leaps down the steps the bales have been stacked into and dashes off to jump on the back of the tractor, grinning at me as I make my way to join the others up there while my heart fills with dread. I wonder what kind of dregs she's scraped from the bottom of the barrel this time.

It isn't long until I find out.

* * *

I was late picking Gilly up, partly because I didn't want to go, and I was holding out for some kind of emergency that would forestall me. Fate did not come to my rescue. Nor would it ever.

We pull up outside a small cottage, situated on its own down a long, narrow lane, and I turn the engine off, unclipping my seatbelt. It's just a short walk into the village where the local pub is. Literally, we just passed it, and it took three minutes to drive here. I don't know why this blind date of mine couldn't have walked and met us there.

Gilly checks her little Nokia phone. Unlike her, I can't afford one. Maybe that's one advantage to being an only child. You get whatever you want. I think I prefer having siblings and no phone. Gilly always seems to be under pressure to reply. To do its bidding.

'We're really late,' she complains. 'Neil's already there and he says he's going to leave if I'm not there in the next five minutes. You wait here and I'll go and grab him.'

I don't understand why we're not meeting this guy at the pub, too.

Gilly is the most disorganised person. Ditzy, I would call her.

I'm just about to tell her to text my blind date and cancel when she flings open the passenger door and leaps out, slamming it behind her hard enough to make my car rock and roll, and takes off down the dirt track lane in the direction we've just come, her voice tinkling with mischievous laughter.

'Best blind date ever. You'll see!'

What the hell?

'Gilly?' I lean my head out of the open window. 'Gilly!'

Stupid cow! What the hell is wrong with her? How does she find this so funny?

I grit my teeth, annoyance getting the better of me. There's no way I'm hanging around here waiting for some stranger to turn up. I'll drive to the pub and if he really wants to meet me, he can walk there. Where it's sensible.

If I catch up with Gilly on the way, I may just mow her down for the fun of it.

I turn the key to fire the engine again, but considering how short her legs are, that girl can move and she's already disappeared around the bend.

Anger burns inside. What an idiot! Me, that is, not her. Why do I fall for her antics?

That's it! I'm not having this any more. She's manipulated me one time too many. I'm not picking up some stranger down a bloody back lane and I'm not going to the pub. Gilly can walk home as far as I'm concerned. Fury pumps my blood through my veins, firing everything up including my temper. How bloody irresponsible of her. This friendship is playing out its last dying throes. I'm done.

As I turn to yank my seatbelt around me once more, the passenger door whips open and my little Renault Clio bounces with the weight of someone flopping onto the front seat next to me, rust grinding as the suspension groans under the weight. A weight a darn sight heavier than little Gilly.

I gasp, whipping around to face my 'blind date'.

My heart stops.

'**Fuck**.'

I barely get that one word out before Craig Lane reaches across and touches something to my neck.

Electricity buzzes through me and my legs jerk. My feet jiggle against the pedals of the car, sending it leapfrogging several metres along the dirt track. My whole body contorts and my face whacks against the steering wheel, sending pain shimmering through my body.

The last conscious thought I have is that I've broken my nose and it's bleeding all over my shorts.

Then there is nothing.

13

PRESENT DAY – FRIDAY, 14 MARCH 2025, 8.45 P.M. – SORIAH

I haven't moved from where I slid down onto the bathroom floor I don't know how long ago.

In one hand I hold my positive pregnancy test and in the other I still stare at the photograph of my husband. My handsome husband with a woman in his arms. She's shorter than me, but most women are. She has long, dark blonde hair that swings loose away from her body as though the photograph was taken with her in motion. It's a partial sideways shot and the back of the woman's head is turned to the camera and the image blurs as I pincer my fingers to expand the screen.

I've done that several times since I've been sitting here.

I need to move. My limbs have stiffened and I'm cold. I shudder a little and then get clumsily to my feet.

Luna is fast asleep on my side of the bed, but when I walk in, she opens one eye to look at me. 'I told you so,' that look says. She's never really taken to Marcus. I'm the one she prefers, even though I bought her for him as a birthday present. Really, only so I could have a cat. It was a bit naughty of me, I suppose, but it worked and he's not unhappy about the situation, merely ambivalent.

I slip out of my clothes and into pyjamas, pulling my thick, fleecy dressing gown over the top.

I'm cold. Colder than I've been all winter. It's not as though the heating isn't on, but being sick and the shock has sent shivers from the core of me outwards until my whole body is racked with the shakes.

I have to stop this. It can't be good for the baby. The baby I've desperately wanted for so long. A baby I thought my husband was also keen on.

Slipping under the bedcovers, I ignore Luna as she huffs at me and moves reluctantly, barely waiting for me to settle before she curls herself into a tight ball between my knees.

My phone lies where I tossed it when I walked out

of the bathroom. Just within my reach. Do I want to look again?

Yes.

I can't resist. I need to look at that image, even though it's branded on my mind.

Marcus's head is tilted down, one hand raised so his finger rests under the chin of the woman whose arms are looped casually around his waist.

There's something familiar there, I'm sure.

I squint at the image.

My heart contracts. That's one of his moves. What Marcus does when he's just about to lean in for a kiss from me. He places his forefinger under my chin and kisses me. I've always found it so endearing. So tender.

I'm much taller than this woman, but he's still taller than me by several inches, so in this photograph he towers over her.

A quiet sob escapes me and I slide further down the bed, making Luna hiss as I disturb her. I edge one leg under her form, despite her soft growls, so I can turn over onto my side as she re-settles herself behind my knees.

Why has this happened?

Why now?

My eyelids slide closed as warmth envelopes me,

Luna's heat seeping through the covers in soothing comfort.

I don't know what I'm going to do, but it's too late to phone Mum tonight. I don't want to upset her. There's no point both of us having a restless night, is there?

I'll speak with her in the morning.

Sleep comes to claim me.

I float down, down, down.

Then I slip off a kerb, my eyes fly open, and I sit bolt upright in bed.

Luna leaps off the bed with an angry hiss, and stalks out of the bedroom door, sick of the continual disturbance, and I stare at the wall opposite for a long moment before the reason I was jolted awake comes back to me. I snatch up my phone and look again.

Marcus is not in Brighton, because that restaurant in the background is one we've been to on several occasions. It's where his main office is in Birmingham, not the hub he uses in Shrewsbury. He wouldn't risk going anywhere too close, but there he is. In Birmingham by The Postbox. Gas Street Basin, it's called, where all the trendy restaurants and bars overlook the canal.

My stomach hitches but doesn't quite heave. I'm

not going to let it. I'm so over being sick. I may be pregnant, but I don't have to suffer.

I swing my feet out of bed and slide them into my old-lady slippers. I pad downstairs and take two dry crackers out of a fresh packet and wrap them in clingfilm, popping them into my dressing gown pocket to take upstairs. I remember my granny telling me that when she was pregnant, she never took a step out of bed until she'd eaten two dry crackers. It may be complete bullshit, but I'm willing to try anything to stop me throwing up.

I take out another two crackers and stand in front of the sink nibbling them.

At the same time, my mind is nibbling at the edges of my dilemma.

There's something off about that whole photograph.

I take my phone out of my pocket and zoom in again.

My mind is screaming.

What the hell is wrong with this scenario?

I type in the hotel name that Marcus is staying at and dial the number.

'Hello, Hotel Regency, how may I help?'

'Hi, could you put me through to Marcus Bentley,

please? I don't think he can get a signal on his phone. This is his wife calling.'

The line goes silent for a while.

'Hello? Mrs Bentley?'

'Speaking.'

'I'm sorry to inform you—'

Blood pounds in my ears and I can barely make out what the man on the other end of the phone is saying.

'I beg your pardon, could you say that again?'

'Sorry, it's a little loud here, lots of background noise. I said I'm sorry I can't disturb him unless it's an emergency as I've just been informed that he's currently up on stage in our main function room making a speech.'

My heartbeat slows down and I sink into the kitchen chair, relief weakening my limbs until I am like a melted pot of caramel. Loose and sticky.

'Thank you. I'm sure he'll call me when he's free. It's nothing urgent.' The rest of what I say tumbles from lips numb and icy.

I tap the red off icon and lower my head to the table.

He's not in Birmingham. He's in Brighton, where he said he would be.

My husband is not currently with another

woman. He's up on stage giving an acceptance speech for being voted Salesman of the Year.

My insides bunch at the cruelty I've just suffered at being led to believe my husband is with another woman.

Who would do that? Who would want to hurt me so much?

I raise my head and stare at my phone screen.

If Marcus is in Brighton, then where did this photograph come from? When was it taken?

Photoshopping is so easy these days. Is it real?

More to the point: who sent it? And what would they gain by hurting me?

14

TWENTY-ONE YEARS EARLIER – AUGUST 2004 – SORIAH

It's dark in here. And silent.

So silent I have no idea where the hell I am.

Except I am half on my side, curled in a ball in a tight space.

The soft caress of something brushing against my face has me jerking upright. A scream lodges in my throat as it has nowhere else go.

Thick, sticky tape covers my mouth, and my panicked breaths can't get out. Air cannot get in.

My nose is stuffed so thick with blood, I can taste it in the back of my throat, but I can't pull in oxygen.

I have to stop!

I have to stop panicking.

Stop struggling.

But I can't and I thrash about, kicking out with my bound feet, elbowing the sides of whatever box I am in. From the echoes, it's wood. I'm in a wooden box.

I'm going to die! I'm going to die!

That thing touches my face again and I freeze.

Stop!

Calm down.

Breathe.

I'm an athlete. My body has been educated to remain in control.

I squeeze my eyes tight and let out a whimper. What a load of shit! I have no control.

White sparks flicker behind my tightly closed eyes. They spring wide open, but it's pitch black.

I turn my face and press my cheek against whatever keeps touching me. Investigate.

Some kind of material.

I hold still and draw more air in through my nose. If I slow down, just concentrate on each breath, then I will survive. If I panic, I will die.

The sparkles dissipate, leaving me alone in the dark.

Alone to think.

I pull in another breath and the musky aroma of the material curls around my senses.

I'm braced on one side, one elbow on the base of

my prison, curled into a foetal position with my cheek squished against one wooden wall and my bum wedged against another. I'm in a wooden box. I rub my face against the material, and it moves. Something above me rattles.

I wriggle until I'm more upright, stopping every few seconds, purely to breathe before I move again, until I'm on my backside instead of my numb hip, propped up against one side of the wooden box. At the movement, my nose drains of snot and blood, flooding my throat until my eyes water. I can't swallow quick enough to get rid of it without choking. But I can't choke, so I swallow, and swallow.

A cool relief floods my nose as suddenly the plug of mucus and snot moves and I can breathe again. I pull air in with deep controlled sniffs, letting it fill my lungs before I release it. I'm an athlete, I chant to myself because I have nothing else I want to concentrate on right now. I know how to do this breathing. It is the only thing I have control of.

The secret is to keep calm. Keep calm.

I stretch my legs and whimper as white-hot pain radiates in pulse waves. Pins and needles shoot through my left foot, and if I could gasp, I would, but my mouth is sealed shut with that sticky tape that's peeled the skin from my lips.

There are more important things to think about though. Like what the hell am I doing here, and how do I escape?

I take a moment to assess my surroundings, shutting off the fear that threatens to rise up and consume me.

I'm in some sort of box. Oh, dear God, don't let it be a coffin.

Adrenaline rushes through me and I'm not sure I can control the fear that's threatening to tip over into hysteria. Everything inside me trembles.

I have to stay calm. I have to take control.

Everything hurts so much, as though a lightning bolt has hit me.

My muscles stiffen and the memory zaps back in.

That's exactly what it was.

I blink hard and Craig's face flashes in my mind's eye, almost blinding me with the intensity. Like an electric shock.

I was hit by a taser. That cowardly bastard hit me with a taser because that's the only way he would have been able to overpower me. I'm fitter, stronger than Craig and on a normal day, I could take him.

He knew that and he chose to take another course of action.

My breath catches in the back of my throat and I

cry out, the sound muffled by the gag covering my mouth.

Pain of a different sort squeezes my heart, and tears trickle down my face.

Oh my God, what did Gilly do? She's supposed to be my best friend and she's abandoned me. Worse. How could she?

She not only led me into a trap, she threw me down a hole and laughed as she walked away.

I can hear that tinkling laughter, as though she'd just played a prank.

Well, this was no prank.

The bitch!

Tears stream from my eyes as I hunch over in the enclosed space. I'm not sure I can bear the thought of what Gilly has done. She's a traitor. For her own amusement and satisfaction, she's literally thrown me to the wolves, or wolf in this case. It's almost as bad as what he's done.

Almost.

Then again...

I raise my head as I become aware of stickiness between my thighs and that thick smell of male hormones that infuses the men's changing room at college, seeping out of the door and along the corridor to the female changing room.

Saliva rushes into my mouth and I freeze, willing myself not to be sick. Being sick could kill me. I could choke to death on my own vomit.

I squeeze my eyes closed. Visions flash in my mind's eye, tormenting me. Craig wrestling my short summer dress up until it covers my face. His own face contorted and maniacal as the material drops away and he is grunting and straining above me, sweat dripping from his forehead into my eyes.

My knickers, torn and useless, lying next to me on a single bed in a small room.

Quiet whimpers slip from my lips against the stickiness of the tape binding them.

I've been raped.

Craig Lane raped me.

Almost worse than that, my best friend facilitated that rape.

I hate him with a vengeance, but I'll never forgive her.

15

PRESENT DAY – SATURDAY, 15 MARCH 2025, 8.45 A.M. – SORIAH

I know I could ring my mum and have a chat, but if I do that, I'll end up telling her I'm pregnant, and that's not fair to Marcus. He should be the first to know.

I can't tell Marcus on two counts. One, he's not even responded to my messages, and two, I don't want to tell him over the phone. This should be a special moment. Something the two of us should share. Quiet, intimate time. I want to see his face, feel his reaction, because honestly, although there's a bubbling anger at the fact I've not heard from him, I'm sure there's a plausible reason and once that's resolved, he's going to be as delighted and excited as I am. I can't even imagine what Marcus is going to say after all this time.

Just as his name slides into my mind, my phone rings.

I jerk so hard, I know I'm not as calm as I'm trying to be.

It's not a number I recognise. Nor is it the number that I was sent the photo from last night.

I stare while the phone buzzes in my hand.

Sod it.

I swipe to answer.

'Hello!' I put on my professional, no-nonsense voice and I'm ready to cut them off if there's that slight pause between them answering which indicates they're calling from an Indian call centre.

'Hello, Soriah?'

'Marcus?' My voice is high-pitched and scratchy.

'Yes, yes, it's me. I tried to get hold of you yesterday, but there was no answer. I had my phone stolen when I stopped at the services on the way here. I've had to jump through hoops to get things sorted. I almost missed my own bloody presentation.'

He's breathless and I can hear the agitation in his voice. 'I went into a phone shop. All I wanted was a bloody replacement phone and they faffed around for bloody ages, kids really, who think they know it all, insisting I had to cancel everything, change everything so that my bloody stolen phone blows up or something before anyone can get into it and access all my worldly goods. What a fucking kerfuffle!'

My lips twitch at the strangeness of that expression. Where on earth has he picked that up?

'Is it all sorted now?' I ask, keeping my voice low and soothing, because this is what Marcus needs right now. He is apt to go off at the deep end and he doesn't need anything from me right now apart from my attention and calmness.

'No, it's bloody not. Apparently, someone got into it before I got it sorted and they've somehow withdrawn money from my bank account.'

My skin goes icy as I lower myself into the kitchen chair.

'How much did they take?'

'A thousand pounds.'

'Jesus!'

'I know!'

'From our joint account?'

'Does it really fucking matter where the money comes from?' he explodes.

I'm silent for a moment while I listen to his heavy breaths down the phone, hoping that he's regretting his outburst because quite honestly, I'm really insulted that he's speaking to me like this.

He's so dramatic. Lately, his temper straddles a line.

Mine is quite under control when I speak. 'It does matter, Marcus, because our credit card bill goes out tomorrow and if we don't have enough to pay it in full, like we do every month—' like I set it up to do because he's useless with money '—then we'll have to pay interest.'

'Fuck the interest.' But his voice has lost its heat. He sighs and I can imagine him running his hand through his hair with frustration. 'No, it wasn't the joint account. It was mine, which is just as well, because I was pretty brassic and they took all I had left in the account plus the overdraft limit. They maxed it before we could stop them.'

'So what happens now?'

'The bank will refund it, but it'll take a while. The guy in the phone shop made me report it to the police, so they gave me an incident number to use when letting everyone know. I think we stopped them just in time before they did hit the joint account.'

I blow out a breath because that would have been a hell of a lot more than a thousand pounds. My salary went into the account two days ago and Marcus's is due – today.

'It could be worse.' I try to reassure him.

'What could be worse, Soriah? I've just been robbed.'

'Yes, but you're going to get it back, you said the bank will sort it.'

'It's ruined my fucking weekend away.'

His weekend away.

'I—' I realise the futility of trying to assuage his misery, knowing there is nothing I say that will make him feel better. I can only thank heavens I didn't mention the baby over the phone.

I don't need any negativity as far as this baby is concerned.

I slip my hand over a flat belly and smile. For now, it's my little secret. Just me and this tiny jellybean that hasn't even developed yet.

'Did you hear me?'

'What?' I jump as Marcus's irritated voice pierces the line.

'No, sorry, I—' I raise my glass of water to my lips and give a slurp as I strain it through my teeth to make a hissing noise. I sometimes use this tactic if my team leader rings me in the evening from work. She can have a few minutes, but I don't get paid any extra for that half hour of my time in the evening. 'Have you moved?' I smile and water drips from my lips. 'The line isn't so good. It's breaking up.' I want to laugh because it's so juvenile of me.

The heavy sigh on the other end of the line certainly doesn't break up.

'Look, I've got to go. They've got all sorts going on today. Apparently, they've arranged for us to have a ride on a flaming Ferris wheel. Who the fuck thought we'd want to do that?'

'Do you mean the Brighton Eye? It's not a Ferris wheel…'

'Anyway, all is fine here.' He cuts me off mid explanation. 'Speak when I get back. Don't wait up.'

I lower my phone to look at the blank screen. He's gone.

He never even asked me how I was. If I was okay.

The whole weekend opens like a yawning mouth ahead of me.

I have nothing to do. Nowhere to go. Not if I want to keep this wonderful secret to myself until I have chance to see Marcus. I feel as though my husband has deprived me of companionship while he's away, because his waspishness has stopped me from telling him our wonderful news.

Luna appears on the kitchen surface next to me, a silent ghost who prowls the house. Never a threat, more of a guard.

She butts her head against my chin.

I smile and lift my phone as she does it again to catch a quick selfie, zapping it through to Mum, who adores Luna. She's the one who Luna always goes to if Marcus and I are on holiday or grabbing a quick weekend away. Luna is quite happy in Mum and Dad's house, her home from home.

An instant reply comes back with a cuddle emoji. This is the kind of contact I have with Mum. Every day we send a quick message. We're both busy – she still works full time as a private carer to a little boy with disabilities. She gives so much more of her time than she's paid for, but she loves him.

She loves her three daughters too, but I know if I don't send a quick message each day, she will worry about me. She worries about me more than my sisters. Still, after all these years. I wish she wouldn't. But she sees the signs when I'm in a decline. She knows what to look out for, unlike anyone else I know.

Carly, my eldest sister, prefers to ignore what happened to me. But that's okay with me. I understand. She never wants to speak about it. I think she lives with the guilt that she wasn't there when I needed her the most. She was backpacking with her friends on her break from university, unable to protect her younger sister. I don't look at it that way. It's not her fault. She needs to live her life and I know that. So we talk on the phone quite often, maybe once a week, and we never, ever mention the past.

Leonie, my younger sister, has two little girls, Sasha, four and Layla, three, and I see the look of fear in her eyes when I visit. Unlike Carly, who I know has a different attitude towards her kids, it's as though what happened to me automatically qualifies Leonie's girls to be affected by it.

Leonie was terribly scarred by what happened to me. She went to counselling for almost as long as I did.

In the end, I figured if I wanted to live my life and not allow Craig to destroy me, then I needed to get on with it. Get out there. Face the world. Not let him dictate my story.

Some days, I can't get past the memories. Or I'm triggered. Most days, though, the thought is on the periphery of my mind, never quite gone, but not dominating either.

That's what Mum looks for in my short messages to her. I've learnt to control that too. I don't want my mum's life to be about me. She's going to be sixty next year.

Strange how sometimes it's these family get-togethers that trigger me. The gathering of the whole family. People who know about my hidden past in more detail than I ever want them to.

I stare at the photo of Luna and me for a moment before I forward it to Marcus's new number.

Nothing.

He's not even read it.

I know he said he needed to get on, but he's away and he never even asked how I am. Unlike my mum, he's oblivious to any emotional trigger points.

Like getting pregnant.

Which he doesn't know about yet, not until I break it to him.

He's going to be so excited. His first baby.

But there's something else he doesn't know.

This is not my first baby. I've been pregnant before.

16

TWENTY-ONE YEARS EARLIER – AUGUST 2004 – SORIAH

With insidious slowness, my muscles tighten as blackness descends, turning what I thought was already a dark box into midnight.

My eyes flutter closed. After all, what's the point of keeping them open when I have no vision?

I list sideways, my head leaning against the rough material of whatever is hanging in the wardrobe.

It smells of him, making me want to vomit, but I'm too tired to care. I've no idea how long I've been here in this stifling box, since the last time he threw open the door, zapped me with the taser, dragging me out, this time only as far as the bedroom floor where he raped me again.

His hot, flushed face filled with sick pleasure as

he pounded inside me, declaring his undying love. His promises to treat me like a prized possession if only I would love him back.

The mistake I made was trying to scream the moment he removed the tape from my mouth to offer me water.

My head pounds from where he smashed it against the floor. My thirst is an anger, burning inside with nothing to extinguish it.

His declaration of love sickens me, as it sickened me the first time I was told by Mr Sharma that Craig only grabbed me and snogged me because he loved me. That's not love, that's obsession, and if that teacher had kept his eyes wide open and witnessed the extent of the obsession, none of this would have happened.

My anger stokes as I think of my best friend. She aided him, also believing it was love.

This is not love.

I can barely raise my head now.

I'd had plans of overpowering him. Craig is not a big guy. He's average size, average height. Under any other circumstances I could have taken him. But for the taser he uses freely and the fact that I am now depleted. Dehydrated in a way I have never been before. Because I'm a runner, I know how to treat my body. It's a temple. Keep it hydrated. Exercise it. Nurture it.

It shouldn't be abused like this.

I'm not saying I've never had sex. I have. Once. I wasn't that keen and there was a lot of blood, sweat and grunting. A bit like Craig. Only it was consensual the time I did it with Olly Featherstone on the back seat of his car.

Why then did he become possessive too? What is it with boys? They seem to want all of you. To control rather than enjoy.

I had to be really harsh with Olly to make him understand I wasn't the one for him. He was tall and handsome, and he went out with Gilly for a short while after, probably having sex with her too. But it wasn't her he wanted and deep down, I think she sensed that. He wanted to go out with her to be close to me. She dumped him pretty quickly.

I wasn't harsh with Craig. We'd barely so much as had a conversation before that day. I have a vague recollection of him on our first day, but that was it. I'd been aware of his furtive looks and long stares, of him undressing me with his eyes. I never had a moment to speak to him after he leapt on me. Kissed me. Assaulted me. Perhaps if I had taken him to one side at that party and had harsh words with him, but he was drunk and stoned out of his mind, slavering all over the place. And violent too. Perhaps if I had laid my cards on the table though, he wouldn't have believed he could get away with it. He's fooled both Mr Sharma and Gilly. Got them on his side.

It just goes to show what a manipulator he is.

But none of that is going to help me now.

Now, I'm crouched in the dark, cramp torturing my legs while I wait for the next time Craig drags me out to declare his undying love for me.

Love! Pah!

The raucous sound of snores fills the air, and I sag with relief. Nothing more is going to happen tonight. He's asleep.

A slow tear trickles down my cheek.

I've peed myself. Not for the first time since I've been in here. I don't know for how long, but I'm desperate again. I need a shit too.

I want to go home and have a shit in my own toilet. Is that too much to ask?

Mum and Dad must wonder where I am. They'll be worried sick. I wonder what Carly will do. Will she race home from university? Will Leonie cry for me?

Will I ever see them again?

As I fall asleep, I know I will wake with a crick in my neck from the angle it's lolling against the wooden panel in the wardrobe. That's the least of my worries. At least now I know for definite that it's a wardrobe as I lay staring up at it from the outside for some time earlier.

I also know he'll be coming for me again. I'm not sure I'll survive it.

When I open eyes thick with dried-on gunk, there's a grainy light squeezing its way through the crack in the wardrobe door.

My head is thick with confusion, but I do know one thing.

Something disturbed me.

'Fuck, fuck, fuck.' His voice is muffled and panicked.

He's awake. My heart gives a pitiful attempt at racing, but it really is weak. I am so weak. I've had nothing to eat or drink in all the time I've been here and I think I'm losing my mind.

How long can a person survive without food and water?

Will I die in here?

Angling my ear against that crack, I listen to what sounds like rustling of bedclothes while fear slices through Craig's voice.

'Yes, I'm here, Mum.'

Mum?

My eyes pop open.

He's talking to his mum. Where the hell did she come from? Has she been here all the time? Does she know about me?

'Hold on, I'm not dressed!' From the frantic tone, I'm guessing she doesn't.

Hope swoops on hurried wings as I jerk upright, a quiver of electricity jolting me awake.

A flurry of activity has me pressing my ear closer.

The swift bang of a door, the yell of Craig's voice joins his mum's higher pitch.

Is she berating him?

'I thought you weren't back until Tuesday.' He sounds harried.

'Your dad's car broke down. We got towed back home last night by the AA. I didn't want to disturb you. We didn't get in until three.'

I wish to God she had disturbed him then, woken him up.

'You're going to be late for college. Get off with you. I'll tell you all about it tonight over dinner.'

'I—' There's doubt in his voice. 'Aren't you going to work?'

'No. I'm not wasting my holiday. It's a bloody nuisance breaking down, we were having such a good time. But I'm going to get some gardening done. Weeds don't pull themselves.'

'Uh, okay—'

I can feel his hesitation, almost visualise him hovering at the door.

'Come on, Craig, get out of here. I'll see you later.'

Her voice fades as I assume she walks away. I want to cry out, but I can't.

I wilt against the side of the wardrobe and the tears I thought I had no more of start again. I am dying.

Monday. It's Monday and I've been missing since Friday night. Why is no one looking for me? Why has no one found me? Why hasn't Gilly said something? She knows who my blind date was. She knows where she left me. God, why hasn't she gone to the police? Why am I still here?

If they don't hurry, I'm going to die alone in this wooden box. I'm never going to see my mum and dad, or my sisters again. Tears track down my face but I haven't the energy to even try to stop them.

I give a slight jolt and realise I must have dozed off.

There's someone in the room. Soft breathing, the words of a song barely forming as though it's under their breath.

'Dear God, what has that boy been up to?'

Is she talking to me? Am I hallucinating?

'Ugh, what is that smell?'

I raise my head in confusion, but I'm trapped in the semi-dark.

There are muffled sounds of Craig's mother moving around the room.

My breath stutters in fast snatches through my nose. I can't cry out, she'll never hear me from inside my prison, but—

I raise my legs as high off the base of the wardrobe as possible, which isn't high given the state of my depleted muscles, and then I allow them to punch down into the far corner.

My sock-covered feet barely make a sound and I whimper in frustration at my feeble attempt.

She's turned on some music and I bet she can't hear me above it.

I slip downwards onto my back and step my feet up the far end wall of the wardrobe, my knees bending at right angles to give me more room as I draw them away from the wall until my knees almost touch my chin.

This time I put my whole energy into the move, imagining I'm kicking that wooden wall down.

I almost do. I don't stop there. I kick and kick and

kick, adrenaline surging to give me the strength I thought I'd lost.

The music clicks off. I scream from behind the tape covering my mouth, but I need to conserve my energy for the more important job of smashing down my prison.

There is silence on the outside and I can't tell if Craig's mum has left, but I'm not stopping.

Suddenly the door springs open and I topple sideways out of the wardrobe, smashing my head on the thin carpet-covered floor.

The face looking down at me fills with a deep, dawning horror as Craig's mother slaps both hands to her face and screams.

17

TWENTY-ONE YEARS EARLIER – AUGUST 2004 – SORIAH

'Water.' The word barely scrapes past my arid throat as Craig's mum drops to her knees, peeling back the strip of tape from my mouth with hands shaking so hard it takes her longer than it should to remove it.

'Water.'

I know it's a cliché but quite frankly, I don't give a shit. I am literally dying of thirst and the reason it's a cliché is because people dying of thirst say it.

I'm trying to suck in air, but my mouth is so parched that my throat has started to stick closed. The skin around my lips stings like it was stripped off along with the sticky tape and the cracks at the corners of my mouth weep with a cold fluid.

The woman staggers to her feet. I'm not sure she's

capable of helping me. Pity stirs in me for this woman, who is the mother of my rapist. She's in shock. I'm in shock. I must be if I can afford pity for the mother of that monster.

I'm too weak to help myself and simply lie there on my side and watch as she makes her wobbly way to the bedroom door, leaving me alone. I want to cry out, to scream for her to come back. To not leave me alone. But my throat is so dry and arid that I am incapable, and she is gone.

She's left me alone.

I close my eyes, defeated, but when I open them, she's returned. She has a phone in one hand, speaking to somebody, and a bottle of water with a sports cap in the other.

Her voice comes from a distance, echoey and faint.

'Police. Yes. And ambulance. Hurry! I've found her. I've found the missing girl. The one who's been on the news. She's right here in my house. Please send the police quickly!' She looks me over. Behind the tears, there's an astuteness as if she is assessing me. Then it makes sense when she explains to the person on the other end of the phone.

'I'm a nurse. She needs urgent medical attention, she's seriously dehydrated. Her pulse is weak and thready. No, I've no idea how long she's been... here.'

Her voice cracks. 'I've just arrived back from holiday, in the early hours.' A sob breaks out. 'I could have helped her so much earlier, if only I'd checked.'

The person on the other end of the line is obviously offering some kind of conciliatory sympathy, but it's not having an effect on this woman.

My hands are unbound but I have no memory of her doing that. Nor of her untying my feet.

She squirts a small quantity of water into my mouth as she supports my head with one hand.

It is the sweetest nectar on earth. Instead of gulping it down, I hold it on my tongue and taste it, letting it slide slowly down my throat. It can't quench my thirst though, nothing will ever be able to do that.

She drops the phone on the floor when she finishes speaking with the emergency services and raises her free hand to cup my face.

I jerk away.

It's one thing to have her hand support my head, another to accept a touch of supposed affection.

I don't want affection. I don't want anyone to touch me like that again.

'It's okay. You're okay. You're safe now.'

Tears dry on her cheeks as she stares into my eyes

and gives a slow blink as though her mind is trying to catch up with what's happening. When she speaks again, it's with low-toned anger that I know without a doubt is not directed at me.

'Oh my God! Oh my God. What's he done? What did he do to you?' Her breath judders in and tears pool in her eyes to flow over as she blinks. 'I can't believe it. I can't believe my son would do this.' Her brow creases and a sudden fury flashes through her eyes. 'He won't get away with this, you know. He's going to pay. I'll make sure he pays.'

I open my lips to reply but choke instead. It doesn't matter what he pays, the price of what he's done to me can never be met.

She drizzles more water into my mouth, and I snatch at it, try to guzzle it but she pulls away. What kind of cruelty is this?

Her voice gentles as she shifts her weight slightly. 'I can't give you too much at a time, it might cause issues. The paramedics will put you on a drip as soon as they arrive. They won't be long, I promise.'

'Name?' I croak as the sound of distant two-tones comes closer.

'Fiona.'

I grasp her wrist, but my fingers are weak. 'Thank you, Fiona.'

She may be *his* mother, but she's just saved my life, and his actions are not her responsibility. Are they?

I close my eyes and when I open them again, I am surrounded by concerned faces: Fiona, a couple of paramedics and—

My vision is blurred but I swear that's Craig poised in the open doorway, staring in horror at the scene in front of him.

'No, no! No!' I raise my hand and point at him, terror streaking through me to send my bowels to water.

Fiona turns in slow motion to where Craig stood a moment before.

She tears out after him, her high-pitched wail breaking through the trance I'd sunk into.

'You bastard! You horrible, filthy bastard!' Her voice shrieks, piercing my ears and there's some kind of commotion beyond the doorway. 'What have you done? What have you done? You're no child of mine!'

I don't know if it's because paramedics work in these circumstances frequently, but neither of them take their attention from me as I stare up at the ceiling listening to the guttural grunts and ear-piercing screeches as Craig's mum seems to be battering him.

Craig's pitiful cries stir no compassion in my heart. She can kill him for all I care.

The police arrive and after an initial furore where they split the pair up, there is silence.

Total, all-consuming silence as I close my eyes and drift off to a safer place.

Only death is good enough for him.

18

TWENTY-ONE YEARS EARLIER – AUGUST 2004 – CRAIG

I heave myself halfway up from the hallway rug as it skids under me. Two police officers have me pinned down, but I'm bucking, and their feet are sliding.

'You fucking bitch!' I scream.

I don't mean Soriah, I mean that cow of a mother of mine.

How could she do this? She's fucking turned me in to the police.

All she had to do was turn a blind eye. I would have sorted it out. I just needed more time with Soriah to convince her that I would never hurt her. That I love her.

One of the pigs loses his footing and falls on top of me. Breath whooshes from my lungs as he knees me in the mouth. Blood gushes onto the cream patterned rug and I stare at it as the puddle grows.

My mum did this.

She'd already thrown a mighty punch and given me a fat lip, followed by a thump in the eye as she pummelled me with flying fists and no direction. Her knee hit home though, and tears are streaming from my eyes. I never expected my own mum to turn on me.

I never expected any of this. I don't deserve it.

I should never have come home.

College was such a drain. I couldn't concentrate. I wanted to see Soriah again, tell her how much I loved her. That I would never hurt her. They don't understand. She's my soulmate. I just want her to understand. I just need more time with her.

When I had my free period just before lunch, I thought I'd skip out and check on Soriah, see if she was okay.

Gilly was in the hallway, but I managed to duck away so she never saw me. I bet she wants to know all the details of how we got on, since I told her Soriah was scared to go home because she'd be in trouble with her parents after it was on the news that she was missing. Gilly thinks it's romantic. She wants to know everything. All the sordid details. If she could have watched, she would have. She's a voyeur. Stupid bitch.

Not as stupid as my mum.

She's in my peripheral vision. Her fists are balled like she's going to have another go, but a woman police officer is holding her back. Consoling her.

My beautiful mum. Her face is ravaged, like she's been destroyed. Deep creases slashing across her cheeks and furrowing her brow as though she's aged ten years in the last few moments.

It's her fault. Not mine. If only she'd kept her nose out of my business.

Hot breath scalds the back of my neck as one of the officers binds my hands together. They flip me over so I'm staring up at them. There's nothing now but the ragged breathing of the five of us in the hallway and Mum's bleating sobs.

I catch her gaze and recoil as she bares her teeth at me and tries to raise a clenched fist.

Mum's never struck me in my life. She's a gentle soul with a heart of gold. She's staring at me now as though she'd love to shove a knife through my ribs.

'I'm sorry.' I gasp the words.

She stops crying. Swallows.

I am sorry. Not for what I've done. I'm sure I could have put that right given enough time to convince

Soriah of my love for her. No, I'm sorry my mum discovered what I'd done. Turned me in before I could put everything right. I will never forgive her.

Her face goes blank, and she struggles to sit up as the police officer lets go of her, keeping their hands outstretched in case she makes another move towards me. After all, they are here for my protection.

With eyes as cold as the winter snow, she glares straight at me.

'Don't ever come near this house again. Keep away from me, keep away from your father. You are a monster. I will never call you "son" again. You sick, sick creature. I hope they lock you up and throw away the key!'

My heart is ripped from my chest.

I'm an only child and my mum and dad have doted on me all my life.

My dad won't desert me.

He's the one who has always told me how good I am. He's built me up, told me I'm better than the rest. He might have told me I'm a loser, but that's his way. He's always been on my side when I needed him. When I was bullied in junior school, my dad is the one who stuck up for me, made me tougher, taught me to fight back. He might have given me a few light slaps to show me how it was done, but it was for my own good. To toughen me up. Look at how he dealt with that hippy guy who turned up on the doorstep.

My dad will understand.

He'll be there for me.

Even if Mum isn't.

Sunlight streams in through the open door to highlight lines that weren't there yesterday but are now deep crevices etched into her skin. Tears streak down a face ravaged with sorrow. I close my eyes against them. I may no longer be her son, but she's dead to me now.

She should have been on my side.

The bitch!

19

PRESENT DAY – SATURDAY, 15 MARCH 2025, 3.45 P.M. – SORIAH

I've cleaned the house from top to bottom and the whole place gives off a crisp lemony scent as I step back inside the front door, fresh from taking a run.

My body is energised, a rush of adrenaline has kicked up my endorphins and my whole being feels great. I am fine.

I checked the NHS website to confirm, if you already exercise, you can carry on while you're pregnant, as long as you don't try to take it up after you become pregnant. As long as I feel fine, I can continue running for a while yet. Which is just as well, as I know how I feel when I run. It centres me so I can think of the good things and push away the bad.

Also, I tried Granny's trick of eating two crackers

before swinging my legs out of bed in the morning, and it worked. Either that, or it's mind over matter as I cannot stand being sick. That also is a trigger and reminds me of other times. Dark times.

Moments that are not to be thought of now.

With a look of self-satisfaction, I smile, gazing around. I've washed all the doors on the kitchen cupboards, cleaned the skirting boards, dusted those tiny cobwebs out of corners we don't even look at. I feel so good about it. It may be nesting behaviour, but I doubt it. It's more that I've had the opportunity to clean while Marcus is away, because he's not the tidiest person in the world and nor is he the tidier. He used to. I'm sure he did. Recently though, it seems the house has become invisible, just as I have become invisible.

I push aside the negative thoughts that try to intrude because this is a whole new chapter we are about to embark on. I race up the stairs, still bounding with energy, and strip quickly before stepping into the shower. The beat of the water on my skin is exhilarating. I rest my hand on my still flat stomach and imagine the baby inside. The baby I want so badly and thought I was being punished for the decision I took previously.

The water stops abruptly as I shut off the tap,

wrenching away the white noise that had filled my mind to keep my senses balanced. I step out of the cubicle, my head swims and I reach out with one hand to grab a huge jazzy-coloured towel off the rail.

I wrap it around me and sit on the loo for a minute. I hope I didn't overdo it. Maybe I turned the heat up too high in the shower. I'm okay now. It was momentary.

I take a minute to acclimatise and look around while I do so. I should take a photo of my pregnancy test for posterity. Or record keeping.

A little ripple of uncertainty hits me.

I swear I left it on the side of the sink because I want to keep it to show to Marcus when he comes home tomorrow evening. I was going to place it in a small box inside some lovely tissue paper I keep in one of the drawers downstairs. A big surprise and a welcome home. Although something tells me that it will be all about him when he arrives home for the first couple of hours, so I will need to bide my time, tamp down on my enthusiasm until the time is right.

I come to my feet and sway a little again. I wander through to my bedroom. Perhaps I should lie down for a few minutes. Or eat something. I've put two crackers on the side of my bed again for the following morning and reach for them as I sink down onto the mattress. While I nibble, I concentrate on picturing where I put that pregnancy test. I'm absolutely positive I left it on the side of the sink. That's the last conscious memory I have of it.

Did I throw it in the bin?

Did it slide in as I was taking the bin from under the sink earlier?

Wouldn't I have noticed?

Am I losing my mind? Surely pregnancy doesn't have that much effect on hormones? Maybe it's because I am so much older now. I'll not be a young mum.

I emptied every bin in the house when I was cleaning, ready for bin collection on Monday.

I want that pregnancy test. It's important. It's all about the excitement of presenting it to Marcus when he comes home. I know I can buy a new one and pee on it again, but that one had special meaning. To me at least. He'd never know, I acknowledge to myself.

I ease my legs off the side of the bed and sit for a while to make sure my head doesn't spin again, then I stand. I'm absolutely fine. Maybe I need to eat a little more frequently. I know you shouldn't eat for two when you're pregnant, but maybe I do need a little more and I shouldn't miss out on meals like I occasionally do when I'm busy. I'm not food driven. I enjoy food to a certain extent, but I'm not one of those people who constantly think about it. Maybe that comes down to my own self-discipline. Now I have someone else to think about, I need to ensure I do this properly.

Once I've checked the bathroom again, I wander downstairs. I peer in each of the bins. I don't know why because I know they're all empty.

I pull on a pair of my rubber washing-up gloves and go out to the bin cupboard. Even though I search through and find the little white bin bag from the bathroom bin, my pregnancy test isn't there.

Strange is an understatement. I feel like I'm going crazy, but that can't be right. I know my hormones raged the last time, but that was a different case, and I had other things to concern myself with back then. Like the stress of a court case. The utter devastation of what had happened to me.

There is no stress this time. Or there shouldn't be, but once again that man has managed to inveigle himself into my thoughts, managing to get let out of prison at exactly the wrong time. How has his fate become so ensnared with my own?

I'm in the hall, pulling off my gloves, which to be honest never got messy anyhow because I pretty much knew what I was searching for and everything

I'd thrown in the bin today was bagged. I strip them off and pause. Listen to the muted mewl of my cat. A soft scratching noise.

'Luna?'

I turn the knob on the door under the stairs and Luna stalks out.

'What the hell...?'

She stares me down and then flicks an angry tail before strutting stiff-legged and full of indignation into the kitchen, presumably so I can reward her by way of food for whatever perceived injustice she has suffered.

'This is ridiculous.'

I hate that cupboard, hate enclosed spaces, but something odd is going on. Luna cannot open doors, she doesn't possess opposable thumbs, and no matter how clever she is, there's no way she got in through that door. I haven't opened it today, and hormonal or not, that's one thing I am entirely sure of. She was on the bed with me all night, I fed her this morning. She prowled the house, played on her cat playing station. I fed her again just before I went for my run. I assumed she was asleep somewhere when I came back. Certainly, she wasn't at the front door to greet me. Not this time.

I frown and crouch down to peer through the gaping entrance of the cupboard.

My heart thrums against my ribcage.

Is there some kind of access from somewhere else?

How could there be?

I lower myself down and edge towards the opening. My throat tightens as every drop of saliva dries up in my mouth. It's dark in there. We really should put one of those lights in, the ones with the sensor that activates with movement. I've asked Marcus so many times.

'When I get round to it, Soriah. You know how busy I am.'

It's not a priority to him because he's not scared of what lurks in dark, enclosed spaces.

I sigh. We're both so busy. Both have full-time jobs.

I consider the sparklingly clean house and deliberate how much of that is down to Marcus.

None of it. He doesn't do domestic chores any more. Not like he did in the beginning. He's always too tired after long days at work and weekends he often spends in the gym. Weekends when I clean the house.

He's going to have to pull his socks up once this

baby comes along, because he's going to have to participate a little more. A lot more. I'm going to expect a commitment from him.

I blow out a breath and swing the door to, then lean forward and turn the knob so the latch clicks into place. I rattle it back and forth. It's not going to move. It's certainly not going to pop open to allow a large cat to make its way inside.

I wander back to the kitchen. The idea of coffee turns my stomach, and the aroma of cat food makes it do double somersaults.

There's nothing I can do to resolve the cat food issue. Luna has to be fed.

I don't need to subject myself to coffee though.

I pour a long glass of water and watch while it clears from the bottom upwards.

Instead of gulping it down, I take long, slow sips. I've trained myself to do this. It's not good to drink something down in one go. I've learnt that. Better if you take it in measured amounts.

Keeping my body hydrated is important.

My phone pings and I sigh.

I've not heard from Marcus all day again. Out of sight, out of mind. For him, in any case.

I hope he's having fun. It would be ungracious of

me to ignore him. It's not in my nature. Then again, I want him to miss me too. Like I miss him.

I reach for my phone and turn it over so it's screen up.

My stomach does another one of those flips as though it's just about to throw its contents all over the kitchen surface again.

Worse, my heart stops beating and ice runs through my veins.

I lower my glass of water to the kitchen surface before it slips from fingers that have turned numb.

Tiny white lights flash in front of my eyes as I stare at the screen. At the words beneath the photograph of a pregnancy test. The small control screen has a thin blue line running vertically through it. The larger screen is filled with a deep blue stripe to indicate a positive pregnancy result.

> The secrets are seeping out now. I don't think your husband will be pleased about this, but just wait until he finds out about the other one.

Black shadows edge my vision, and I reach for a kitchen chair, knowing I'm about to faint.

I go boneless just as I manage to heave it towards me, slumping into it and laying my head on arms I've crossed like a cradle. I give a gentle shudder as I shut my eyes, unable to contemplate the gravity of my situation.

Nobody knows.

No one. Except...

My eyes fly open.

There is one other person.

20

TWENTY YEARS EARLIER – FEBRUARY 2005 – SORIAH

I wrap the soft, baggy cardigan tight around me and hug myself as I sit between my mum and dad in the courtroom to listen to Gilly's sentencing. My mum reaches for my icy hand, tucking hers into my sleeve to touch me. I wrap my fingers around hers and settle both our hands on my thigh, feeling her warmth saturate through my clothes.

This is what love is.

She's barely left my side since the police brought her into the hospital to be with me. Her high cheekbones are more prominent from weight she's lost over the past few months while we've attended court together. She laughingly tells me she needed to lose a few pounds. Those pounds have turned to almost two stone.

She meets my eyes with hazel ones that have turned green with distress. They glow preternaturally under the electric lights.

I've inherited my eyes from her. Light green against my dark skin which causes some people to do a double take.

Everything else I've inherited from my Barbadian dad. My long limbs, my skin tone, my thick hair.

He sits upright and dignified beside me. His world torn apart by the rape of his child. A child he can do nothing to help, because there is nothing to do.

He wasn't there. That's his biggest sin in his eyes.

I don't blame him, but I can't help that he blames himself. No assurance I give him changes things.

Brown eyes, so much darker than mine, bare a soul that is destroyed inside. Afro-textured hair is cut close to his scalp these days instead of the dreadlocks he always wore when I was younger and steel grey shows through, especially at his temples.

The black suit, white shirt and black tie sits uncomfortably on the broad shoulders of a man who is used to wearing navy scrubs in his job as a hospital porter. He refuses to turn his head and look across the courtroom at Craig Lane's mother, a woman he has worked in the same hospital with for five years. Shame stiffens him. Rage quivers through his body.

It's not her fault. She saved my life, according to the doctors. If it hadn't been for her quick actions and professionalism in dealing with me and liaising with the paramedics, I could have died.

Sometimes I think that would have been for the best.

For the most part, I just want this over. One way or another.

I'm surprised to see Craig's mum here, in the back row of the gallery. Her son won't be sentenced for another few weeks. Maybe she wants to ensure justice is served all round, because when she found out what my best friend did, she was incandescent according to the police.

My best friend.

I force myself to look at her, but she doesn't return my gaze.

Gilly Houston is paler than her usual cool colour, like the life has slowly seeped from her.

There's a stirring of sympathy as she cries. She's not stopped crying since the day the police picked her up, I believe. The day Craig's mum discovered me in his wardrobe. Battered and raped. Yet I have not cried since.

Crying is for those with something still to lose.

I have already lost everything and yet there is more heartache to come. Something I know is going to rock the foundations of my family, as it rocked mine when I realised this morning.

A creeping sensation pricks at my skin, raising goosebumps all over, despite the temperature in the overheated courtroom. This is going to be so, so hard.

Gilly's mum sits in the front row of the gallery. She's shredded her third tissue and we've only been waiting for the judge to enter and pronounce sentencing. There's been a distinct absence of Gilly's dad. He never came to the hearing either.

I'm lucky to have a dad who will stand by me. At least, I hope he will stand by me once he finds out what more we have to face.

Gilly's hair is wispy and flyaway as though she washed it this morning and blasted it with a hairdryer without trying to tame it with a brush. It's too long for her elfin face and gives her the look of a mad professor.

She's chewed at her lips and even from this distance they look torn and ragged.

Not once has she looked at me. Nor tried to contact me, although in her defence it may be that her solicitor and the police have warned her off trying.

She's shown no remorse. Not truly, in my opinion.

Oh, she's cried and she's said she was sorry it happened to me, sorry Craig did what he did, but not once has she told everyone that without her interference, her encouragement, none of this would have happened. She blatantly egged Craig on. Reinforced his belief that I might be interested in him.

He is guilty of kidnap and rape, but Gilly was the catalyst. The conductor.

'All rise. All rise.'

As the judge enters the chambers, we all come to our feet. Mum's hand squeezes mine and I find comfort there. Dad wraps an arm around me and despite my assurance that I'm done crying, hot tears prick at the back of my eyes. For no other reason than that I am loved. I will always be loved.

We sit and my parents each take one of my hands. Their knuckles brush with each other's across my lap and once again, I'm reassured of this close-knit unit I belong to. Both my sisters wanted to be here, but Carly is sitting start-of-term exams and Leonie should not be witness to this. She's at school. They've both been there for me during the Christmas holidays, but I can barely remember any of it. We never celebrated. Not as we normally would. It was quiet. Subdued.

The judge takes a moment to refer to his notes and then raises his head, his thin nose giving a little flare at the end to indicate his dissatisfaction with the case.

'Gillian Maureen Houston, please stand.' The court clerk's words ring clear in the virtually empty room. In deference to Gilly's age, the judge has ruled that it will be a closed court. There are no reporters, no public. Just the few of us involved.

Judge Beaman breathes through his nose and then stares at Gilly, who crumples against the rail she's supposed to be standing erect in front of.

I feel my sneer break through and pull myself more upright in my seat.

Where is this girl's pride?

She lets loose a sob.

'Gillian Maureen Houston, you have been found guilty of conspiracy to kidnap, and for perverting the course of justice by your actions of keeping secret the whereabouts of someone you claim to be your best friend.' He glares directly at her from under thick grey eyebrows and her fear comes out as a plaintive wail.

'I have taken all the evidence into consideration in deciding your sentence. By your own admission, you knowingly and recklessly led your friend into a dangerous situation, even to the extent of deserting her at a most crucial point, when she needed you most. You left her alone with someone you already knew was obsessed by her. You did nothing to avert the consequences of your actions. You failed to return to check on her when she didn't appear at the pub you were supposed to meet in. A mere half hour from the time you left her.'

Gilly is shaking her head as though in denial, but all the evidence has been heard. Evidence I gave under oath myself. Evidence I know to be true. There had been more evidence to give. Information about my relationship with my best friend, about her abuse of me. The pinching, the persuasion, the manipulation. I felt stupid at the time when I was telling the police officer, spewing out all the lurid details while I lay in a hospital bed. I now know that what she did was wrong. All of it.

Judge Beaman is unmoved by Gilly's distress. He probably sees it so much but has to plough on with his summation, his voice raised above hers. 'Indeed, you then went on to consciously make a decision to withhold information from the victim's parents of her whereabouts when they called to enquire, thereby adding to their distress and to the length of time your *best friend* was incarcerated in the hands of a *monster*.' He stresses the last word.

Judge Beaman raises his head and stares with furious intent down his nose at Gilly and if she could ball up any smaller, I'm sure she would. One direct look from this imposing man and I'm certain I'd do the same. But he'd been gentle with me. Just as they all have. I am the victim. Before that day, I'd never considered myself a victim, but it seems I already was.

Even Mr Sharma hasn't got away unscathed. Although he did nothing illegal, not like Gilly, he was guilty of feeding Craig's superiority complex, and the prosecutor made that clear when Mr Sharma was called as a witness to Craig's conduct. When I testified about that step in the long, winding events culminating in my kidnap and rape.

The judge had been merciless then, slashing at Mr Sharma's poor grasp of the situation.

That same judge shows no mercy now to Gilly, and nor can I feel any in my heart as I hear once more the step-by-step precis of Gilly's part in my kidnap. What she did to me.

I will never know for sure if Gilly was aware of the possibility of Craig raping me, but I do know unquestionably that she was oblivious to my safety and put her own sick sense of entertainment first.

'Your counsel has tried to convince the jury that you are a young, innocent woman, incapable of causing such serious devastation with deliberation. I disagree. Young, you may be. Innocent of these crimes, you are not. Considering the facts laid out before me, the information we have received from Craig Lane's counsel in trying to justify his actions, and evidence from the victim herself of your past conduct and manipulative nature, it is obvious to me that you had guilty knowledge and intent. You made a premeditated decision to put someone you termed as your best friend into the hands of a monster. You let your jealousy take precedence over your friendship, which I find woeful, and I find the coercive control you used to get your own way abhorrent.' He pauses a beat, glaring at her over the top of his glasses. 'Taking into consideration that you were a mere two weeks off your eighteenth birthday when this crime was committed and due to the severity of the crime, I have no alternative but to sentence you as an adult.' There is a sharp gasp as the entire courtroom sits to attention. 'The term for this is seven years in prison.'

I lean forward and strain to hear his words as Gilly's screeches reach a crescendo. Before she fully collapses on the floor, the two courtroom officers flanking her leap forward and scoop her up, holding her limp body between them.

I turn as Gilly's mum wails and screams almost as loudly as her daughter. I've always thought the woman to be so lovely, so kind and thoughtful, but she spoilt her daughter to such a degree that Gilly turned her spite and vileness on others, thinking there would never be any retribution, because she was the golden girl. Me included. I rethink that as the memory of tiny bruises on the inside of my arms and my thighs come to mind. Me in particular.

As my gaze drifts back to see Gilly being led out of the dock and down the stairs by the court officials, I wonder what made this girl hate so much that her petty jealousy rose to swallow any humanity.

With Dad's arm around my shoulders, I slip my free arm under the soft cardigan and slide a hand over the gentle swelling of my belly. Something I've only this morning come to realise. Or at least acknowledge.

One more consequence of Gilly's narcissistic nature. Something the judge can't bring into consideration, because it's not something I would ever tell the court.

Tears prick at my eyes, but I refuse to let them fall. What am I going to do?

21

PRESENT DAY – SATURDAY, 15 MARCH 2025, 5.55 P.M. – SORIAH

I pull up outside Mum and Dad's house and take a moment before switching off the engine. I know I wanted to avoid Mum, but it's hard. We don't keep secrets from each other.

Perhaps it's unfair to Marcus, but he's not here and I need some support. I know I do. I know when I reach that point. The point when memories resurface and panic sets in.

That letter is responsible for all of this. I'm losing my mind, and it's all because of that letter. Then again, who the hell is sending me messages and photographs? A photo of something that was in my house. Assuming it was the same one. I'm positive it was.

My mind might be playing tricks on me, but even if I did put my pregnancy test in the bin, that means someone went through my bins. Why would they do that? How would they know?

Unless they'd been watching.

I glance over my shoulder and Luna opens her mouth, letting out a plaintive yowl which she's done every twenty seconds since I put her in there. She hates the car, always has, but I'm not leaving her in the house while I stay overnight at Mum and Dad's. I'm not comfortable that whoever locked her in the cupboard won't come back and do something more serious.

As I clamber out of the car, Mum opens the front door and wraps her arms under her bosom. Her greeny-hazel eyes are narrowed so I know there's no way I'm getting out of this.

I lean into the back seat and haul out my weekend case, followed by Luna in her pet carrier.

Mum is already behind me as I turn, and she takes Luna from me then leans in for a tight hug.

'Everything all right?'

I nod, feeling emotion bubble inside my chest.

'Yes.' I duck my head in the pretence of picking up my case. 'Marcus is away, so I thought I'd come and spend some time with you and Dad.' I raise my head, lock the car and by the time I face her, I have a smile plastered on my face. A smile I know she can see straight through, but she allows me some space, giving a little head jerk to indicate where I imagine my dad is inside the house.

'He's in a lot of pain, but he's not going to admit that to you. He's too much of a man.'

'Any news on his hip replacement?'

We reach the front door and step inside.

An icy finger steps its way down my spine, and I spin around, one hand braced on the door as I squint into the falling darkness. Searching.

My breath catches in my throat.

Across the road, a dark figure slides into the shadows and the hair on the back of my neck prickles.

Is someone out there watching me? Have they followed me?

A shudder runs through me, but I make a move to step back outside, to challenge, bravery coating me, knowing my parents are there to back me up.

The form melts away and is gone.

'Soriah, shut the door, love. You're letting all the heat out.'

I push it closed behind me as Mum bends to let Luna out of her cat basket.

Should I mention it? Without the other details, it's going to sound stupid and weak. Once I start to tell her, where do I stop?

I wet my dry lips and say nothing.

Mum scoops Luna into her arms and the cat starts a loud purr immediately.

Mum's voice is low as she strokes the cat and snuggles her face in Luna's thick fur. 'The results came in from your dad's MRI scan, they're going to have to operate urgently, the whole ball has crumbled inside the socket of his hip. They say there's nothing left of it. No wonder he's in such pain.' Her mouth tightens and I recognise that stony-eyed stare. She's trying not to cry and the last thing I want is to upset her more than she already is, so I'll keep my concerns to myself.

After all, it's probably nothing. Just an overactive imagination triggered by being alone in my house.

Yeah, but what about the messages on my phone? There's no imagination involved there.

I touch my hand to my pocket where I slid my phone. It's okay, though. I've blocked the number and hopefully I won't hear from them again. Some cruel joke. A coincidence I don't wish to discuss now.

I reach out to cuddle Mum. She seems to have shrunk in the last few years. I know I get my height from my dad, but she is definitely not as tall as she used to be. Her shoulders have rounded, and she's developed a slight stoop. It grieves me that this has been brought about by my circumstances. Her devastation at what happened to me.

We've all moved on, we live with the events of that weekend, but it doesn't mean we're no longer affected. But we are survivors. Not just me, but the rest of my family. After all, we don't have a choice. Life goes on.

I hold her against me and Luna grumbles a protest as I squish her between us, before she scrambles up Mum's chest and leaps over the top of her shoulder onto the windowsill at the bottom of the stairs, making a short skid before she leaps off there and shoots up the stairs.

Mum chuckles as she buries a hot face in my neck.

'Dad'll be all right, Mum.'

She nods, her voice muffled. 'I know. He will be, provided they bloody well get on with it.' She pulls back and looks into my face. 'I can't understand how they put people through such agony, having to wait so long that it's too late by the time they operate. He's really not as strong as he was four months ago. How is that supposed to help his recovery time?'

I hold her shoulders and she loops loose arms around my waist.

'Do you have a date?'

She shakes her head. 'No. It's a waiting game. They know he's in a bad way, but I bet they'll wait until he falls down the stairs and then admit him as an emergency, telling us how surprised they all are that his hip has deteriorated so quickly.'

'Ha!'

We turn and walk from the hallway to the sitting room together.

Dad's normally beautiful conker-coloured skin has dimmed, and is dull and greying around the edges of his face. His normally clean-shaven cheeks and chin are peppered with coarse white stubble. The only other time I've not known him to shave was just after I was raped. When he couldn't rationalise what had happened. When he spiralled into depression so far, he never realised that not shaving was an outward sign.

I can't help the worry in my voice as I drop to my knees beside his chair, so he's not obliged to struggle to his feet.

'Oh, Dad.' I put one hand on his arm, the other on his knee. 'Why didn't you say how bad you've got? I would have come around and given you a hand.'

'A hand with what? Mum is handling things just fine.' His Bajan accent rolls stronger with the pain he's in.

I glance up at Mum's weary face. They've been hiding this from me. Probably from Carly and Leonie too. I can see it's too much for them to cope without help, but both Mum and Dad have pride enough to bowl us over if we try to interfere.

All the same, I'll speak with both my sisters later from the privacy of my childhood bedroom. The one I shared with Carly once Leonie came along as we were closer in age. She got to have the tiny box bedroom all to herself that just about fit a single bed and a small dressing table together with a thin built-in wardrobe that was too narrow for a door. A bright orange slick of material covered it, strung up with a length of white net curtain-expanding wire which droops in the middle with the weight of the curtain. It's still the same one after all these years, faded and thinning, with a wire that is yellowed and stretched. Splashes of green and purple daub bedding that Mum washes every couple of weeks just in case Leonie comes to stay. It's not so easy now she has her kids, but they share my old room, and she only tends to visit without her husband as there simply isn't enough room. Mum and Dad tend to go to their five-bedroom house more often.

I glance around at the living room, divided down the middle by a brightly coloured bead curtain my mum insisted on having despite none of us liking the clacking noises it made as we walked through to the dining area. Nothing changes in this home of my youth.

'Dinner will be ten minutes. I've already put the rice on.' Mum turns her back to walk into the kitchen and I come to my feet, then scooch next to my dad on the sofa, making sure not to jolt him. I link my arm through his and lean my head on his shoulder.

'This is tough, Dad. Are you taking any painkillers?'

'I've hit the morphine patches.'

I raise my head and smile. 'How's that working for you?'

'It's rubbish, girl, but I'll get by. I'm worried 'bout your mum, though. She's taking it hard.'

I smile. It's a sad smile though. I can't imagine anyone loving me the way my dad loves my mum. Marcus doesn't. Oh, he loves me, but it's not that all-encompassing desire to do anything to please me. Marcus pleases himself and I'm secondary in our marriage.

Then again, maybe I never encouraged anything more as I'm so terrified of triggering that one thing that could be bubbling under the surface. Obsession.

My gaze flicks up to the sitting room windows and I push up from the sofa and make my way over. As I draw the curtains closed, I stare out into the dusky night again. A featherlight dust of fear strokes my skin and I shiver.

There's someone out there. Isn't there?

'Everything all right, sugar?'

I whip the curtains closed so the wooden rings rattle on the rail, then turn back to my dad.

'I thought I saw someone, it's nothing.'

I know I have to plaster on a smile so he doesn't catch the anxiety rising in me, but his nutmeg eyes contemplate me with a wisdom I don't believe I will ever possess.

I step from one foot to the other, ever a child in his presence.

There's a gentle reassurance as he speaks but we both know it's not the truth. 'That'll be old Mrs Jackson. She'll have seen your car arrive and she's not satisfied with curtain twitching, she'll have sneaked down the side of her neighbour's house, like she does to catch a closer look. It wouldn't surprise me if she tiptoes over the road here just to see how new your car is. Nosy old bat.'

I laugh, but it's slightly forced. We both know it's not true. He's soothing my paranoia, and I'm pretending to be soothed. Because it's not paranoia if it's really happening.

'Dinner's ready.' Mum's voice breaks the moment, and I turn, dashing to take laden plates from her through to the dining table.

I turn as Dad comes unsteadily to his feet and rush back to lend assistance.

He waves me away with a certain degree of affection, but I know he hates to give up his independence. Hopefully it will only be for a short while.

I watch him though as he hobbles, aided by a cane, to the table.

'I brought wine,' I chirp, trying to keep everything light-hearted. I know my parents don't keep alcohol in the house, but they never object to a glass or two when I bring some.

I make my way back to the hallway where I've left my weekend bag and slip two bottles of red wine from it, resisting the urge to peep outside again. I'm safe here tonight.

I switch off the hall light and turn toward the sitting room when I hear a faint noise. I whirl around.

My heart hammers so hard I go lightheaded and raise my hand to lean against the wall.

A white envelope is pushed through the letterbox and lands with a soft thunk on the hallway carpet.

Horrified, I freeze, a terrible sense of foreboding invading me, making my limbs turn numb. I knew with a visceral instinct that shadow over the road was there for me.

'Soriah? Hurry up, love. Your dinner will get cold.'

I tuck one bottle under my arm and swipe the envelope from the floor, tilting it so the light from the sitting room catches it. With a quick check, I can see it has my name scrawled across the front.

In my heart, I knew it would. Knew it was for me.

'Soriah?' My mum's voice is louder now. Is she coming to find me?

I stuff the envelope in my overnight bag and straighten as Mum walks into the darkened hallway.

'What are you doing? You surely can't see what you're doing in the dark.'

She smacks the switch on the wall and light floods through the hallway, leaving me blinking. 'It's okay, Mum.' I can hear the warble in my own voice. 'I thought I'd bring both bottles, save coming back for another one later.'

She takes one from me and strides back through

the sitting room to the dining room. 'You planning on drinking all of this? Because your daddy and I won't have that much.'

It's at that point I realise I can't drink. I shouldn't drink. But bringing wine is a habit. One they'd be suspicious of if I didn't. I can't remember the last time I turned up at their house without bringing at least one bottle. But I can't drink it this time.

I'm pregnant and I can't tell anyone yet. No one but me knows.

I turn and glance at my weekend bag, just beyond the open hall doorway.

My stomach clenches, sickness stirring in the pit of it.

Someone else does know.

They know much more than that too.

It's just a question of how much do they know?

22

TWENTY YEARS EARLIER – APRIL 2005 – SORIAH

I glance across the courtroom at Judge Beaman, the same one who sentenced Gilly.

His demeanour is anything but soft, but I don't quite understand. Surely when a sentence is passed, life means life, but in this case, life means something in the region of twenty years.

Is twenty years enough for what Craig Lane did to me?

I place my hand on my swollen belly. He might have twenty years, but I truly have life.

Or do I?

I have a choice. Not the choice I should have been able to make. Due to my own stupidity and *naïveté* I didn't even notice I was pregnant until the day Gilly Houston was sentenced.

How ignorant was that?

My mum's reaction couldn't have been more shocked. She was knocked off her feet. Literally. When I told her, she slid to the floor. My poor, dear mum. Stoic throughout everything. That was the blow that hit her the hardest.

'Have you told your sisters?'

I shook my head. 'No.'

'Then don't,' she hissed in my ear. 'One life ruined is enough.'

Even now, I'm not quite sure I understand what she meant with those words. It's not like they could become pregnant too, by osmosis, or some such thing. But I did as my mum requested and when she took me to the abortion clinic and explained to the doctor there why I needed an abortion, I went along with that too.

What I refused to go along with was the actual abortion. Once that doctor told me that at twenty-two weeks, that baby was fully developed in my womb with eyes that were just about opening and ears that could hear, there was no way I could in all good conscience kill a living being.

How could I abort something real? A human. A

baby who never deserved to be murdered just because neither of its parents wanted it.

I certainly don't want it.

The mere thought of holding a baby from that evil creature turns my stomach. But so does murder.

I'm now thirty-two weeks pregnant, but because of my physique, there really isn't much on show still. Apparently, my stomach muscles are supreme according to my gynaecologist. All the running and athletics, I assume. It makes for tight stomach muscles.

I'm wearing a baggy sweatshirt to court, over jeans made specifically for pregnant women. No one would know to look at me, unless they knew me really well. My sweatshirt covers the small swelling of my belly, but I now have breasts which are so obvious to me. Hopefully not to others. My face has plumped out so that when I look in the mirror, the definition of my jawline has softened, but again unless someone looks very closely, they wouldn't know.

The attention isn't so much on me, but Craig. Still, I'm really cautious. We've kept it so private.

I certainly don't want the press to find out. We've already been hounded to give our side of the story. Our side! I wouldn't tell them anything if they offered me a new house in a secret location. They're feral and untrustworthy. They'll bleed you dry and leave you dying in the gutter. That's why they're called the gutter press. They don't want a story so the victim gains empathy resulting in communities banding together. No, they want to sensationalise every single thing. Because of my age at the time, nothing should have hit the newspapers, but of course they linked my disappearance with Craig's arrest. He gets anonymity because of his age, though.

My face was already splashed all over the papers by that time.

Missing teenager found. Family distraught.

Distraught. They have no idea.

Imagine if it was revealed I was having Craig's baby. That would stir up a shitstorm.

I give a small shudder as the judge enters the courtroom. Mum is holding my hand, but Dad remains seated, head bowed. Shame has hit him hard.

Despite being of the same opinion as me, that it would be wrong to murder any kind of life form, let alone an innocent baby, he's not coping well with the idea that his middle daughter will be giving birth to a baby. A baby conceived with a monster. It's not ideal. I know it's not. For the life of me, I can't think past this.

The court case has stripped me of everything. I've

had to relive every step, from the very first time I caught Craig noticing me. My feelings.

My feelings are the worst to deal with because instinctively I'm not the type of person to attribute blame. But I can't ignore the fact that Gilly was at best stupid, childish and irresponsible in her actions. At worst, she was spiteful and vindictive, and she set me up for a fall she was fully complicit in. The court chose to see it as the latter. I'm glad they agreed with me.

Mr Sharma's reputation has also been smeared. Not quite ruined as it could have been as the college have taken the 'lessons will be learned' route, which means nothing to anyone. Except Mr Sharma didn't lose his job, nor have to be put on any remedial course. He received a slap on the wrist and his apology was accepted.

Dad wanted far more justice, but when the judge named Mr Sharma in his summing up, there was no doubt of his opinion of the teacher.

I don't blame him, but there is a discomfort that Mr Sharma sided with Craig and guilted me. Admittedly, how was he to know what Craig would then go on to do? I'm sure if at any time he'd suspected foul play, his attitude would have been different, but what Mr Sharma saw was a young woman wearing what he considered inappropriate clothing. His attention was focused so much on that, he missed the monster stalking that young woman.

Unlike Gilly, his actions weren't illegal, but they were irresponsible. Thoughtless. You can't go to jail for that, and although I don't consider he should, I can never forgive him for not protecting me. If only he had reported Craig's actions on that day, maybe Craig's mum and dad would have stepped in, taken action. The police would have been made aware. Maybe that would have been enough to deter Craig from taking the next step.

Who knows?

I don't want to dwell on the ifs, buts and maybes any longer.

I wasn't required, nor even advised to come along to the sentencing, but for me, this is closure. I want to know what punishment is being meted out.

From my point of view, it's not enough.

Craig will only be thirty-eight when he is released. Still a young man. That's not life.

The baby gives a hard kick inside as though it's aware of the emotional turmoil in the courtroom. I grasp my mum's hand and give it a hard squeeze, knowing she understands.

I won't be keeping this baby. That much I have

already decided. It would be unfair to keep a child I could never love because it reminds me of the father who raped me.

Every day of that baby's life will be a trial. And that's not just unfair on me and my family, but on the child. I wish it no harm, but nor do I want it in my life. The mature couple we've chosen to adopt the baby will give it the best life. They are desperate for a child and have been trying for several years. The baby will be adored by them, and the circumstances of its conception will be known by no one, but Mum, Dad and me. Even my sisters are completely unaware and will remain so for their own sanity.

Craig stands in the dock, his ill-fitting suit hanging from narrow shoulders and a frame that has become skinny over the past few months. Is that remorse? I think not.

I don't trust him.

Throughout the entire procedure he has acted in what could be called an exemplary manner. Not once has he become flustered. Apart from pleading not guilty and telling copious amounts of lies that left me breathless. His composure was stoic. Luckily, the judge and jury saw through him. His ability to manipulate lessened throughout the prosecution.

He turns his head and stares directly at me. It's

the first time since the court case started that he's even tried to look at me, and he's caught me off guard. He's never looked at me before.

I squeeze my mum's hand again, barely able to swallow, caught in the headlights of his gaze. Hypnotised like a mouse in a snake's thrall.

'Do you have anything to say, young man?' The judge peers over his glasses, his face stern.

Craig never turns his attention away from me but holds my gaze with his.

My breath stutters in my throat and black clouds swarm my vision.

'I love you, Soriah.'

A court official steps up behind him and tries to lead him away with a tug on his elbow, but Craig shrugs the hand from his arm and raising his voice, he yells, 'Nothing will ever stop me from loving you, no matter how far apart we are! No matter how long it takes, I know you want to love me too.'

I press my hand over my mouth and throw myself back against the hard wooden bench in the courtroom as they drag him out of the dock, a mess of arms and legs entangled together as two guards fall on top of him. He struggles, slim, wiry and unexpected, and they hit the floor.

Tears roll down my cheeks.

One guard wraps an arm around Craig's neck as he raises his head.

His gaze crashes into mine.

'Soriah!' He screams my name with the passion of a dying man. 'Don't let them do this to me. Tell them. Tell them the truth. That you love me.' His face contorts with agony and tears shimmer on his cheeks. 'Wait for me. Wait until I get out. I'll never forget you. I love you!'

23

PRESENT DAY – SATURDAY, 15 MARCH 2025, 10.45 P.M. – SORIAH

Exhaustion should have dragged me down into the depths of comforting sleep, but I stare blank eyed above me as lights from passing cars track along the ceiling and then down the walls.

I can't be bothered to get up and tug the curtains closed tighter. It's a triangle towards the top that's fallen open. They're not the heavily lined curtains of my youth, but Mum has updated, gone cheap and cheerful in the absence of her children who rarely stay overnight.

We have no need, normally.

Mum sleeps over at Carly's and Leonie's when she babysits their children as it's easier and the kids have their own space, and Dad isn't worn out with them charging around from early morning until late at night.

Our bedroom is very different from when we lived here. Mum has modernised it and it's clean and fresh.

Somehow, it still has the same scent.

I tuck my nose under the covers and persuade my eyes to close.

The words on the letter swim through my mind. It's no good. I can't sleep.

I swing my legs out of bed and sit on the side. God, it's freezing in here, but Mum has hot flushes sufficient to keep her own bedroom warm enough, thereby keeping Dad toasty too and she refuses to stick the central heating on at night. Now they'll no longer have their winter fuel allowance, perhaps I should buy them an electric blanket. One of those ones where you can heat up one side or the other. Feet or body.

I'm sure Dad will appreciate it after his operation, he'll need it even if Mum expires of heat.

For now, I slip my feet into a pair of Carly's slippers that she keeps for when she visits. I dig the letter from my bag and snuggle on my bed, wrapping the quilt around me.

Worn, yellowed paper crackles as I unfold it, wondering where on earth it came from. It's so old I can smell the mustiness. The handwriting is poor, spider scrawls across the page.

Dear Soriah,

I hope you read this letter and don't simply throw it away.

All I ask is a chance.

I recently received a letter from Victim Support and assume you have too.

It scares me that Craig is out in the world now after all this time. I'm sure you are safe from him, but I feel that he may seek retribution from me.

So many years have passed and there isn't a day that goes by when you're not on my mind. I occasionally detour past your mum and dad's house and have once or twice seen them in the front garden. I've never stopped. My shame is too deep and I wouldn't know what to say.

It came as a shock to see you arrive tonight as I was passing. It's the first time I've seen you since the court case. Of course, I was detained for three and a half years and then let out on licence.

I wouldn't expect you to want anything to

do with me. I wondered, though, if you would agree to meet up. Just the two of us. I understand if you say no, but I want the opportunity to speak with you, face to face. To apologise. I'm a changed person and I want your forgiveness, if that is possible, because until you forgive me, I can never forgive myself.

I was young, I was foolish. I see that now.

If you could, I will be at Pinegates Garden Centre tomorrow from 10 a.m. when they open. I'll be there all day, and hope that you will come.

My sincere thanks for reading this.

In everlasting hope.

Gilly

I suck in my breath as tears roll down my cheeks.

I knew someone was watching me. Is she the only one? What about the feeling that someone was in my house? What about the messages from the unknown number? The flowers without a message. Was that my pregnancy test they'd photographed, or did they take a shot at the fact that I would be pregnant? A long shot. How in hell's name would anyone know? I barely knew myself.

Is that all a figment of my imagination, or a coincidence?

Are my hormones driving me crazy or is someone really stalking me?

Is it Gilly?

It doesn't seem logical. She says in her letter she just saw me for the first time since she went to prison. Maybe she knows something. Perhaps Craig has tried to contact her too. That letter from Victim Support could certainly be the trigger.

I wipe my nose with the back of my hand.

What am I supposed to do?

I don't really want to meet her. It's the last thing on my bucket list.

Logically speaking, though, if I meet up with her, I can establish if it's me or her who is going mad. She wouldn't have sent me flowers. Would she? She's the only person who would know exactly what type of flowers Craig had left in my locker that day. It was brought up in court, of course, but did they mention the variety? The colours?

It makes sense she dropped the note through my parents' door, because she doesn't know where I live. As far as I'm concerned, she doesn't know my married name either. I'm assuming all of this, but I may be wrong.

Maybe I need to find out what she does know.

I fold the note and slip it back into my overnight bag. It's best not to tell Mum and Dad. They have enough right now to deal with and I don't need to upset them. It's a meeting, in a public place. That's all. I'll be perfectly safe.

It might make me feel better about myself. Clear some things up.

I'm not sure if I want to give Gilly absolution, but then again perhaps she's suffered enough.

We were both so young back then. Maybe I was too harsh. Time and distance have imbued me with a far more mature outlook.

I no longer hold such a grudge against Mr Sharma. Yes, he was wrong, but I now see he was in a tough position. Craig easily manipulated him, although I believe Mr Sharma's own blinkered view took precedence. I wonder if he learned his lesson. I don't think he was a young man at the time. He could even be retired by now.

Was Gilly also in the same situation? I don't think she was. She was young, immature, stupid. But was it her intention to be evil?

The only way I can find out is to meet her.

There's no chance Mum is going to let me get away before Sunday lunch tomorrow, but she always serves it at one o'clock on the dot. I can get away by two-thirty. Three at the latest.

I reach for my phone and check. The garden centre tea rooms are open until 4 p.m. Gilly did say she was willing to wait all day if she needed to.

Would she?

I snuggle back down in the bed, toeing the slippers from my feet and letting them drop to the pink bedroom carpet before I curl into a tight ball and tuck my face into the quilt. It's bloody cold in this house. How have I never noticed before?

Or is it just icicles running through my veins with thoughts of what tomorrow will bring?

24

TWENTY YEARS EARLIER – MAY 2006 – CRAIG

It's bloody cold under this thin blanket.

Dark, too.

I thought it would be light in prison but it looks like I got the darkest room on the planet.

I blink the pitch black from my eyes, but I can see nothing.

Hear nothing but the deep even breathing of the lad on the bunk below me. It's not quite a snore, but it's louder than I've been used to. More of a Darth Vader sound.

I'm an only child. Dad never snored. Nor did Mum. It was always quiet at night in our three-bedroom house. Too quiet for me. Or so I thought at the time.

I couldn't wait to escape, to run footloose in amongst all the kids at college, the parties, the people. Even if I didn't have any close friends to speak of. It was company.

Now all I want is for the door to be locked at the end of the day and Garth and me to settle down for the night.

I hate being amongst the milling crowd of demons. Men, boys really, like me. I turned eighteen before my trial, which was unfortunate for me. These lot have more savvy, more strength, more meanness than I could ever imagine.

Garth is a few months older than me, but he's been here for six months longer than I have. For stabbing his stepfather, who sounds like he needed stabbing. Unfortunately, the guy didn't die. Fortunately, that means Garth only gets attempted murder, instead of murder, and should be out in a few years. Three to five, I think he said. If he behaves himself and doesn't commit GBH inside, earning himself another sentence. Generally, he does behave himself. He toes the line. Mostly. And when he doesn't, no one sees.

Mitigating circumstances played in his favour. And the fact that his stepdad is still breathing.

Wanker.

That's what Garth called him, in any case. Apparently, further mitigating circumstances were the fact that his stepdad was attempting to bash his brains out at the time with a rolling pin.

Who the hell keeps a rolling pin in their house these days? No one rolls out pastry. You can buy that shit ready rolled. I know because my mum used it all the time when she made meat pies for my dad and me.

My heart squeezes at the thought of my mum, and her wonderful meat pies with their thick, dark gravy. I can almost smell them as I lie here in the blackness, imagining a time when I get out. It's a long way off.

I won't be getting out early. No matter how well I behave.

There were no real mitigating circumstances in my case, despite my dad's absolute conviction that I would get away with it. He even swapped my solicitor just before the case because he believed the new one he'd found would do a better job.

I'm not exactly sure what kind of job he imagined he could do. Maybe if they could have convinced the jury I was a complete basket case, then I would have got off lightly.

I wasn't up for that.

There's nothing wrong with me. Nothing mentally, in any case.

Nothing that couldn't be put right if only I was with Soriah.

Even my mum doesn't understand.

Especially my mum doesn't understand.

She won't come and see me. Hasn't even spoken to me since the day she beat the shit out of me in front of everyone in our front hallway.

I'll never forgive her for turning on me like that. It was humiliating.

I'll never forgive Soriah either, for causing that rift between me and my mum.

If it wasn't for her…

I sniff, feeling the warm trickle of tears leak from my eyes and run down my temples and into my hairline.

'Are you fucking crying?'

The voice in the dark startles me and I almost jump from my top bunk.

'Fuck off. I'm not!'

'You are! You woke me up with your snivels.'

'That's 'cos I can't sleep with your fucking heavy breathing.'

'Aw, mate...' His voice vibrates with disappointment in me.

We lie in silence, and I scrub away the tears from my face, drawing my fingers down to stretch my skin. My nose is stuffed up now so I have no choice but to sniff hard, giving myself away.

'You awright?' Garth's voice is quiet now. Gentle.

Tears well up again but I refuse to let them fall.

'I was just thinking of my mum.'

I know Garth's mum died just before he stabbed his stepdad. That was the issue. She was no longer there to protect him against the violence of a big man, and they were still living in the same house, neither of them knowing what to do while they waited for her funeral to take place.

It's silent in the bunk below.

I turn over onto my side and let out a sigh. 'Do you miss her?'

'Who? Me mam? Nah, she was an old cow.'

But I hear the loss in his voice, the bravado that masks his sadness.

'Mine won't talk to me.' I've told him this before, but what else is there to talk about in here?

'Mate, it's no loss. She sounds like a cow, too.'

But she wasn't. She never lifted a finger to me. She gave up her last everything, just to make me happy.

If I wanted something, she let me have it.

'I miss her.'

'Mate, you're going to be in here for a long stretch. You gotta let it go, or it'll drive you crazy.'

'I know.' The past two months already feel like a lifetime. Just another nineteen years and ten months to go, less the time I spent in custody, which was almost eight months. 'At least you'll be getting out pretty soon, compared to me.'

'Yeah.' He snorts and bitterness floats on the air.

'What will you do when you get released?' I'm curious to know, but I'm pretty certain of his answer.

'What will I do? Mate, I'm going to fucking go and finish the job I started.'

I laugh. It's not often I laugh, but Garth can coax it out of me.

'How about you?'

His question makes me pause.

We've never discussed my life after prison before, because it's too far away. But, if there's one thing I know, I won't change my mind.

I smile.

'I'm going to fucking go and finish the job I started, too.'

'Ha!' Garth lets out a hoot of laughter. 'Well, you've got plenty of time to think about it, so how about you close your eyes now and let us both get some fucking sleep?'

There's a smile on my face as I close my eyes and drift off, knowing I'm deadly serious. Just over nineteen years is a long time to construct the perfect plan.

25

PRESENT DAY – SUNDAY, 16 MARCH 2025, 3.25 P.M. – SORIAH

I swear Mum knows something's not right. Especially as I only ended up having half a glass of wine with my dinner last night. At least I could decline today without suspicion as neither Mum nor Dad approve of drinking anything if driving. Not surprising in their case, they're such lightweights, it would be like sticking them in bumper cars.

Mum's face was already flushed with one glass of wine last night.

Dad had two very large glasses. Slugged them down like they were Ribena. According to Mum, he never even felt the pain in his hip as he hauled himself upstairs and then collapsed on the bed. Best night's sleep he's had in weeks.

I left the second bottle for them for tonight.

Not that I'm advocating alcohol to resolve his problems, but if it gave him a good night's sleep for a change, then so be it. Once in a blue moon won't kill him. He had a bit of a headache this morning, so I gave him a couple of my stronger ibuprofen/paracetamol mix and he seemed remarkably better than when I arrived the previous day. Maybe my presence under their roof helped too.

'You know, Dad, you really need to take more painkillers, just until after your operation. It won't hurt.'

His smile was benign, which means he doesn't intend to take any more than he has been doing. He wouldn't be on the morphine patches if Mum didn't insist on putting them on his shoulder for him where he's not aware of it, and at least that way, he's not consciously swallowing 'poison', as he terms it, every few hours.

Mum's gaze is deep and searching as I stand on the doorstep and hug her goodbye.

She knows.

Not what, just that there is something I'm hiding. If only she could see inside my brain, she'd have reason to be worried.

She cups my face in warm hands and studies me.

'If you need anything, anything at all, Soriah, just ask. We're here if you need us. You can tell us anything, you know.'

I place my hands over hers, turn my face and press a kiss on her palm and then draw her hands away.

'I know, and I will, when I feel the need.'

I'm not exactly lying to her, but I am avoiding the truth and for now, I know my mum will settle for that.

She's never pushed me to reveal my feelings when I'm not ready to. She simply reassures me that she's there. This is the deal we both understand. If she pushes, I run.

Guilt is a slippery snake deep in the pit of my belly, but I can't tell her what's going on. For her own sake. It would just upset her.

As for the business about the baby, how can I put my mum before my husband?

I hesitate. Almost stutter it out.

No, it's not fair.

I can't put Marcus second. He would be so insulted if he thought Mum and Dad knew before him. He'll be home tonight and once I've told him, I'll drive back over again tomorrow night after work to break the news to Mum and Dad. They're going to be absolutely thrilled to bits. I think. I hope. But it does stir up other memories. Not just for me, but them too.

Still, it leaves me with an utterly dreadful feeling as though I've been somehow disloyal, or deceptive. Which I have. But with good reason.

Mum stands on the doorstep and waves as I reverse my car out of the drive, Luna unhappily ensconced in her crate on the back seat. She'll hate this, but I have no option. She's going to have to stay in the car while I meet Gilly. I couldn't leave her with Mum, then there would be questions. Too many and I can't cope with that right now.

Fifteen minutes, thirty tops for me to meet with Gilly and see what the hell she wants.

Is she behind the messages to my phone?

It seems odd she would drop a handwritten note through my parents' door, though, if that was the case. Why not just message me again?

That's the issue here.

What if Gilly is the person sending the messages? How did she get hold of my pregnancy test?

My mind is in a whirl. There are too many questions that have no answers. None that I know of in any case.

I realise I'm breathing way too quickly and my head is spinning.

I concentrate on slowing everything down, breathe in to the count of five and out to the count of five, hold my breath at the top for the count of one. My counsellor taught me this when I was eighteen and I've got out of the habit of using it, until recently.

It's not that being kidnapped and raped will ever leave me and I don't want to trivialise it, but I need to get on with my life and on occasion, a really good day means that the memories are distant and faded as though it never happened to me, that it was someone else. A story I heard. It's a survival technique.

And I am a survivor.

When I arrive, I've been so distracted, I barely remember the journey to the garden centre, but I pull into the car park and realise there's only a bike that looks like it's been dumped along the pitted dust track and one other car as well as mine here. Is that Gilly's? Or did she walk? Does she live close? Is that why she chose this place?

It's kind of out in the middle of nowhere with a few old farmhands' cottages set back from the road just at the entrance to a long, winding driveway.

It's incredibly quiet.

Where is everyone else?

I know it's a chilly Sunday afternoon, but don't people come out to garden centres any more? Maybe it's a little too late in the day, and a little too early in the year.

I spare a quick look at the garden centre building which is separate from the cafe and there's a young man serving an elderly lady, but she appears to be the last of the customers from what I can see, unless there are more people lurking down the long aisles that look virtually empty of product.

Maybe that's why no one is here. Perhaps it's the changeover season for plants. Once the frost is gone, this place will possibly be burgeoning with spring plants – pansies, begonias and petunias. Although it does look a little sad, as though the owners have lost interest, or hope.

There's another bike propped up outside under the overhang to protect it from the weather and it may be presumptuous of me, but I assume it belongs to the young man as it has all the traits of a trail bike.

I turn my back on the garden centre, circling around to the other side of the building that houses the cafe and glance at the notice on the door with the opening times. It closes at 4 p.m. Just thirty minutes, which may not be a bad thing as it limits my time with Gilly and means she needs to get straight to the point.

I want to know why she's been spying on me, how long has she been doing this, and I want to know now.

We're not teenagers any longer. We're both grown women, surely she can't have the same spoilt, entitled attitude she had back then, especially considering the time she spent in prison. Wouldn't that change her? It would change anyone, I imagine.

Perhaps she's more of an adult now. Her letter certainly seemed mature, asking to meet so she can apologise.

What if she asks me to forgive her. Could I?

It's something that's rolled around in my mind since I read the note.

We were teenagers, not children back then, or at least I considered myself reasonably mature being the middle child. Certainly mature enough to make the right decisions. I didn't drink and drive. It was a decision only I could make, no matter what my parents said. I could have gone wrong, made the wrong choices. I chose not to.

Gilly had those choices too and she chose to take the wrong path.

Has that childishness been stripped from her?

Did she learn anything in prison?

Is she sorry? Really?

My fingers are already cold as I push inside to the sound of a chirpy bell announcing my arrival, and find the place empty.

She said she would wait, but in all fairness, I have left it until the eleventh hour. Not so much out of disrespect, but because I could hardly rush Mum with her three-course Sunday dinner she'd put on especially because I'd come to stay. She likes to feed me up. Mum has always been a nurturer. It makes her feel good too to know she's still allowed to take care of us. The transition hasn't yet happened into role reversal. She's still a strong, capable woman, clinging on to that for as long as she can.

I was hardly about to rush off and cause her more concern.

I wander over to the counter at the far end of the cafe, turning my back to lean against it while I scan the empty room.

Condensation mists the windows and drips down, leaving jagged lines to the outside world. A world where nothing is going on.

Where is everyone?

Has the place closed early because there are no customers?

Have the staff all gone home, too?

Surely, if that was the case, they would have locked up.

This is bizarre.

Faint music plays through crackling speakers which gives the place a haunted feel.

My heart trips over itself and the volume of its beats escalates inside my ears, easily overpowering the tinny music.

I grip onto the counter as panic seizes me. Instinct kicks in.

Run! Run, now!

I clench my teeth together and crush down on the desire to streak through the cafe, fling open the outside door and charge to my car.

This is ridiculous.

There's nobody here.

Nobody but me.

A faint scratching noise has me whipping around.

There's a bell on the counter and I hammer the heel of my hand on it, breaking the heavy atmosphere with deliberation.

I glance at the swing door into what I assume is a kitchen.

With one hand on my chest, I reach forward and push.

It gives easily.

Unbelieving, I stare at the heap on the floor.

I press my hand against my mouth to stop myself from screaming.

A small, plump woman, dirty blonde hair fluffed wildly around elfin features, lies on her side, curled up as though she tried to tuck herself into a foetal position but couldn't quite make it before death stole her.

Blood pools around her, congealing at the edges like a spot of heated jam.

Both hands with slackened fingers are curled around the handle of what looks like a chef's knife plunged hilt deep into the centre of her body.

I gag, pressing my hand harder against my mouth. It's Gilly.

I may not have seen her for the past twenty years, but her facial features are distinctive.

Still holding the door, I glance back into the cafe but there is no one. No one to help, no one to call.

Something shuffles in the kitchen, and without looking behind, I run.

Desperately scrabbling for my phone, I fling open the outer door, my scream piercing through the silent, deserted car park as I race towards the garden centre and the safety of the only two people I've seen here.

As the young man bursts from the garden centre and rushes towards me, my knees melt from under me and my world turns black.

26

PRESENT DAY – SUNDAY, 16 MARCH 2025, 5.45 P.M. – THE FOX

Bloody Gilly Houston. Silly cow.

She'd been more than willing to entrap Soriah all those years ago. When it suited her. When she would have benefited from it.

According to the court papers, she'd said she was looking to help her friend settle down into a serious relationship. She made it sound as though she was doing Soriah a favour, but it was because Gilly needed her own friend out of the way, leaving the field clear for her to have her choice of boys who really wanted Soriah more than her.

Poor fucking Gilly!

All she wanted was for her friend to be happy, she claimed. Content.

Boo-fucking-hoo!

She didn't though, did she? It was all just a means to an end. Her end. Her selfish, childlike wants and needs. She never saw beyond her own self-satisfaction. That's obvious.

All she can do is whine about how Soriah ruined her life by dobbing her in to the police, which meant she had to go to prison for three and a half years. She absolutely does not understand that her demise was down to her own juvenile stupidity.

She got off lightly there, in my opinion, but it meant that despite her intelligence, according to her, she could never get a job of any worth. Not with a police record.

So what made her decline to help me now? To get her own back?

Was it because none of it benefited her?

Despite her time inside, or maybe because of it, this woman is still a user. She uses her own family, for God's sake. She has no fucking pride. She begged them for a job working in their garden centre cafe, and they gave her one. They've looked after her and I'm not sure she deserves it.

Maybe it suits their purposes as well as hers.

I would have thought I could persuade her,

though, given what I told her, but I think she saw 'prison sentence' flash through her head once more.

I didn't ask her to do much. Just write a fucking letter. That's all. It was hardly an effort, but she reckoned once she put something in writing, she was doomed.

I can see her point.

She could have sent her a text if I'd given her Soriah's phone number, but all things considered, that could have complicated things.

That's not the result I needed though.

The moment I saw Soriah bundling her precious cargo into her car, pretty kitty Luna, I knew she was on her way to her parents'. I've followed her several times. Mostly she doesn't take that moggy and only stays a short while, but I know if she takes the cat basket with her, she intends on staying overnight.

I took a couple of shortcuts, because that's what I do. I know these streets like the back of my hand. I parked up the street from her. I don't know if she's a slow driver, or she stopped to fill up with petrol, but I'd started to doubt myself after waiting for her for over fifteen minutes.

Relief coursed through me. I thought I'd wasted my time, but in the end it turned out quite useful setting myself in position for a good view of her parents' house.

It was ideal timing.

I just needed all my ducks in a row.

She couldn't see me, but I know she suspected my presence. She lifted her head, nose in the air as if she could smell me, but I can melt into the shadows.

It gave me a sense of satisfaction to know I'd disturbed her. Given her a feeling of unease.

When I was a kid, I watched a documentary that showed how city foxes observe their prey for weeks, sometimes for months on end before they make a move. By that time, they've figured out every aspect of the prey's moves, every entrance and exit of their houses. Where the guinea pigs are kept, how safe the chicken coop is, or which bedroom the baby sleeps in.

I'm that fox.

I know everything there is to know about Soriah, and her cheating husband, Marcus. The sneaky bastard. I even know who he's cheating on her with. But that's my secret for now. I'll bide my time, wait for the right moment to make the big reveal, because that will be a real mindfuck.

The real golden nugget was finding that pregnancy test.

Fucking bitch doesn't deserve a baby.

Look what she did with the last one.

Now, my hands are shaking as I scrub them clean of blood I can no longer see, but I know it's still there.

The shower steams up the cold bathroom and still I stand under the torrent of water.

I never intended to hurt Gilly. Not really.

Just like the fox, it's my nature to check things out. I'd visited the garden centre on numerous occasions. By foot, by car, by bike. The bike is a quick getaway, but on foot can be less noticeable. If I do that, I park my car down the long lane where there's an animal rescue centre and one extra car will never be noticed in amongst the dozens that are strewn along there, people walking stray and abandoned dogs. Adopting them. I can't think of anything worse than having a dirty, flea-bitten animal. But I pretend I'm visiting there as I park up.

I wish I'd done that today.

People don't notice me. I've realised that. I duck my head as I enter the garden centre and tuck my hands into my hoodie pockets, looking for all the world as though I'm studying the flowers, the trees, the plants or the bags of compost. I've never gone inside during the day to look at the stupid garden ornaments, handbags and cards.

That's where a couple of the cameras are located. One panning the shop, on the look-out for shoplifters, and another concentrating on the till.

There aren't many cameras throughout. It's a garden centre after all, but it is privately owned so they take a little more care than mainstream garden centres.

There's one camera on the main entrance into the car park, one on the exit and one that pans around the car park in case anyone is shovelling more compost into their boot than they paid for.

The final one is focused on the till in the cafe.

That's why I don't go near the till. Have never been near the till.

I'm a city fox. I circumnavigate all the perils. Plan my route. Find my exits. And they're not by the official routes. I've learnt I can squeeze my way past the loose fence panels along the narrow dirt drive between the magnolia tree and the giant camellia bush, coming out the other side into the ornate garden whose path meanders past several small interconnecting ponds with carp of varying colours.

The gardens are overgrown and ready for a hard prune back this winter. I learnt that from one of the brothers who works here. That was a month ago. I've made sure I don't run into him a second time. I may be a city fox, but not a grey one, indistinct and shadowy, I am memorable in some ways, and the fact that we spoke may just trigger his memory if he sees me again.

Three brothers run the place with their dad, but it's the old girl who owns it, and she's a sly old fox herself. You have to keep a close eye that she doesn't spot you, because she'll make a beeline for you.

She did yesterday when I was talking to Gilly. Maybe I would have got further with Gilly if the old battleaxe hadn't spotted me and come over halfway through our conversation. If she'd minded her own business, I could have had more time, used my powers of persuasion, because Gilly is not the kind of woman who is averse to a flirtation, I can tell you.

Having entered the side door which leads out through the gardens where I'd prowled unnoticed for twenty minutes waiting for the last of the straggling customers to leave the cafe, I was standing by the swing door that opens into the kitchen and I'm pretty sure that one camera covers that angle so I stayed with my back to it. I don't need my face showing, but a grey hoodie from Asda can't be identified. I'm no snob. I don't need to wear designer clothing. Unless it serves a purpose.

'Is there an issue here?'

The old girl says the word issue with a hissing ess instead of with a sh. 'Iss-you.' I bet she thinks it makes her sound posh. Chances are, she says 'appre-seeate' too. Silly bitch.

I smile, enough to satisfy her, but not enough to attract her attention as Gilly gave a guilty start.

'Not at all. Just saying what a good bacon butty she does here.'

I rolled my shoulders forward in a defensive stance and ambled away, hoping she'd dismiss me from her mind, because she'd seen my face.

That's when the idea of using Gilly without her knowledge came to me.

My mind is quick and adaptable.

I didn't need her after all. My mistake. One I quickly rectified.

After making my way out through the garden, I'd scaled the wall of the flat-roofed garage from the unmonitored side and hauled myself through the narrow opening of the bathroom window. I've done this loads of times too. I'm a fox.

I'd helped myself to a few bits and pieces here and there, although there's very little that appeals to me. On occasion though, the old girl has put aside some cash before she places the rest in the safe overnight. One of the boys collects the main haul in the morning and away it goes to be banked. There's not normally much cash, not worth me drawing attention to myself for. Although I do know the combination as she's not too clever these days and keeps it written down.

Most customers pay by card. Sometimes though, I just nick a couple of twenties and wonder what she thinks when she counts it through and finds herself short.

Does she think she's going senile?

Or maybe she believes one of her lads has taken it. Swiped a few quid because from what I can see, she doesn't exactly pay them well for all the hours they put in. Minimum wage, at best. I have no idea why they continue to work for her, except they're probably hanging on waiting for their inheritance to drop. A place like this, with all this land, must be worth a fortune, acres of greenhouses full of crap at this time of year.

Tight bitch.

I wouldn't blame them if they did skim a little off the top.

Whichever, I don't believe she'd admit to losing a bit of money, twenty here, forty there, just in case they accuse of her being senile and stick her in a home.

I get that vibe when I've been lurking in the potting area listening to them talking about how much longer she can live on her own. No one else lives on site. Not even Gilly. I suspect because they don't want her to inveigle her way into the old girl's good books and steal their inheritance. They may be family, and Gilly's aunt gave her a job a number of years ago because no one else would, but that's as far as she gets her foot in the doorway as far as those boys, her cousins, are concerned.

They all go home to their families once they lock everything up, thinking the place is secure because they have a few cameras and a couple of locks.

Secretly, I think the big guy, Paul is his name, wants the house. Not in the state it's in. He'll probably gut it. One of them will have it as it can hardly be sold separately. The garden centre and cafe are their livelihoods.

The time will come when she pops off and things will change. Who knows, they might even sell the whole place off to a builder for a new housing estate. Just imagine how much she'd get if they sold it with planning permission for a few dozen houses.

Right now, the scent of mould and dead skin cells

lies heavy on the air, thick and cloying. She's closed all the doors and windows except that top one which she always leaves off the latch. I expect it's so the bathroom doesn't get too steamed up and create more of the black mould that lines the window.

I found what I was looking for relatively quickly. She keeps a small walnut writing bureau, and I delved inside. When I found it, I locked up and got out of there. She's a nosy old biddy and loves to spend her time cruising around the entire centre, interfering here and checking there, but I wouldn't put it past her to slip back home.

When I arrived back, I took my time composing the note, then slipped it through the letterbox of Soriah's parents' house. And fuck me, but I almost got caught. But I'm the fox and I slipped into the night.

I'm pretty sure Soriah never saw me.

Now, I step out of the shower and, grabbing a towel, I rub vigorously all over my skin, making it prickle and burn.

I drag clean joggers and a hoodie on and then sit on the closed toilet seat.

I close my eyes and lean forward, cupping my head in my hands.

There's a touch of elation beneath the pure terror.

A self-satisfied smile spreads over my face as I wind my mind back and let the memories rush in.

Shit. I've never killed anyone before.

That was horrific.

That was brilliant.

27

PRESENT DAY – SUNDAY, 16 MARCH 2025, 3.25 P.M. – THE FOX

I poke my head inside the door and do a quick scan just to make sure there's no one there but her.

'Gilly,' I whisper to grab her attention.

She spins around, one hand on her heart, the other pointing the blade of a long carving knife at me. It gleams with evil intent, but her face is slack with shock, and I know she's not about to use it on me. She trusts me. She's got no reason not to.

It was an instinctive reaction.

'Shh.' I put my finger up to my lips and duck my head slightly as I let the door swing closed behind me. There's just the two of us in the kitchen now. I made sure of that, waiting until she told the two young waitresses to go home early.

There's a north-east wind blowing, bitter and biting, sending people scuttling back home to turn on their heating, pour a drink or make a hot chocolate and stick the telly on.

That's what I would like to do. Instead, I'm stuck here, waiting. Waiting. Waiting. All fucking day I've waited. As I said I would. My own stupid fault, I should have put a time limit on the arrangement.

My stomach rumbles at the sight of all the food piled up on the side that Gilly's preparing for tomorrow. I've not eaten all day because I didn't dare risk being seen in here. There's nowhere in a ten-mile radius to get food.

This place is the arse end of nowhere.

I curl stiff fingers into balls, taking advantage of the heat of the kitchen where the savoury scent of meat pies almost knocks me off my feet. I'll be having some of those before I leave.

My feet are like blocks of ice, and Soriah, the bitch, has decided not to put in an appearance. I don't know why I thought she would. She owes Gilly nothing. According to Gilly, she does, but that's a whole different ball game.

'Gilly.'

She turns her back and places the carving knife down on the heavy wooden chopping board and then turns to face me, wiping her hands on the tea towel at her waist before removing it and placing it next to the knife.

'What do you want this time?' Her face hardens and there's a steely glint in her eyes.

'I've got Soriah's telephone number.' I hold out my burner phone and waggle it invitingly at the woman. It's all very well writing a letter supposedly from Gilly, but I can hardly make myself sound like this little woman.

She shakes her head and her dirty blonde hair drifts around her little face like the dying embers of a dandelion clock and I fully expect it to float away at the lightest gust of wind.

'I don't want it. I want nothing to do with her. Nor you. Go away. You're just shit-stirring. There's absolutely nothing about the past that can be changed, and I don't want to be this woman's friend in the future. She'd never agree to it in any case.'

'Don't you want forgiveness?'

Her eyes flare and she takes a step towards me. Looking into my face, she growls up at me. 'I don't need forgiveness from that woman. I did nothing wrong, so fuck off with your forgiveness prattle. If I'm guilty of anything it was being too good a friend, if you ask me.'

My mouth quirks up in a smile.

'That's not what the judge and jury found.'

'They're knobs. All of them.'

My burst of laughter takes us both by surprise.

Evidently, any kind of rehabilitation she's gone through has fallen by the wayside. This woman isn't rehabilitated. She still seems to think the world owes her something.

I cross my arms over my chest and circle around so I can lean on the counter. My stomach protests at the deprivation of food, and I reach for one of the sausage rolls cooling on the far side of the counter.

She slaps my hand, but it's too late. I already have hold of one and grin as I take a huge bite.

'Fuck! Fuck!' The fast burn of it scalds my tongue and I puff out steam as tears spring to my eyes. I think it's taking a layer off the inside of my mouth, but I don't spit it out, I keep huffing in and out to cool it before I begin to chew.

It's her turn to laugh, but it's hard and bitter. 'Serves you right, you thieving bastard. You think you can take what you want? That I won't say anything, just because of who you are?'

I shake my head, but as my mouth is full, she takes advantage.

'If you want to see her—' she pokes her finger towards me, and she's lucky it doesn't come in contact or she's likely to lose it '—you see her on your terms, but it's nothing to do with me. The past is the past, but if you want a bright, shiny new future with her, you take the step. Not me. Don't involve me.'

'But—' I want nothing of the sort and she's beginning to irritate me now.

'But nothing.' She imitates my previous move and crosses her arms. Her large chest wobbles like an underset jelly, I suspect because her bra doesn't come anywhere near fitting properly and she's bulging out of the sides.

She narrows her eyes as though she can hear my thoughts. 'It's not in my best interest to call her.'

I blow on the sausage roll and risk another big bite. Chewing noisily so I can suck in air and cool it quicker, I continue to badger her. 'Look, just get her here so I can talk with her.' My irritation is rolling over into anger. It's building like the embers of a dying fire someone has resurrected.

'Why? What's in it for me?'

And I can't for the life of me think what that would be.

'You get hold of her. But not here! I want nothing to do with it. Now, fuck off.' She waves her hand as if swatting away a fly and I catch it mid-air. She's already smacked me once and that was more than I'd normally tolerate.

She jerks backwards, but I hold firm to her wrist.

Surprise quickly turns to fury, and she swipes out with her free hand, catching my face with an angry wallop. The bite of sausage roll sticks in my throat and I almost choke. Coughing it up, I stare at her as she laughs like a loon, narrowed eyes filled with reckless insanity.

Shocked, I raise my hand to my burning cheek, but before it touches, I change direction and backhand her. No one touches me. I've never allowed it and I'm not going to start now.

She staggers back a step, and I follow, unsure if I want to walk away or slap her again.

She takes that decision from me.

With a screech high pitched enough to burst my eardrums, Gilly launches herself at me, clawed fingers swiping at my face as I raise my hands to defend myself. She slams up against me and I stagger back, surprised at the unexpected power. Losing my footing, I go down against the bench and crack one elbow hard enough it echoes through my ears.

I try to push her away, but she's crazy. Incensed.

I can't quite get my footing, and she won't stop screaming.

She needs to shut the fuck up or her cousins will come running from the far end of the garden centre.

I ram my hand against her mouth, shock zapping through me like an electric current as she clamps her teeth shut on the plump flesh at the base of my thumb. I scream, jerking my hand away, and my elbow catches something behind me, making it rattle against the surface of the bench.

I reach back. Grapple with it. I feel the handle of the knife in my hand and snatch it up just as Gilly launches herself at me again, teeth bared, eyes blazing.

The blade plunges deep into her plump little body, helped by her furious forward motion.

Astonishment fills her eyes. Horror. The snarl drops from her lips and we are frozen in time for a long moment as we stare at each other, locked like lovers in an embrace.

I step back, my fingers loosening their hold on the shaft of the knife. The whole blade is embedded inside her. Blood oozes from between my fingers and I grab for the tea towel Gilly had placed on the side, quickly swiping it up and down the handle of the knife, rubbing at any fingerprints it might have along the shaft.

A noise in the main cafe stops me dead, the light,

ironic tinkling of the doorbell. I grab Gilly's shoulders to stabilise her, lowering her to the floor before she even has a chance to fall.

A gurgling noise emits from her throat, but no words come from her mouth as blood bubbles up and dribbles from her lips. She's not dead. Not yet. But her eyes are glazed with a faraway look.

There's nothing more I can do here. It's too late.

'Mummy.'

At least I think that's what she mutters.

I take hold of the hilt of the knife with the tea towel, intent on wrenching it out and driving it straight through her heart this time to make sure the job is finished, but it doesn't budge. It's lodged deep between her ribs. The bright red bubbles spewing from her mouth are most likely from her lungs.

'Mumm—' Her eyes are wide and staring as I step back.

She's done for.

'Hello. Hellloo?' A woman's voice calls out.

Someone hits the little bell on the cafe serving counter right next to the swing door I'm standing in front of, jarring my senses and scraping my nerves raw. If they look through now, they're going to spot me.

My bowel spasms and I let out a sharp gasp. Fuck! I nearly shit myself.

I'm stronger than that though.

I'm the fox.

I don't know why, maybe because I'm in shock and the last cohesive thought I'd had was that I wanted them, but I scoop up three sausage rolls, stuffing them into the large front pocket of my hoodie as I make a quick decision.

I sprint to the back of the kitchen, hit the emergency exit bar on the door and push it down. I fly through, barely taking the time to check if anyone else is around, but I'm in luck and I race along the back of the building, through the thick vegetation. I push my way out of the wooden panels, leaving behind a bloodied handprint I can do nothing about.

My breath is heaving from lungs that are on fire as I reach the bike I'd partially hidden at the entrance to the garden centre, a bike that no one would think twice about seeing. I spin the dial on the safety lock and spring it open.

Head down, I power along the long narrow lane leading to the main road. It's around three miles and normally takes me about fifteen minutes, but I'm charging along, thigh muscles burning.

Just as I reach the rescue centre, the sound of blaring horns and sirens blast from the main road.

I slam on my brakes, my heart still racing faster than the wheels of the bike ever could. I leap off and push my bike behind the hedgerow near the turning to the centre. They're closed now, but I know there's a camera at their gates too. I keep my head lowered and risk moving off the road, close to the ditch and hedgerow as police cars fly past with an ambulance hot on their tail.

Dogs set up a unified howling, barking, whining cacophony and I push closer to the hedgerow, hoping like hell no one spots me as I cower, shock setting in, draining all of the adrenaline from me.

My legs shake and I lower myself to the ground, curling into a ball.

I can't stay here. The police won't hang around before they start searching. I know that. They'll spread out in an ever-widening circle.

I force myself up just as another police car flies past in the opposite direction.

I wait, listening for the sirens to fade and make sure there are no more.

I need to move.

I am the fox!

I sling my leg over the bike and force myself to

bear down on each of the pedals, one and then the other. Once the rhythm starts, the bike glides along, no longer a panicked rush, but a calm evening bike ride. I snort. If you believe that, you'll believe anything.

One glance at the sleeve of my grey hoodie, and I know I can't stay on the main road.

Blood soaks the cuff and swirls in bright splashes over my chest where I held Gilly to me as I lowered her to the floor so she wouldn't make a sound. That was a mistake.

Who knew there could be so much blood from just one stab wound?

I've always believed it had to be a frenzied attack to produce that much. It wasn't so much a frenzy as a really lucky jab deep into her chest, assisted by her own lunge forward.

I cross the main road and take the overgrown public footpath that runs alongside it, hoping I won't meet some random dog walker who has decided to venture this far. Not many do as the footpath leads nowhere and it's hardly a balmy evening as the rain turns torrential in my favour.

I lower my head, squinting against the driving rain, and cycle as fast as I can, determined to reach home without anyone seeing me.

My hoodie weighs heavy against my skin, soaking my already cold flesh until it turns to ice. My teeth rattle with the cold as shock sets in.

The memory of a bright voice echoes in my head, so clear she could almost be saying it in my ear.

'Hello? Helloo—'

I brake suddenly and come to a stop, my heart is straining with exertion and something else.

Fury. Frustration.

At the lost opportunity.

Because the voice I recall hearing was Soriah's.

She did come. All that effort, all that waiting and she came.

And I missed her.

I fucking missed her.

28

PRESENT DAY – SUNDAY, 16 MARCH 2025, 3.55 P.M. – SORIAH

Tears fall on my face, and I struggle to break free. Free of the confines of the box I'm trapped in, drowning in my claustrophobia.

I kick and kick but no one hears, no one comes.

He's here!

He's going to...

I drag in a breath and bolt upright, slapping at the arms that are holding me.

'Get off! Get off me!'

But the arms are gentle.

'It's all right, it's all right. I've got you. You fainted.'

My heart is hammering, and I shoot a look over at the cafe where the door stands open.

'Call the police. Call an ambulance,' I gasp out.

The elderly lady I saw earlier bends over me, and I realise the young lad and I are both on the shingle ground of the car park. My backside is in a puddle and icy rainwater soaks through my black leggings, transporting me to that place long ago when it wasn't fresh rainwater, but my own urine turning cold and soaking through.

Panic slices through me. 'Help!' Echoes of another time and place won't shake off.

'Are you all right, my lovely? You were lucky Adam caught you there, otherwise you would have taken a proper tumble.'

I struggle to my feet, moving out of the arms that although trying to help are restrictive and suffocating.

I grapple in my pocket for my phone, desperate to get help. I can barely breathe, let alone talk.

Adam hands it to me, briefly dusting himself off and then holding out his hands. 'You dropped it when you fainted. I'm sorry, I had to lower you to the ground. Should you be standing? I think we'll take you into the cafe and sit you down. Gillian can bring you a cup of tea.'

I shake my head furiously. 'She can't.'

I stab my finger against the numerical pad once the phone unlocks and dial 999, holding up my hand for both Adam and the old lady to keep quiet.

I haven't got time to explain myself or repeat it twice.

'Hello, yes. Police. Ambulance.' I'm pretty sure it's too late for the ambulance, but the police are certainly going to be needed.

A dawning look of horror crosses Adam's face and he makes a move towards the cafe. I snag at the sleeve of his fleece and shake my head again. 'Don't,' I mouth to him and raise my hand for him to stay.

'I've just arrived at a garden centre.' I reel off the address and have to repeat it as I've spoken too quickly. It's a wonder I've retained the address in my muddled mind, but I plugged it into my satnav at my parents' place, and managed to remember it.

'I went into the cafe to meet someone. There was no one there. I heard a noise and looked into the kitchen. There's a woman on the floor. I—She's got a knife in her stomach and there's blood. So much blood.' Black clouds rush through my vision, but I know I have to get this done.

I glance at the old lady and see her hands go to her mouth. She's turned a strange shade of grey. Watery blue eyes stare into mine and the moment of recognition hits both of us at the same time.

It may have been twenty-one years ago and the lady in front of me is no longer the smart, erect person I knew back then. Her hair is pure wiry grey and her shoulders are rounded, giving her a stoop I don't recall, but I recognise those eyes as they meet mine.

The phone slips from my hand, crunching onto the ground, and Adam snatches at me as my bones turn to water again.

'Soriah!' The word whispers from the old lady's lips as she, too, staggers.

Panic slashes over Adam's face and he wraps an arm around her as well as we stand in a huddle.

'Help!' Adam's voice booms out across the car park. 'Help!'

Two large men dressed in green overalls and wellies round the corner of the garden centre at the same time as each other and charge towards us, their combined weight making the ground shudder.

Adam gently hands the old lady off to the younger of the two men. 'Sean, Gillian's been stabbed. The police are on their way. We can't go into the cafe, but we need to find a chair for Aunty Anne, Paul.'

His eyes narrow as he turns back to me. The arm that encircles my waist tightens.

My gaze skitters away from his and I glance down at the phone on the ground. The screen is lit up, which means we're still connected, and the call handler is listening in. I don't know what to say.

This woman is Gilly's great-aunt on her mother's side of the family. We spent as much time at her house as we did Gilly's own in that year or so we were together. She was the owner of the strawberry farm we worked at during the summer which was how Gilly had managed to swing a last-minute job.

Recognition had taken a while on both sides, but I never knew there was a family connection to this place. I've never realised Gilly worked here. That was obviously why she said she could wait all day for my arrival.

I wonder if this young man has heard our story. If it has even touched him. The cool blue eyes indicate it has. There's no mistaking a name like Soriah. It is reasonably unusual.

He's not unkind as he steadies me and then guides me under the overhanging shelter to one of the two chairs Paul has retrieved from behind the garden centre counter. His whole body has stiffened, though, and I realise he knows Gilly's side of the story, although he could only have been a baby when it happened, it's possibly been often repeated.

The distant sound of sirens gets louder and still I can't move, not even to lean forward and retrieve my phone. Adam must have picked it up and he puts his ear to it.

'Hello? Yes, she's all right. We're here with her.' He glances at the older woman who has virtually been carried to the shelter and lowered into the second chair. Her wrinkled face has crumpled in on itself.

'You might want to send another ambulance, my aunty has taken quite a fright, and she's got a dickie heart. She's going to need checking over. Yeah, she's a real funny colour.'

Frosty eyes turn on me, giving me a quick scan, presumably in response to a question from the call handler. 'No, *she'll* be fine.' His voice, a moment ago soft and gentle, turns hard and unforgiving.

I want to point out that I would never have been here if Gilly hadn't sent for me, but nothing I say is going to help. Not at this point.

Tears well up and I turn my face from him. I don't need this kind of distrust. I never stabbed Gilly.

As the thought hits me, I drag in a breath. My head is still spinning, and bright spots explode behind my eyes.

I tuck one arm around my stomach, almost crying out as I think of my baby, and pray the stress doesn't kill it. I'm only in the very early stages, but it's taken us so long to conceive.

I lower my head to my knees, close my eyes and let the quiet of the men's voices drift over the top of my head.

This way I don't have to answer any of their questions. I'll wait for the police to come and I'll tell them everything I know. Like I did last time.

I let out a quiet whimper.

Will the police think I killed Gilly?

I want to raise my head as the loud wail of sirens indicates more than one police car is screaming down the drive towards us, but I'm not sure I have the strength.

I squeeze my eyes tighter as tears leak from between my eyelids.

Please don't let me lose my baby.

I want this baby. I really do. This one is so important to me.

29

TWENTY YEARS EARLIER – MAY 2006 – SORIAH

'One more time, Soriah. Push, now.'

I'm too exhausted to push, but my body seems to have ideas of its own. I'm barely in control as I bear down, grunting with the effort.

'Good girl. That's it, Soriah, that's it.'

A sharp pain rips through my vagina, and I let out a visceral growl as a popping sensation is followed by the fast slither and whoosh as my body expels the child.

Tears track down my face and I gasp in breath after breath.

I want to cry out for my mum, but I keep quiet. Nothing I say can change things now.

My heart feels as though it's been ripped from my chest, along with the baby from my womb.

'That's it, Soriah. It's nearly over now.'

What does she mean 'nearly'? Surely to God that's it? I don't think I can take any more.

'Congratulations. You have a little boy. Would you like to hold him?'

I turn my face away. From the baby. From the judgement I don't want to witness in the midwife's eyes. 'No. Don't bring him near me. I don't want to see him.'

It's not until that moment my decision is cemented in my mind.

I know I already committed to giving the baby up for adoption, but maybe, just maybe had it been a girl, I might have changed my mind. Not now.

I can't imagine looking into the face of a child who will grow up looking exactly like my rapist.

I know it's not the baby's fault, but that doesn't influence me one iota.

I didn't want to know the sex while I was carrying it. Better not to know.

Because of Craig, I have to live with the lies I've told, the decisions I've made and the heartbreak I've caused.

I've spent the last four months with a friend of my mum's down in Devon, pretending to my sisters that I'm finishing college elsewhere as I can't bear the thought of returning to my old college, my old friends.

The truth is, I didn't want my sisters to judge me. Not for the fact that I was raped. I know for a certainty that they are totally on my side. There's no hiding those facts from them and they never blame me for what happened. But they might have a different opinion if a child was involved. If they knew there was a baby on the way, they'd want me to keep it.

I couldn't.

The only other people who knew were my parents, and Mum was supposed to be here. But she's not. She never made it in time.

'Thank you. Thank you, Soriah.'

I look up and Denise hovers over me. Petite and slender with eyes of rain-soaked moss and rich, dark hair neatly pulled back from a heart-shaped face. Her eyes are wet with tears.

Her husband, Kai, is outside the delivery room as, although we share a bond, I really wasn't ready for a man to witness me giving birth.

Mum and I spent a considerable amount of time

choosing the right parents for this child that I can never love, but ironically never harm.

Kai is of mixed race, like me, so that makes it easier all round. Just because I'm my mum's daughter doesn't mean to say she understood originally about Afro-Caribbean hair, which is so different from her fine, straight bob. But my dad does. He taught her. Thank God.

On the contrary, my eldest sister has hair more like my mum's. It still has that wiriness, but it's more manageable.

At the very least, I want that for this child. Understanding, acceptance, even if I can't bring myself to love him. I want somebody to. It's not his fault his father is a monster. I have done the best I can for him.

I'm thankful for the opportunity they are giving him and vice versa. It's rare anyone gives up a newborn. It's rare that a child doesn't enter the adoption process not already having been traumatised.

This baby hasn't suffered any trauma and nor do I intend him to. I wish him the best life possible. I just don't want him to touch my life any more than he already has.

I hold out my hand and Denise squeezes it.

'I hope you have a wonderful life together.' My voice is hoarse and husky and I accredit that to all the abnormal, animalistic sounds that have come from my throat for the past couple of hours.

Relief washes over her features and only then do I realise all this time she's been holding on, hoping I wouldn't change my mind.

I still have time, but I'm not going to.

The smile I give her is weary as I wonder when my mum will arrive. We thought there'd be plenty of time between me starting labour and giving birth. Barely three and a half hours since my contractions started. It's like my body couldn't wait to expel him once his time came.

The midwife mentioned that it was because my body was young, fit and healthy. I'm not so sure. It's certainly not as healthy as it used to be. I've not run for ages. Partly because my belly was too big, but mainly because I don't feel safe. Running is a solitary pursuit mostly. I don't want to be alone. Nor could I have joined a club. I don't want the attention, the questions about a pregnancy I don't want to discuss.

Kath, Mum's friend, has been the ideal companion. She's a counsellor for grief and trauma. That's the whole reason my mum chose her. She seems to instinctively know when I want company and when I want to be left alone. She'd have come, if I'd asked, but Denise and the midwife were the only people I wanted if I couldn't have my mum. After all, it's not a circus.

I wanted the least fuss possible. No drama. Drama is definitely not my thing.

Mum should be here any time now. I almost don't want her to get here too quickly now, I'd rather she didn't see the baby. Just as I didn't want to have the opportunity to bond, nor do I want Mum to.

'Would you like to know what we're going to call him?'

I close my eyes. 'No, thank you. I'd rather not.'

'I understand.'

I know she does.

Denise gives one last squeeze and then slides her hand from mine as the midwife calls her name.

The room is suddenly empty and I'm alone with my thoughts.

I know, for both our sakes, I have done the right thing.

So why does it feel so wrong?

30

PRESENT DAY – SUNDAY, 16 MARCH 2025, 7.25 P.M. – SORIAH

Mum's face has turned to stone. She's sitting opposite me in the hospital cubicle as I lie on the bed and let the doctors complete their checks.

I don't want to look at her for fear of the disillusionment I'll see in the depths of her gaze, so I close my eyes and wait. I don't need to pretend I'm exhausted because I am totally wiped out.

When Mum and Dad arrived at the garden centre after the police called them, I handed them my car keys so my car, with Luna in it, could be taken back to their house. At least that's one responsibility I have off my hands. At least I know she is safe there.

Mum had to drive my car as Dad is only able to drive their automatic and mine is a manual.

I open my eyes as a lady in blue scrubs pops her head around the thin blue paper curtains.

'Soriah?'

'Yes.' I struggle upright.

The woman slips through the curtain and glances at my mum and then expectantly back at me.

'It's okay. This is my mum. She can stay.' I almost say she knows everything, but she doesn't. Not yet.

The woman gives a brief nod and then quickly analyses the notes she has brought in with her.

'I'm Dr Winter, head of obstetrics. I'm very pleased to say that despite the trauma you've suffered, your baby appears to be in a satisfactory condition.' She leans over and presses a couple of buttons on the beeping monitor and sends me a tight smile.

'Your vitals are absolutely fine, now, but when you first came in your blood pressure and heart rate were fairly high.'

Racing, she meant. I can see it in her expression, but she's being subtle, not wanting to raise my BPM again.

She reaches out and touches the back of my wrist. I think she's about to take my pulse rate, but it's not required as I'm already wired up. Then I realise it's a small sign of affection and empathy.

'We're going to send you home, but if you have

any concerns, there'll be a telephone number on your discharge papers, don't hesitate to ring my ward. I suggest you get some bed rest.' She looks up at my mum. 'Will you be able to stay with Soriah?'

My mum takes in a breath, but I know she's going to worry about Dad if she leaves him alone with his gammy hip.

I reach out. 'Marcus is due home later.'

Mum snaps her head around. 'Is he? Really? Where is he now, Soriah? Because he's not with his pregnant wife when she needs him.'

'Mum.'

'It's true—'

'No. That's not fair, I knew he was going away this weekend for the work awards presentations.' I feel it's only right to correct her, to defend him, especially in front of a doctor who is possibly thinking the worst. 'Mum, I only found out yesterday that I was pregnant.'

I sigh and drop my head. 'I wanted Marcus to be the first to know, then I was going to tell you and Dad.'

'How did that work out for you?'

I let out a soft snort as my mum's face breaks into a wobbly smile and she holds out a hand for me to grasp and then hauls me halfway off the bed into her arms.

The moment her grip on me tightens, I let out a sob and wrap my arms around her.

'Oh, Mum.'

'There, there. Let it all out, now. You've been through a lot over the last couple of days.'

As I pull back and Mum reaches up her sleeve, producing the ever-handy tissue for me to blow my nose and wipe my eyes, I notice the doctor has made a discreet exit to leave us alone.

I sniff. 'The police want to talk to me again. I told them everything I knew, but they said they'll call around to see me tomorrow and go through my statement again. Once I'm not so shaken. I think the paramedics just wanted to get me out of there and the police were scared the shock would cause me to miscarry once they realised I was pregnant.' I shake my head. 'Mum, it was horrible.' I look into my mum's eyes and see the pity, and much more, there's curiosity there too. 'There was so much blood. So much.' I swipe the tissue under my nose and then turn it in on itself, fiddling so my mind doesn't dwell for too long on the vision that insists on embedding itself inside my mind's eye.

Gilly's body, blood oozing.

'You never mentioned you were going to the garden centre. I would have come with you if I'd known.'

I raise my head and stare at her. 'How long have you known about Gilly working there?'

She presses her lips together. 'She's been there years. Her great-aunty owns the place. I thought you knew. She's the one whose strawberry farm you worked at… that summer.'

She lowers herself into the chair beside my bed, her voice quiet as though any reminder of 'that summer' might upset me. I can't be any more upset than I already am.

I can't move until the nurse comes and removes all the wires in any case, so I lean back.

'I never considered it her aunt's fault what Gilly did, and when she was in prison, I used to visit the garden centre. It's a nice place, and local. We never spoke, particularly. But we acknowledged one another.' Mum ducks her head as though remembering. 'One day, I walked into the cafe and there was Gilly. I turned around, walked out and I've never gone back.'

'You said you would have come with me.'

She nods. 'I would have. But I would also have made sure you knew what you were walking into. Gilly's not—*wasn't* popular with her cousins, but by all accounts, she was a hard worker and using the skills she learned in the prison kitchens, she was doing well in the cafe. I saw her aunt afterwards and I asked her why she'd not told me Gilly worked there. She said everyone deserved a second chance.'

Mum's lips quirk up at one side. 'Not with me they don't. I've never returned.'

'Mum.'

'Were you going to give her a second chance? Is that why you were there?'

I think her anger still boils hotter than mine inside. Is that because she's a mum?

I shake my head and reach for my bag on the small bedside cabinet. 'I don't know.'

My head swims as I bend forward so I jerk upright again. I delve in the small bag I now balance on my stomach and pass the handwritten note to my mum. 'She sent this last night.'

She frowns as she takes it. 'Where to? Our house?'

I nod.

'How—?'

'She must have posted it through the letterbox. I thought I heard something, a noise, I saw a shadow. Then there was the letter and it was addressed to me. I never mentioned it, because—' My shoulders sag. 'I didn't want to worry you, Mum. You've enough to worry about with Dad.'

There's silence but for the hustle and bustle on the outside of the curtains that enclose us. When she's read it, she folds it neatly and hands it back.

'How come you still have it? Didn't the police want to keep it?'

I shake my head. 'I never told them.'

She leans forward, eyes bulging. 'Why not?' she asks in an urgent whisper.

I want to say, because it would complicate things even further. Because they're going to think it was me who killed Gilly.

She reads it in my eyes and lets out a groan. 'Tell them. Now.' She picks up her phone and hands it to me.

'I have my own phone. Mum, it's complicated—'

'Not as complicated as a poor innocent woman lying dead in a pool of blood.'

I gasp. 'Muuuum!'

Hardly innocent, I know, but not deserving of murder, I have to admit to myself.

'I may not have ever forgiven her for her part in what happened to you, but I would never wish her dead.'

I nod as tears fill my eyes again. 'Nor me, Mum.'

'It's not you the police are after, Soriah, you're not covered in blood. You would be if you'd murdered someone. They already know it wasn't you, or you wouldn't be lying in this bed without being handcuffed to it.'

She pauses, her eyes going wide. 'What if the person there was out to get you and not Gilly?'

I draw in a breath because that's exactly what I'd been thinking, but I haven't told her Craig Lane has been released, because that's another secret I've been keeping from her.

'I know. I know.'

'Then ring the police and ask them to meet us at home. You're staying the night with me where I can keep an eye on you. Luna's already there in any case.'

'But Marcus—'

'But Marcus, nothing. If he wants to come and see his pregnant wife, he can jump in the car and come to my house.' One slim eyebrow raises, and she gives a little chin jerk in my direction. 'I know he's not comfortable with us, but I'm your mother and you're not going to be out of my sight until I'm sure you're well enough, and safe enough. Now, phone that number the nice police officer gave you and ask him to meet us at home.'

I pick up my own phone and find the number the

officer put in for me earlier when I was too much in shock to even speak, let alone process a telephone number.

I dial and wait for the reply.

Mum's right.

This is important.

What if the person who murdered Gilly made a mistake?

What if she got in their way, and they were really after me?

31

ONE YEAR EARLIER – SATURDAY, 17 FEBRUARY 2024, 11.25 A.M. – CRAIG

Being in prison can be so knackering.

My yawn almost cracks my jaw as I lean against the cell door watching the dull day drag on. Some days the inmates are full of energy and high jinks, but every so often the whole place drops into misery.

Today is one of those days.

It's not just about the weather, although that can be a factor.

Sometimes there's a valid reason. Like when Tommy Durrant got slashed by one of the cokeheads who'd managed to get hold of drugs after a year of abstinence. He went off his rocker and killed his so-called best friend, Tommy, in the shower. The butter knife he'd smuggled from the kitchens and sharpened to a lethal edge himself sliced through Tommy's soft round abdomen, spilling his guts on the filthy shower floor while he watched, his brain not yet processing his body had died.

Tommy had been a good 'un. He made us all laugh.

Once you witness something like that though, you need time out to consider how fragile life is. Even more so when you're inside.

Keith Hammett died the day he was due to be released after serving eighteen years for armed robbery. His wife, who'd visited him every week for his entire sentence, waited for three hours in the car park outside thinking they were taking their time releasing him. When she got word he'd died of a heart attack, she drove to their favourite dating spot, drank the entire litre bottle of whisky she'd bought for their celebrations and swallowed a month's supply of her arthritis tablets. That would do the trick.

You'd think.

Only she ended up in ICU on life support. Poor old cow.

Those were the times morale dropped.

Today, I couldn't tell you what the reason is, but it

hangs thick in the air like the stench of stale spicy food.

Something's coming.

I fold my arms over my chest and squint as I track movements. The inmates, the prison officers.

I don't worry about me. Not any more. I've looked after myself in here. Kept fit, exercised. Unlike loads of the guys, my belly is flat and my shoulders are broad from lifting weights.

I was only a kid, my body barely developed, tall and stringy when I was first sentenced. I've found I love the physical. Something I brought with me from the outside. That connection to Soriah, watching her run, jump, throw. I want to be fit when I'm released. And the time is coming. The more I can do, the closer I feel to her. The happier it makes me.

Unlike this place.

I stare across at the landing opposite and then slip into my own cell.

I don't need to see this. I've witnessed enough over my time here and it still turns my stomach.

Retribution.

It's doled out inside for the most inconspicuous slight.

If you know what you're looking for, you can see it coming.

Fat Billy Carson is going to have that new young lad before the morning is done.

Billy, fat bastard and top dog in this section. We've never come to blows, the two of us, as we have a quiet respect for each other. I don't do drugs. I think too much of my body to do that. I had a go in the beginning and soon realised it was a fool's game. I was one of the lucky ones who never got hooked.

The young lad, I forget his name. Tyrone, maybe. They come, they go. He won't last long. He'll be out before we know it, one way or another, escorted in cuffs somewhere else for his own protection, or on a stretcher. The latter is more likely.

Word is Fat Billy Carson took a dislike from the moment the cocky young lad came in, swaggering for all the world to see he was a hard man.

He's not hard. Billy will prove that.

I turn my back and walk away. Some fights are worth seeing. Some aren't. Others just sicken you to your stomach. This will be one of them.

'Lane.'

I whip around, hand clenched into a fist, prepared to do battle myself. You don't sneak up on each other in here. It could cost you your life. But it's Weasel. The skinny, balding little guy who delivers the post. If ever we have a meltdown in this pot, he's going to be one of the first to go. It would be my pleasure.

He's one of the screws but no one knows how he got the job. Maybe his mummy is the governor. The only thing he has going for him is he's slimy and he knows everyone's business. For a price.

That's probably because he delivers the mail to the cells.

He's not supposed to. That's not how it works.

In fact, I'm not even sure how he keeps this job, but once the mail is scanned and any contraband removed – which he probably takes for his own – Weasel brings letters around. Only the interesting stuff. Most the other stuff these days is scanned, but on occasion the scanner breaks down. Call me cynical, but I think it's whenever there's something juicy in the mail.

Not that I ever receive mail from anyone.

As he holds it out to me, I frown.

I've not had a letter in years.

I've written dozens, but never received a reply.

Weasel smirks as I take it, holds on to it for a millisecond longer than needed, just to show his power. 'This one's a killer, mate. You might want to take a seat. Who'd have thought?'

My forehead creases in a frown as I look from the

single sheet of paper in my hand back up to Weasel who seems to have made himself comfortable in the doorway, looking as though he can't wait for me to read the letter.

I want to tell him to piss off, but that's not a wise move. Him and Fat Billy are as close as you can get in this kind of environment. I don't need that sort of trouble.

I read the first line and risk a glance at Weasel, who sends a crooked, expectant grin my way, as though he can't wait for me to read on.

A rush of heat engulfs me, swallowing my face in a fiery glow.

'Fuck.'

I lower myself onto the bottom bunk.

'Fuck.'

I rest my head on my hand.

'You want me to read it to you?' Weasel laughs and I want to punch him in the face, but I'm known for my good behaviour and I'm not spoiling that when I have less than a year to go before I get out.

'Fuck off.' But I say it without heat. I'm too floored by the first couple of words.

Dear Dad,

Sweat breaks out on my upper lip. I barely have the strength to wipe it away. Every muscle has turned to water.

Dear Dad,
 This may come as a shock to you.

No shit, Sherlock!

For the past eighteen years I have lived under the misapprehension that the people who have raised me are my parents, when in fact they are not.
 I'm sure you can imagine the shock I had recently on the death of my mother, when I discovered the truth from my dad.
 Under the influence of antidepressants, the truth came out and has caused a rift in our relationship.
 Their reasoning for not telling me was, he said, because they always felt I was theirs and that my biological parents had given up the right to have anything to do with me when they handed me over.
 I disagree. And apparently, so do the authorities. I contacted them.

> *I have for the past few months sent letters to my biological mother, Soriah, to gain information without any reply or acknowledgement. I'm not sure my letters reach her as apparently the address was an old one and she may have moved.*
>
> *Your name was not registered on my birth certificate but in amongst papers I found in my 'mum's' drawers, I came across a letter from Soriah to my mum confirming you as my father. Apparently, there was some question when I was a baby that needed a genetic check.*
>
> *There is nothing to confirm whether or not you are aware of me, but I think it only right and fair that we are given the opportunity to become acquainted.*
>
> *I hope you find it in you to reply. My birth mother did not.*
>
> *In anticipation,*
> *Your son*

I stare at the name on the bottom of the letter while my eyes fill with tears.

Soriah and I made a son together.

Weasel's laughter is distant and echoey in my head.

My tongue is stuck to the roof of my mouth, too dry for me to swallow.

Fuck! I never knew. I never knew any of this.

Soriah.

Rage is building in the pit of my belly like a furnace being stoked.

How could she do this? I've been a dad all this time and would never have known except for this lad who has contacted me.

What a fucking bitch. The ultimate punishment. Far worse than being imprisoned all this time.

The paper in my hand starts to shake uncontrollably.

'Mate.' Weasel's voice is faint, as though coming from a great distance, overwhelmed by the thudding of my own heart, wrapped in the white noise that has become my world.

I'm barely able to raise my head and my eyes swim with tears. His laughter has dried up. 'Mate. You all right? You've gone a right funny colour.'

My breath jams hard in my throat.

I want to reply, if only to tell him to fuck off again, but this is serious.

I can't even think how fate is a bitch, depriving me of seeing the son I never knew I had.

There's a pain in my chest sending licks of fire

down my left arm. The letter trembles in my numb fingers and then flutters to the floor as though it has a life of its own.

Fuck.

This is it.

I'm having a heart attack.

32

PRESENT DAY – MONDAY, 17 MARCH 2025, 3.05 A.M. – THE FOX

I've fucked up!

I bolt upright in bed, the covers sliding down to pool around my hips.

It was never my intention to murder the chubby little bitch.

It was never my intention to leave any evidence.

But I have.

Assuming Soriah still has that letter I wrote to her.

In my handwriting, not Gilly's. There was a reason I wanted that stupid cow to write it.

Fuck!

My chest tightens and panic slices through me.

I scissor my legs to kick off the bedding and leap

out of bed. Grabbing the neat pile of clothing I folded the night before, I tiptoe into the shower room and tug everything on. I remove the panel on the side of the bath and drag out the black bin liner containing my soggy clothes from the day before. I can't risk wearing them again, there's so much blood soaked into the sweatshirt and streaked down the trackie bottoms. I can't risk sticking them in the wash, even. Not in this place. They're all too savvy here. Which is hardly surprising.

I'm pretty sure I left fingerprints back at the garden centre, I know that, but I don't need that extra layer of evidence rearing its head if ever I get caught. There was nothing on the knife, I'm pretty sure, but I left a print on that back fence panel, it's well-hidden so long as they don't follow that route, and hopefully the rain will have washed the evidence away. If luck is on my side, it will have done. Then again, they may be doing a fingertip search of the entire place.

I'm sure I'll hear something later. The whole place will be talking about it. Gossips all of them at work.

Then there's the letter. That could show premeditation. That I deliberately lured Soriah to the garden centre. Which I did. It's my handwriting.

The connection between Soriah and Gilly is

strong. I did use Gilly. Admittedly. But I wouldn't necessarily want to admit that to the cops.

Sweat beads on my brow as I drag on my socks and trainers. I can't afford another pair of trainers, so they will have to do. I'm not exactly badly paid, but I've no one else to support me. I have to stand on my own two feet, pay rent and contribute to the heating and electricity here, which seems to be on twenty-four hours a day, and my bloody little car has just cost me a fortune when it failed its MOT. Definitely not buying trainers anytime soon.

No worries, I don't think I stood in any of the blood as it spread from Gilly's body in a widening pool.

I blink away the image.

My stomach gives a sickly lurch, especially when I reenact in my head that moment the blade pierced Gilly's body, giving almost a popping sensation as her skin split, allowing the knife to slide in deep. I never knew it would be so simple, so easy. I thought there would be resistance, but with the aid of her momentum, that knife glided through her body like it was soft butter.

The flood of warm blood over icy fingers still hovers in my memory, the sharp metallic scent of it clinging to my nostrils, no matter how long I stood in that shower. Until someone hammered on the door, and I needed to vacate.

I'm at once revolted and thrilled.

Who knew taking a life could be so easy? So satisfying.

Gilly had been an irritant from the first moment we started to communicate. What a whiny, whingy little woman she was. I've never known anyone blame her fate on another person so much.

Soriah ruined my life.

I wish I'd never met Soriah.

I see Soriah is living her best life, married now to a handsome man, with a good job.

I had to settle for being a glorified waitress because of Soriah.

I can't even get a good man. The last one I hooked up with beat the living shit out of me. Just because of Soriah.

My life could have been so much better if not for Soriah.

I could have been someone.

Gilly was never destined to be anyone. She was too much of a narcissist. Forever blaming everyone else for her shortfalls.

She never even sees her own parents since she went to prison. What kind of person cuts family off? Despicable, that's what. She's not the only one to do that. Admittedly, from the sound of it, it was a two-way thing for her and her parents.

You can be angry with someone, but surely you can forgive family anything. If the circumstances change, personalities shift. Forgiveness is a blessing. We all deserve it, and we are all capable of change.

Apparently not Gilly, though.

She had the most irritating habit of pinching a little bit of skin on the inside of my elbow between her fingers and twisting it as soon as she became excited about anything. I almost knocked her sideways the first time she did it. But I needed her then. Or so I thought. Too late for regrets now, but I got my own back. No more nasty little pinches from her.

I snatch up my rucksack and slip from the house, pulling the door shut behind me. In the silence it sounds like a gunshot.

I freeze.

I don't want to attract attention or wake the two lads who are still asleep. I lower my head and set off at a trot down the road to where there's a load of industrial work going on with enormous skips, far bigger than ones used on domestic projects.

I lob the bag over, mourning the loss of the clothes inside, but it can't be helped. I daren't risk it.

Once I've rid myself of that burden, I jog on a

little faster. I don't want to use the bike this time. Don't want it seen in case someone recognises it from the garden centre, or I was heard taking it from the house. Strictly speaking, it doesn't belong to me. It's Ken's but he never uses it in the winter. He's a fair-weather cyclist and he's never noticed before when I've borrowed it.

By the time I approach Soriah's house, my chest is burning with the amount of cold air I've sucked in, and I bend at the waist, resting my hands on my knees for a short while as I gather myself.

The soft tremor in the pit of my belly has grown, spreading outwards until my fingers tremble and my knees weaken. I need food. I've not eaten since I stabbed Gilly. The cold sausage rolls are in a little zip-sealed bag under my bed so no one else snaffles them. I thought I would eat them late last night but at the thought of them nausea rose in a ball of acid into my throat.

I need something now. My sugar levels have dropped to rock bottom.

I blow out a breath as I contemplate what Soriah might have in her kitchen. Perhaps I can grab something out of her breadbin, or cupboard. Stuff a few things in my backpack to keep me going for a few days. Just until I get paid again. I know it won't always be like this, but I'm not that well-paid right now, not until I build some experience. I've run out of money and there's virtually no food left. The other guys are like scavengers. The slightest scent of anything edible and they're on it like flies on shit. There's no respect for personal belongings.

Maybe I can stock up. I took a litre of milk last time and a new box of Weetabix she had stashed behind an open one. She was never going to miss those. Perhaps I can forage. Provided I don't wake them.

And it is *them* this time. Much riskier.

Marcus, the knobhead, is back home from his sojourn away.

I don't know what it is about him I dislike. Really, there's very little reason I should object about him playing away from home. None of my business, certainly.

I can't help myself though. It irks me.

What irks me more is that he's home. And that makes it more difficult to shimmy into their house with the risk of the two of them. He's a big guy. I don't want a confrontation with him.

Before anything, though, I have to open the key safe and get the key.

Then I have to tackle that fucking awful cat again.

I think it likes me. It sets up a pitiful yowl when it sees me, like I'm its long-lost reincarnated mate.

The first time it sidled up to me, I nearly shit myself. I was inside that cupboard on my hands and knees trying to see if there was anything interesting I should know about in there. That's what I'd come for after all. Like a box with documents in, or some clue to the life this woman leads. I was simply being nosy.

A noise like a crying baby had me freezing where I was until that cat sidled up against me, tail high in the air, rubbing itself against my hip, slowly sidling up to my shoulder.

I shot out of the cupboard and slammed the door. My heart raced.

Last time I chucked a piece of roast chicken from Soriah's fridge into the understairs cupboard to get it out of my way before it had the chance to take me by surprise.

It won't leave me alone.

Don't get me wrong, I'm not a cat hater. I wouldn't set out to harm furry bundles.

I'm not a monster.

It's just I am massively allergic to anything with feathers or fur. They only need to brush up against me, or for me to inhale some of the dust from their skin. My eyes swell shut within minutes and I sound like an eighty-a-day smoker using a CPAP machine when there's been a power cut.

Even being in the house for a short time makes my skin itch.

I always carry a little bottle of prescription Piriton with me though, for just such occasions. It's not a miracle worker, but it takes the edge off. The best method is to avoid animals altogether.

This time I have no choice though. I need to get hold of that incriminating letter.

I creep around to the long, dark passageway edging the side wall of the house, feeling for what I want in the pitch black and punch in the code to the key safe by touch. The front drops down and I reach into the tiny, dark cavern, not daring to turn on my flashlight. I feel around with tips of fingers that are almost numb with the cold.

Fuck!

It's not there.

Clever girl.

She's not changed the keycode, that would have been too simple. She's removed the key altogether. Which, let's give Soriah her due, is the intelligent thing to do if you know someone has broken into your house to send you photographs of your own positive pregnancy test.

She's just made it that much harder for me. Not impossible. Just more difficult.

I try the latch on the back gate, and she's bolted that too.

I wonder how scared she is.

I grin.

Does she think I'm coming after her, like I did Gilly?

I'm not sure I'd want to repeat that level of violence, but now I've done it once, maybe the second time won't be so hard.

I reach up and hoist myself over the side gate, using my feet to walk part way up. I land on the other side a little harder than I anticipated, and sharp bursts of heat flash up my ankle as my foot turns.

Shit!

I hobble to the back door into the utility room, hoping she at least made this easy by leaving the door unlocked.

I turn the handle and push, bracing my shoulder against the door to absorb the sound.

No chance.

This woman is not stupid. There's a certain pride in that discovery.

I rummage in my rucksack and pull out a box of miniature screwdrivers. I used to have to do this all the time when I was a kid, as Mum always said I could wait until she got home before I was allowed in the house. She never gave me a key because she didn't trust me not to lose it. I had done so twice. She learnt not to stick it under a plant pot, or again I would use it, then either leave it in the outside of the lock or lose it.

Her mistrust of my reliability means I know how to scale fences and pick locks.

I slide the smallest of the screwdrivers in the lock and fiddle around blindly in the pitch black.

I can't do this.

I need light.

As I delve into my pocket to retrieve my torch, ironically, the very thing I need – light – blazes from the kitchen window, casting its long finger to point me out.

I hit the ground, the unlit torch rolling away from me as I ball up as small as I can to make myself invisible in the darkness next to the wall.

Terror streaks through me and I tuck my face almost into my knees.

If anyone cares to look, they're going see me, rolled up on their patio, soaked to the skin. There's not a single excuse I can find as to why I would be behind the locked gate into their garden, at their back door, while it's pissing it down with rain.

In the night, it is silent.

I raise my head and risk a glance.

I don't think I've been seen.

I push to my feet and sidle along the short stretch of wall between the utility door and the kitchen window, pressing myself tight against it, my breath barely leaving my mouth.

I roll my shoulders and peer into the kitchen.

Well, fuck me.

Soriah is there.

She's on her own.

33

PRESENT DAY – MONDAY, 17 MARCH 2025, 3.55 A.M. – SORIAH

I understand why Marcus didn't want to sleep over at my parents'. I really do. For a start, there's no way the two of us can share a bed. They're way too small. And even if Marcus took one bed and I had the other, his feet would dangle off the end unless he curled up on his side. Marcus is not a side-sleeper. He likes to stretch out full length.

Did he need to cause an atmosphere, though? Honestly, Mum only wanted what was best for me. She wanted to keep me close and cosset me. Truth be told, I wanted to be cosseted.

Marcus didn't, nor apparently did he want me to be.

Marcus got his way. As usual.

Now, he's fast asleep, stretched out full length on his back doing that heavy breathing that borders on a snore.

I touch my wrist where it's tender. I can pretend to others that it was from when I fell at the garden centre, but the two of us know the truth. It was when Marcus grabbed me when Mum and Dad weren't looking and squeezed so hard I whimpered.

It's the first time he's physically hurt me. I think.

And then I remember my nightmare where a weight was pressing down on my chest. Could he have done that? Would he?

He has no reason, and I am catastrophising. My mind in a desperate whirl thinking of everything I can to distract myself from the real threat.

I'm staring unseeing at the ceiling, terrified to close my eyes because I know the vision I'll see will be Gilly. The handle of that long knife sticking out of her stomach, blood oozing until it coagulates in a pool around her.

I slip from under the covers and pad to the bathroom on bare feet. I shrug into my dressing gown and slip toes that are already turning chilly into thick bootie socks and then sneak downstairs. I don't want to wake Marcus. He was already sulking before we went to bed, he'll be worse if I disturb him.

Apparently, my mother's call spoilt his whole weekend, even though he was due to come back in any case.

The kettle sounds loud in the quiet of the kitchen as it comes to the boil, then clicks off, plunging me into deadly silence.

I can't be bothered to move.

I've not felt like this since Craig raped me.

It's hard to put my finger on it, but a kind of numbness creeping over me until my mind stops thinking. Or is it? It's cloaked in cottonwool, everything dulled down so nothing can hurt me.

Like when the GP put me on antidepressants. They never stopped the depression, just dimmed it, like draping material over a lampshade to subdue the lighting. When you remove it, everything seems even brighter and sharper than before.

It's possibly the shock.

Is this what happens when you keep secrets, though?

I've not told Marcus about the baby, although I know Mum really wanted me to. Not just because she thinks he'll be thrilled but she wants him to take good care of me. Protect me.

I'm not sure he ever has. I'm the caretaker, the nurturer.

Marcus expects it.

Maybe things will change once I let him know. But the timing could not have been worse.

It's my surprise though. I want the timing to be right so Marcus and I can celebrate properly together.

It feels obscene somehow in the face of Gilly's death to suddenly announce this new life.

A death that, although Marcus was shocked about me witnessing, didn't seem to impact him very much.

Admittedly, despite my mum's glowering at me, I never mentioned the connection between Gilly and myself.

Because how could I do that without the whole story coming out? A story I've never told him. So, as far as he's concerned, I walked into a cafe and found a woman dead on the floor.

I wonder how he would react if he found a freshly dead body.

I'm sure he'd freak right out. But somehow he seemed to think I would cope. Like I always cope. So, no, he hasn't really offered up a huge amount of comfort. Except as he turned his back on me when we first went to bed.

'Y'all right?' he said.

'Not really.'

'Hmm.' His words faded as sleep took him down. 'You'll feel better after a good night's sleep.'

Like that was the cure for everything.

I change my mind about the cup of tea I was about to make and reach instead for a tub of hot chocolate I keep in the kitchen cupboard. I spoon three heaped spoonfuls into my mug and then open the fridge to take the milk out.

I blink.

Where the hell is the milk?

I bought a fresh one on Friday, didn't I? And because Marcus hasn't been here, I've not used it. Or have I?

I scan the inside of the fridge, moving containers to one side to double check. It's not there. This is unbelievable. There's about half an inch in the bottom of the old carton. No new one. Bizarre.

I bought one.

Definitely.

Or did I?

Shit, I'm losing my mind. Is that what baby brain does? All those hormones charging around like a stampede of wild horses. Filling me with panic.

I let the fridge door drift closed and pour boiled water onto the chocolate powder. I know you can use just water, but it's never the same. Milk is always better. Certainly, when you find out you're pregnant.

I stir the hot chocolate. Round and round and round. Chocolate powder forms lumps which float to the surface and keep on spinning long after I stop stirring.

Like the thoughts in my head. Some of them clumped together, others flying apart, but all of them spinning in the same direction until eventually the centrifugal force forms a whirlpool, tugging all those little clumps into the vortex until they're dragged to the bottom to disperse.

My thoughts are intent on dispersing too, but I wrestle them back from the edge of that precipice.

I pick up my mug and cradle it in my hands while I stare into space.

What reason did anyone have to kill Gilly? Just stab her straight through the stomach like that. I don't want to think about this, but I can't help myself.

It's too much of a coincidence that she wrote me that note, pleaded with me to meet her, then just happens to get killed on the same afternoon I'm due to meet her. Was it someone who knew of our meeting? Why would anyone want to kill Gilly? To stop her talking to me?

I can't imagine for one moment anyone would have a reason to stop her speaking with me.

I take a sip of my hot chocolate and realise how much time has passed as I've sat here, it's not terrifically hot.

I frown.

The letter.

I take another sip of my hot chocolate and then put it on the kitchen counter. Leaning forward, I unloop the strap of my handbag from the back of the chair and draw it towards me.

I know I have a photograph of it on my phone, but it's not quite the same, so I take the letter out and spread it on the kitchen surface, flattening the creases. I know I'm giving it up to the police later this morning, but I've opened it before, read it, screwed it up into a ball so many times I'm sure there won't be fingerprints other than my own on the paper. And Mum's. I must mention that.

I stare at the writing.

There's a trickle of recognition, but I can't quite—

How would I know if it's Gilly's or not? It's been years since I saw her writing. We'd sit next to each other during lessons, and she had what I thought then beautiful, unique writing with perfectly formed script, each of the tailed letters, or descenders, cut short to perfection so the text was uniform.

This writing is fluid, slanted forward, with curling tails and flamboyant ticks. Slightly scruffy. But it could have been rushed.

How am I supposed to know?

It's completely different in my mind to Gilly's.

Then again, what would I know?

We were teenagers.

Now we're women. Well, we were.

Only Gilly is no longer alive.

Can a person's writing change that drastically?

I think not.

So what does this all mean?

If that's not Gilly's writing, then someone else wrote the note. Why would anyone pretend to be Gilly? Unless they wanted to entice the recipient of the letter. To trick them.

I pick up my hot chocolate and finish it off. No matter how well wrapped up I am in my dressing gown, a chill skitters over my skin so I'm covered in goosebumps.

Why would anyone want to come after me? I've done nothing.

There's a stir of unease deep inside, because that's

not quite true. I have done something and that comes back to haunt me.

From the bag, I draw out the other letter I slipped inside when I was at Mum and Dad's house. One of the many I keep in the bottom of my dresser. The ones I never answered.

I compare the writing, my hands trembling as I hold the letters side by side, a streak of terror shooting through me. Am I mistaken, or is there a similarity?

I need to speak with the police in the morning.

They need to know.

I think Gilly was killed because of me. Which means I'm being stalked.

I blow out a breath and stand up. This time I fold the letters neatly and slip them inside my handbag. I don't want Marcus to know, but how can I keep this from him? All the dark secrets of my past. Will it change his opinion of me? Does it matter?

I raise my head and watch rain streaking down the window, my reflection staring back at me. There's absolutely nothing I can do tonight.

I need to go to bed.

Tomorrow I'll deal with all of this, but exhaustion is dragging at my limbs. I'm done.

I walk to the sink and reach to turn the tap on to rinse my mug out.

A shadow flits across my peripheral vision, and I gasp.

I take a step back from the window, and then another. I reach for the kitchen light and plunge myself into darkness and then charge into the utility, skidding through the door just as the shadow flows past the door to the garden gate, a hulking dark silhouette streaming out of my view before I can fully focus.

I reach for the door handle and freeze.

Do I really want to do this?

34

PRESENT DAY – MONDAY, 17 MARCH 2025, 10.25 A.M. – THE FOX

Well, well, well.

Who knew?

I let out a brief burst of wild laughter.

Well, shit. This is going to surprise her.

I take a photograph and don't even hesitate as I forward it to Soriah.

> SNAP!

This game is getting ever more exciting.

I thought I'd fucked it up last night. Who knew she could be so hostile? So fucking fast. I thought she was coming out the back door after me.

I look both ways before I close the front door behind me and start off down the street, a grin plastered on my face, despite everything, because that has to be the best, most ironic news ever.

Just wait until she finds out. Soriah is going to hit the roof and I want to be there when the penny drops. I really do.

I check my hands where I scraped them raw as I scrabbled to get over the fence last night. The burn is a bitch, but I let out a laugh. This is insane. Bizarre.

I wasn't willing to take on Soriah. Not under those circumstances. She looked like she was about to do battle and she's no Gilly. No, Soriah is tall, athletic. Regal. Most of all, she looked like a lioness about to go to battle to protect her cub.

Oh, the irony!

Wouldn't you think she'd be cowed by her past? Not a warrior! I can't help but admire that in her.

I'm going to have to be a lot wilier though.

Truthfully, in my defence I was not expecting her to be in the kitchen last night at the exact time I was about to break in. Just like I wasn't expecting Gilly to attack me. Self-defence. That's what it was when that knife ran through her.

I'm not sure I can get away with that reasoning twice.

I don't even want to. I don't want to kill Soriah,

that was never my game. I simply want to see her ruined for what she did to me. What she put me through. It's simply justice. An eye for an eye. Or in this case, a ruined life for a ruined life.

I want to watch her suffer.

Besides, I'm actually having fun.

I hunch my shoulders up near my ears to ward off the cold. I borrowed one of the lads' puffa coats, but the wind whips through it, providing no protection at all. Cheap, nasty knock-off. But I want to look different each time I come along this street in case I get caught on someone's Ring doorbell or some such shit. I know how these things work. One little misstep and you're all over social media for everyone to judge your guilt.

The general public don't think it's appropriate to contact the police directly these days. No, they slap it on Facebook or their local WhatsApp group and ask every other fucker's opinion but the one that counts.

I pause at the end of Soriah's street and tug my baseball cap lower on my head, hitch the collar up and groan as it flops back down again, letting the icy blast of wind sneak in through the gap at my neck.

Her car's gone, which I half expected because it's a workday. Then again, I did wonder if she'd take the day off, like dear Marcus has done. Sly little git.

I recognise the other car parked slightly further along the street and I perk up instantly.

Oh, this really could be interesting.

I slide my burner phone from my pocket and take a shot of the royal blue VW Golf. Distinctive even without looking at the registration plate.

A tremble of excitement rushes through me just as another car slides by. This one a white Audi A3.

It pulls into the drive and after several taut moments, Soriah steps out.

I grin.

Oh, I want to be the fly on the wall. Puhlease!

35

PRESENT DAY – MONDAY, 17 MARCH 2025, 10.35 A.M. – SORIAH

I pull into the drive, edging my car close up behind Marcus's.

That's odd. I know I didn't tell Marcus I wasn't going to work today, because I wanted to sort things out with the police first, myself second. But he never told me he wasn't going in either. I would have thought he'd mention it. Although, admittedly everything was quite fractious last night and I was not myself after my experience at the garden centre.

What is concerning me is how little empathy Marcus showed.

I'd just witnessed a horrific murder.

He didn't show any compassion. Almost as

though he was uninterested, distracted by his own thoughts.

On the contrary, I was surprised my boss was as sympathetic as she was when I called her first thing this morning just as I arrived at the police station.

'Take the day off, Soriah, take a couple of days if you need it. Oh my God! I can't believe it. I saw the local news this morning about the woman being stabbed. That's my local garden centre. I know her. I recognised her face. Isn't she called Gilly? Oh, poor Soriah. You must be in terrible shock.'

This has to be the most Fenella has actually ever said to me and it's all a little over-exaggerated and icky.

'I'm sorry to let you down, but I'm just about to go into the police station to go over the statement I made yesterday. I was in too much shock, I think, for it to make sense.'

'No, don't worry. I'll handle things this end.'

This is so out of character for Fenella I almost stutter in my reply, wondering if she's putting on a bit of a performance. Maybe she's with the HR director.

'I'm sure Nola can handle the meeting. We made sure it was all set up on Friday before we left.' I reassure her.

'Nola's not here. Her mum is still poorly. She's having an extra day, taking it as holiday while she gets things in place for her mum. She'll be back tomorrow. I am sure we'll manage without you both for one day.'

There's a trickle of guilt as I realise I've not even messaged Nola to ask her how her mum is. If that makes me a bad friend, then so be it. I'm sure Nola won't think so, once I tell her what's been happening in my life. I'll take her for lunch when we're both back in the office together to make it up to her. She'll understand.

I glance at my phone as it pings a second time to signal a message coming in. I never took any notice the first time as I was driving.

I frown at the one word in capitals.

SNAP!

A second notification comes through and I blink. This time it's a photograph.

Puzzled, I stare at the screen with an image of a positive pregnancy test. It's not mine. Mine was blue lines on an all-white stick. This one is a white and pink stick with pink lines.

'What the hell?'

I don't understand. So is this a woman messaging me? Who could that be?

I gave the police officer the letters. All of them. Even the ones I've had hidden for years in my old bedroom at Mum and Dad's house together with the ones I've received more recently. All of which I've ignored. Mum simply rubbed my arm when I dashed home early this morning to collect them and asked if I wanted her to come with me.

I didn't.

Sometimes you have to do these things alone. It gave me the freedom to say what I needed to without being conscious of upsetting or insulting my mum. It's a delicate balance. I know she will never forgive herself that her little girl was raped. It was never, could never be her fault. But she takes the blame. That is human nature. She loves me unconditionally. I don't need her to be hurt any more than necessary.

Maybe it would have been better if she'd come. She may have prompted me. Although I've not told her about the text messages. They slipped my mind in amongst everything else. I forgot to tell the police officer too.

After all, I've not really had that many.

I'll call her after I've had a cup of tea and something to eat. My stomach is churning, but I know I need something. I've escaped morning sickness because I have been careful what I eat. Not today.

I've been sitting with my engine idling for several minutes, so I press the button to switch off. I unclip my seatbelt and swing the door open. Biting wind tries to force it closed again but I win the short battle and let the door slam behind me as I dash past Marcus's car to the front door.

Maybe this is an opportune moment in that case. He's home.

Having spoken with the police officer, I'm far more confident now about addressing this – all of this – with Marcus. It's only fair I let him know. The whole story. Fair for him, fair for me. It's time. He needs my honesty. I need his support.

Soft music drifts down from upstairs and I smile. This is our music, beautiful, romantic. I change my initial idea of tactics. This is just perfect to share with him the news of my pregnancy, our baby.

The rest can wait.

I've spent almost two hours with an incredibly insightful woman police officer. I made a statement and then we discussed in detail all my reservations and doubts about letting Marcus into my past.

She's right. I need to let him know. How can you

have a relationship without complete honesty? This way he can help protect me, share in my anxiety and soothe my fears.

I slip my shoes off and sneak up the stairs, a wide smile on my face. I'll surprise him first, then let him have the good news. What an opportunity.

If he's home all day, we can take some well-deserved time out to discuss everything. I can't wait to see his face.

I pause at the partially open door. A sudden seed of doubt makes my chest burn as the noises beyond have a familiarity that stops the breath in my throat.

With one finger, I push the door wide and take a step inside the bedroom. My bedroom. Where my husband is having sex with someone in my bed.

'Fuck!'

I breathe the word out on air that was stuck in my throat and both bodies freeze mid-writhe.

A woman's head pokes out from beneath my husband's shoulder. Shock registers on her face, but there's also a sly narrowing of her eyes.

Marcus leaps from the bed, his naked body on full display.

SNAP!

Now I understand.

I don't take my eyes from the woman as she hauls

my bedding up around her chest, dragging it off Marcus so he snatches at it.

My mouth is dry, but I have to know.

'Hello, Nola. When did you discover you were pregnant with my husband's baby?'

36

PRESENT DAY – MONDAY, 17 MARCH 2025, 5.55 P.M. – SORIAH

Silence drapes over me like damp velvet.

I haven't moved in hours.

Luna warms my lap with her sturdy body and thick fur.

I need to move.

I need to pee.

All I can think of is Nola and Marcus.

And their baby.

'When did you discover you were pregnant with my husband's baby?'

Nola's eyes had gone wide at that, and so too had Marcus's. She whipped her head around and stared at him. 'I thought you said you'd not told her.'

'I haven't.'

'He hasn't.'

We say the words together. Like we've always spoken the same thing together at the same time. That's what a partnership is, isn't it? Being in complete synchronicity.

Only he's no longer my partner, but hers.

Marcus reached for my dressing gown and paused mid-stretch.

Maybe it was the feral growl I let loose at the thought of him wearing my thick, fleecy dressing gown. No way. Never again.

'You messaged me a photograph of the pregnancy test.' My fingers tremble as I swipe my screen and tap on the photograph with the word 'SNAP!' above it.

I hold it out for them to see.

Nola's forehead wrinkled and Marcus opened a drawer and dragged on a thick pair of charcoal tracksuit bottoms. The ones I bought for his birthday last month.

'Not me. I only found out this weekend.'

I raised my hand to my mouth as the penny dropped and scrolled back through to the original photograph. The one with my husband about to kiss another woman. About to kiss Nola.

It was Nola.

I never recognised her. Maybe I only saw what I

wanted to see, and never thought of Nola, who always wears her hair up for work. Call me naïve but I never expected to see my friend in the arms of my husband. Why would I?

I don't know when that photograph was taken. I don't care.

Then I close my eyes. Of course I do. Of course I know. Nola left work early on Friday to tend to her 'sick' mother. Marcus was at the Birmingham head office until mid-afternoon before travelling to Brighton. She joined him. They travelled in his car to Brighton. To spend the weekend together in a top-notch hotel, where only employees were supposed to be.

God, I'm so stupid. So naïve. How did I not see this?

I was too stunned to react. To scream. To cry.

Now, I tug the neckline of that dressing gown around me. I wipe cheeks I'd not noticed were wet from tears streaking down them.

I never even told him. They didn't even question the word 'SNAP!' Why would they?

They were too absorbed in their own drama.

Secretly I don't think Nola was even upset. From the sly look in her eye, she was thrilled she got her man.

While I have nothing.

No man. No best friend. No work. Because I cannot work with Nola. No way. She's got to be crazy if she thinks I would.

If I was truly feeling spiteful, I could possibly email Fenella and let her know Nola isn't sitting by her mother's sick bed, instead she's rolling around in *my* bed with *my* very much alive husband.

Or she was. Until they left and I stripped the bed and rammed it all in the washing machine. I'm not sure I can use it ever again, but what choice do I have right now?

Now I'm all alone in this house.

Me and my little baby whose daddy doesn't even know it exists. May never know, depending on whether I decide to tell him.

That would be one step too cruel. Wouldn't it?

The circumstances are different, but I wonder now whether the steps I took with my first baby were the right ones.

I may have handed over all my letters to the police officer this morning, but I remember them still. The earlier ones from Craig, each begging for my forgiveness, for my love. That he would never forget me, never stop loving me.

One every year from the moment he was convicted.

I don't know why I kept them.

More recently those other ones.

From the young man who claims I'm his mother.

I lower my head into my hands and allow those tears to flow.

How do I deserve to be a mother?

Regrets? Of course I have. A million.

My biggest one, possibly, giving away my son.

I scrabble in my pocket for a tissue, dislodging Luna as I delve my hand underneath her bottom to reach it. With a disgruntled grumble, she leaps off my lap only for me to discover I have no tissue.

I push to my feet and make for the hall table where I know there will be tissues. My teeth chatter as I rattle open the drawer.

I'm so cold.

I blow my nose and wipe my tears, catching the reflection of myself in the hallway mirror. I can't remember a time when I looked so horrendous.

I hold still, check my face out, coming closer to the mirror.

Yes, I can.

I will never look as horrendous as I did then. I close my eyes and bring back the image of me.

Broken nose, left eye swollen closed, split, bleeding lip, braids of hair ripped out from my scalp.

I draw myself up, straightening my spine and stare back into sea-green eyes brighter than usual, thick black lashes spiky with tears, dark purple painted underneath. Nose swollen from wiping it.

Yes, I've seen worse.

I did not survive that only to fall apart now.

I pull my phone from my dressing gown pocket, tap my household app and boost the heating for a couple of hours. I'm not willing to sit here in the cold. I have no idea what the future will hold. Whether I will keep this house, or if I have to sell it, but right now my priority is to look after myself, look after my baby. It's still so tiny there's always a chance it won't survive. But I will, and I'll do my very best to keep it safe.

I tuck my phone back in my pocket, blow my nose once more and then hear the muffled sound of footsteps approaching the house.

I've asked Marcus time and again to set up that Ring doorbell I ordered, but like everything else, he's not got around to it. My lips twist in a bitter smile. He's not likely to now.

Now I wait in the darkened hallway, relieved I never switched on the light.

Whoever it is on the doorstep doesn't know I'm here. Has no idea how close I am.

I draw in a soft breath, reach out and wrap my hand around the base of the tall lamp on the narrow hall table.

I wait.

Should I call the police? Am I being paranoid? With everything that's been going on lately, is it all just a figment of my imagination?

I wait and listen.

Nothing.

It is just my imagination. Surely.

Or is it?

I reach for the latch on the door and twist, wrenching it open in one quick move.

Breath slams into the back of my throat as I choke on a scream, slapping a hand to my chest as a black figure steps forward, arm raised.

37

PRESENT DAY – MONDAY, 17 MARCH 2025, 6.15 P.M. – SORIAH

Arm raised, hand fisted, the young police officer's eyes are as wide with shock as mine, I imagine.

Stepping back, he drops the threatening arm and a smile spreads over his shadowed face.

'Sorry, I was looking for a doorbell but couldn't find one. I was about to knock.' He waggles a loose fist down by his side to demonstrate his point.

I flick on the porch light and he flinches, screwing his eyes shut against the brightness of it and raising his arm once more to deflect it. He's very tall and the light must have caught him straight in the eye.

'Oh, sorry, sorry.'

But I don't switch the light off.

He smiles again and removes his peaked police

cap that gives me a glimpse of short, tar-black hair and green eyes almost as bright as mine, except for the light hazel flecks that dapple them as they crinkle at the edges. His straight white teeth bright against smooth cappuccino skin.

The instant relief at a friendly, if babyish face, makes me sag against the doorframe.

He reaches out a hand and touches my elbow with the tip of his fingers, ready to catch me, I suppose in case I drop to the floor. I don't recoil, which I normally would, but somehow, I have nothing left with which to respond. Nothing else can happen today that can be worse than I've already been through. Nothing I haven't already imagined. Can it?

I mean, I was fully expecting a knife-wielding monster in the image of Craig on the doorstep.

'Shall we start again?' His voice ripples with underlying amusement. 'Hi, I'm PC Kelvin Morey. Sergeant O'Dwyer asked me to call around and check on you. She says you're concerned about your safety.'

I immediately recognise the name of the woman police officer I spoke to earlier that morning and move back to allow the PC to enter. My breathing is still heavy, and I let out a self-conscious laugh.

'I'm sorry, I've had quite a day. Quite a few days, to be honest.'

'So I understand.'

But he can't understand, because he doesn't know the half of it.

He steps inside and pushes the door closed behind him, plunging us into darkness as his tall frame blocks out the porch light. I never turned on the hall light.

I slap at the light switch, panic rising as the walls start to close in on me. The police officer reaches out and calmly switches on the light, his fingers lightly brushing mine aside.

'It's okay. There's no need to worry. The dark never hurt anyone.'

I study the face of this youngster, this child, and wonder what experiences he's been through that can give him the confidence to say that. Evidently, he's never been locked in a wardrobe for almost three days.

I push back against that memory and concentrate on the here and now.

Isn't there a saying that you know you're getting older when the police officers start to look young? This one looks like he should still be in school.

I force a smile. 'It's not the dark that worries me, but the monsters that hide in its shadows.'

His eyebrow twitches in a high curve to give me a

strange sense of familiarity. 'Well, I'm here to keep the monsters away for a while. Is it okay if I come through?'

'Umm, yes. Fine.' I tug at the belt of my dressing gown, tightening it, and wonder whether I should run upstairs and get changed, but I carry on walking through to the kitchen. I really can't be bothered.

'Can I get you a drink? Coffee, tea?'

'Tea would be nice.'

He slips his cap onto the kitchen surface and makes a quick scan of the room before he pulls out a chair and takes a seat, his hefty uniform with its full utility belt creaking and groaning as he settles. He's quiet for a moment as I fill the kettle and switch it on.

'Sergeant O'Dwyer tells me you've had some trouble. You reported someone loitering in your garden last night, I believe.'

I nod and point at the window. 'I thought I saw something out there, a quick flash of movement. Then I ran through to the utility and there was a dark figure...' I send him a quick ironic smile. 'When I reached the back door, the person had gone. Over the back gate.'

'And you're sure it was a person, not just—?'

'A figment of my imagination brought about by witnessing the violent death of a woman I once knew?' I turn back to reach for the teabags, hoping he didn't catch the irritation in my voice. I plop one teabag in each of the mugs I've put by the kettle and turn back to him, tempted to apologise for my snappish behaviour. But I don't. That would be the old me, the one who allows her guilt to rise up and take priority. Not any more.

'No. I don't think it would be that, but maybe an exaggeration of something you thought you saw? You've been under a lot of pressure by the sounds of it. I thought you might have seen something and not quite caught what it was. Maybe a cat. A fox. Did you get a good look at their face? It was definitely a person, yes?'

I dip my head in acknowledgement. 'Yes. It was definitely someone, but no, I never so much as caught a glimpse of their face. I heard them scramble over the fence. And then they were gone.'

'And you say you almost went out to challenge them? I wouldn't advise confronting an intruder, you're much better off calling the police. That's what we're here for.'

I let out a light snort. 'Yes. Foolish, I know. I stopped myself in time. Who knows what might have happened?'

It briefly occurs to me that it's precisely what I just

did when I flung open the door to this young police officer. I didn't know who was there, I didn't stop and think.

He's right, of course. It's not advisable, but I'm sick of this hide-and-seek game that seems to be dragging on. Tormenting me.

He nods. 'And where was your husband?'

I sigh. 'In bed, asleep. It was just after three in the morning, and I couldn't sleep after what I witnessed yesterday.'

Only yesterday, yet it feels like a lifetime ago.

'Sugar? Milk?' I ask over my shoulder.

'Three sugars, just a little milk.'

I fish the teabags from the mugs and dump them in the little caddy I use to collect them, slosh in a little milk, add the sugar to his and give it a rigorous stir, then turn and place a mug in front of him. My stomach gives a loud rumble.

'Would you like a biscuit?'

He smiles, a little lopsidedly, and spreads his hands. 'I wear uniform, of course I'd like a biscuit.' He chuckles as I reach for the biscuit barrel and rather than get a few out and place them on a plate, I simply remove the lid and slide it across the small table to him.

He reaches in and, choosing one of the chocolate

biscuits, takes a bite, letting out a quiet hum of approval.

I readjust my dressing gown and sit opposite him, choosing a plain biscuit for myself.

I'm not ready yet to tell the police that my cheating husband left with my best friend who is pregnant with his baby. His other baby. Christ, you couldn't make this stuff up.

A quick rush of emotion floods my system, and I hold back the tears by sheer dint of will. I don't want to cry any more, but with everything going on including bouncing hormones, I'm not sure I can hold back the tears.

What I want is to call my mum and tell her what's happened. She's going to want to come over and be with me. Maybe my dad could come too, although I think he'd struggle with our stairs, they're quite a bit steeper than theirs and there's only a handrail on one side.

The police officer, Kelvin, rubs at eyes that suddenly look as tearful as mine feel, scrubs at the end of his nose and then reaches into his pocket to pull out a small brown bottle with a prescription label on the front. He rattles out a tiny yellow tablet and puts it on the end of his tongue, dry swallowing it before he takes another bite of his biscuit, almost casually as if he's used to doing that at any given time without fuss.

'Are you okay?' I'm not sure why I should be concerned about him, but it's human nature to ask, isn't it?

'Yes. I'm just allergic to your cat. This should fix it, provided I don't actually stroke her.'

The bite of biscuit dries to dust in my mouth and I find I can't swallow. I pick up my tea and take a sip of the scalding liquid to wash it down before I can speak.

'How do you know I have a cat?' I croak out.

Confusion races across his face for a moment before his frown clears and he breaks into a smile. 'I assume that was your cat at the top of the stairs when I came in? Smoky grey colour.'

'Blue,' I reply, feeling properly foolish. What an idiot.

'Blue?'

'Yes, she's a pedigree. British Blue Shorthair.' My heart softens and I grace him with a smile. 'She's called Luna.'

'Luna. Pretty name. Even without seeing her, I'd know you had a cat in any case, this reaction is exclusive to them. And rabbits, but people rarely keep rabbits loose in their houses.'

'How did you know I don't have a dog?'

'I'm not quite as reactive with them. In any case, dogs normally make themselves known. I'm used to it, visiting people's houses.' He pats his pocket, where he returned the small bottle. 'That's why I keep these to hand. It's not that I don't like animals, I just can't have contact with them.'

He settles against the back of his seat, everything rattling and creaking from his ridiculously expansive uniform. As he takes a sip of his tea, he sighs.

A bitter chuckle slips from my lips. 'I know that feeling. Like you just want the day to come to an end. Actually, this whole week can bugger off.'

He mirrors my rueful smile.

'It's been a tough week all round. Tougher on you than most. I know you've spoken to my gaffer, but would you like to talk it through? It might make you feel better.'

And just like that, I find myself repeating the events I've related to his sergeant earlier in the day.

'You never touched anything when you found your friend, Gilly?'

'I never said she was a friend,' I correct him. 'In fact, quite the opposite.'

His uniform creaks again as he moves forward to rest his forearms on the table, leaning into me with such intense interest that I'm obliged to expand my statement.

'Gilly was... She was a friend of mine at college. We knew each other fairly well, when she did something horrible.'

'Horrible? In what way?'

I don't hesitate to reply. They say not to speak ill of the dead, but I couldn't speak well of her when she was alive, so why would this be any different?

'She lured me into a situation which resulted in me getting—' Even now, after all these years, all the counselling, it's still not easy to force that word from my lips. But this man is a police officer, even if he's young enough to be my son. He knows all about these things and he's here to help. That's what he told me.

I pull the collar of the dressing gown snug around my throat. 'What she did resulted in me getting raped.'

'Wow!' His lips puff out as he says the word. 'That's no friend.'

His green eyes bore into mine with incredible sympathy. 'I'm very sorry. You must be devastated. On all counts.'

I wonder what he means but before I can ask, he expands.

'You not only suffered devastating abuse, but you lost a friend. Presumably a really good one.'

I ponder his words. Was Gilly a really good friend? Now she's dead, do I soften my memory of her?

I shake my head. If there's one thing all those counselling sessions taught me it's to be honest with myself. 'We weren't as close as we seemed at the time. If I'm honest, I was trying to distance myself from her when it happened.'

'How did you allow yourself to get in that situation?'

I snort out a bitter laugh. What does he know? This young man with years of experience yet to come. He may be a police officer, but there's nothing that could prepare anyone for what happened to me.

I rest my elbow on the table and point a finger in his face.

'There was a time I would never have called you out on that statement, because I was young, and I didn't appreciate the significance. I am not to blame. I did not "allow" myself to get into any situation. The truth is, if there weren't predators out there, there would be no victims to shame, to share the blame, because that's how human nature works.'

'I didn't mean—' He leans back, holding up both hands, palm outwards in a defensive move.

'Nobody does.' I'm not cutting him any slack here, I'm having my say, because there's a fury bubbling underneath the surface of all the injustice and blame I have endured.

'I will tell you—' I waggle my finger '—had I not been guilted and shamed by the head of year at college, my life would be so different now. If my so-called best friend had not put me in that situation by *guilting* me, again, would I have been raped?' I shrug, dropping my hand to wrap it around my mug.

'Bad things happen because bad people do bad things, and if we blamed the bad people instead of making the victims somehow a guilty part of the whole thing, perhaps we would fare better. Girls should not be blamed for wearing skirts too short, tops too low, heels too high. They might be lambasted for not taking more responsibility for their own safety. But bad people are the ones to blame.'

I draw in a breath, calming myself. Kelvin hasn't moved, he's quietly listening.

Heat races up my neck and into my face.

'Sorry, I'll get off my soapbox.'

If the truth be told, would I handle it any differently today than I did back then when I was green and innocent? Possibly. But hindsight is a luxury I don't have. It happened to me. In that moment. At that age.

He rubs his fingers over his lips and my gaze zeros in on them. They've become puffy, like he's just undergone fillers, poor guy, and here I am giving him a lecture.

'Are you okay?'

'Hmm.' He reaches in his pocket and pops another pill in his mouth as Luna winds her way past him, arching her back to rub against his leg as she passes him by. With one effortless bound, she leaps up onto the kitchen table, flicking her tail so it reaches out to caress his cheek in a sign of affection, making her contented 'brrrrddd, brrrddd' sound as though she's happy to see him.

'Whoa!' He whips to his feet so fast, he almost upends the chair.

Panic flashes over his features and he makes his way to the door. 'I think I'd better go.'

He sneezes and I fumble to my feet, too.

'I'm sorry.'

'No.' He holds up one hand, sneezes again, and then again and again while he scrabbles in his pocket and pulls out an old-fashioned handkerchief which he holds over a face that looks as though it's rapidly swelling. 'I have to go.'

He sneezes yet again, then once more as he backs out of the door and takes off down the garden pathway to his police car.

Bemused, I stand in the sudden silence and wonder what the hell is going on with my life. How has every single element of it become so crazy?

A plaintive cry from Luna makes me look down.

To the left of the doorstep, a large bouquet of brilliantly coloured gerberas is propped against the porch wall.

I gasp, wilting against the doorjamb, barely able to move as the burn of scalding sick rises in a wave from my stomach to my throat.

38

PRESENT DAY – TUESDAY, 18 MARCH 2025, 8.20 A.M. – SORIAH

Muted sounds come from the kitchen as I walk cautiously down the stairs, pausing in the hall before I enter.

'Morning, sleepyhead. How did you sleep?'

I smile at Mum as she opens her arms wide for me to step into. I dip my head and bury my face in her neck. She holds still, the warmth of her arms wrapped around me a comfort beyond words.

As I raise my head, I give her a wobbly smile, ready to cry all over again. 'Not bad.'

She breaks into a smile. 'Liar.'

She leans back to study my face but keeps her arms loosely around me. From the look in her eye, I know what she's going to say as she raises a hand to cup my cheek.

'Bastard.'

Actually, no, I never saw that one coming. That's not what I was expecting, Mum doesn't swear under normal circumstances, but hey, who said anything about these circumstances being normal?

'I can't believe he would get another woman pregnant while you were both trying for a baby yourselves. How effing inconsiderate.'

I can't even comprehend how Marcus could do that. I've known for some time that he's been withdrawn and moody, but I thought it was the pressure that trying to have a baby together was bringing. Instead, he was spending all the time between work and home at the gym, working out, getting fit and the rest of his leisure time between the sheets, showing just how fit he had become.

This should be the happiest time of my life, instead I'm numbed by all the events. It's as though my emotions have been put on hold.

We drop our arms from around each other and Mum moves to the kettle to make tea while I take slices of wholemeal bread from the breadbin and drop them into the toaster. We don't need to speak about what we're doing, we know each other's rhythm.

'Even more effing inconsiderate that it was with a friend of mine. Who'd believe she'd do this to me?'

My dad is sitting at the table, and I lean in for a hug, kissing the top of his grey wiry hair. He's already got the Weetabix Mum brought along especially for him because I was damned if I could find the extra pack I always keep in the back of the cupboard for him.

'She's no friend. The worst enemy you can have is one in your own camp.'

I'm inclined to agree.

'That's twice it's happened.'

'Well, once is understandable, twice is sheer carelessness.'

Mum gasps at Dad's words until I laugh. Oh God. I need to laugh just to escape the pure horror story that is currently my life.

'I'm going to work on that skillset, Dad.'

He smiles and hunches over slightly as he puts another spoonful of Weetabix in his mouth, unconsciously giving away the pain he's in as his face twists.

He raises his head to meet my eyes, his own narrowing to slits. 'Do you want me to go and kick that boy's ass for him?'

I grin again, but I suspect if I said yes, he probably would attempt it.

'I think I'm okay to handle it, thanks, Dad. He's not worth the prison sentence.'

As the toaster pops up, I grab the hot slices of toast and butter them on the breadboard, letting the butter soak in before I pop them on a plate in the middle of the table where there's a little jar of jam for us to share.

Mum hands me a mug of tea and reaches over to refill Dad's mug with steaming black coffee. The only hot drink he would dream of having.

We all huddle together, knees touching under my small round kitchen table. I've only room for two chairs normally, but we've managed to squish another one in, taking it from beneath the stairs where I have the spare two stacked. Mum did that for me. She never even asked. Unlike Marcus, she knows the basis of my fears. That's the advantage of having someone who not only loves you but knows you too.

'What will you tell your manager?' Dad places his spoon back into his empty dish and reaches for the slice of toast Mum is offering him. They're like a well-oiled machine, my parents.

I glance at the time on my phone. I'll have to call her shortly.

'The truth.' My mouth turns down at the edges. 'How can I work with the woman who's stolen my husband? The woman who is pregnant by him. How can that be fair in anyone's world?'

'But if you leave, you're not going to get paid any kind of maternity allowance, even if you manage to get a new job while you're pregnant.'

I raise my hand to my forehead. 'Dad, I don't know what's going to happen. It's too early yet to know. Employers can't discriminate against pregnant women, so I'm sure I can get another job.'

He gives me a long, pensive look. 'You don't believe that, do you? Employers can find any kind of reason to not employ a pregnant woman.' He exchanges a look with Mum. 'Even these days. Isn't that right, Gayle?'

'Your dad is right, but also I think we're getting ahead of ourselves. After all, Nola may be the one to leave. She's the one with someone else's husband who can keep her while she's on maternity leave. You have no one.'

'Don't pull those punches, Mum.'

Her face creases as she takes my hand in both of hers. 'I don't want to upset you. But it would be unfair if you have to leave and she gets everything.'

'I'm not ready yet to deal with it. It's too much.

What I'm going to do is ask for some personal days for the rest of the week, then I'll have time to get my head in some sort of order. To think.'

Mum nods her agreement and I reach for a slice of toast, feeling my stomach lurch at the thought of that sticky red jam.

'Thanks for coming over last night.'

I notice the slightest wince from Dad as he can't hide the pain that stabs at him each time he moves.

I pretend not to notice. He's a proud man and he doesn't want his daughter fussing.

'We'll stay again tonight—'

'No, Mum.' I cut her off, placing my hand over hers so she knows it's not an insult. 'I'll need to live on my own. I have to get on with my life.'

'But those flowers on your doorstep. It's not right.'

'I've told the police, Mum. They're aware.'

'And what good were the police last night? You had one of them in your house at the time the flowers were delivered. What good was he? Heh? Someone must have walked right up to your doorstep and placed them there and he never even heard.'

'Neither of us heard.'

'Well, perhaps he should have. That's his job. It's sick, I tell you. If they've released that Craig Lane and he's stalking you—'

'They're sending someone around this morning to check on him. The officer I spoke to confirmed Craig has stuck to all of his conditions of release. I don't know much about it, maybe I'll telephone Victim Support, but I don't think he's released straight into the community, he has to stay in some kind of hostel where they can check on him at regular intervals. He's not allowed within so many miles of where I live, and he has to report in twice a week. Apparently, he's been sticking to that.'

'Apart from when he sneaks out to buy you flowers and personally deliver them to your doorstep because that isn't within the nine-to-five working hours he's supposed to check in at.' Mum's tone drips with sarcasm.

I can't disagree. It has to be him.

'And he murdered that woman when you were supposed to meet up with her.' Dad speaks around a mouthful of toast. 'How did he know about that?'

Mum has evidently told him everything. I should expect nothing less. Their marriage may not always be perfect, but they are good communicators. With three girls, they have to be.

'There's no evidence it was him who murdered her.' I try to placate him.

He lets out a derisive snort. 'Don't be naïve, child, they must suspect him.'

'They absolutely do, which is why they are checking up on his whereabouts. I imagine they'll have him in to the station and interview him. I'm sure they'll keep me informed.'

I look to Mum for some help as I feel myself getting bogged down in an ever-decreasing circle of what-ifs.

Her face brightens, like she has the best news. 'Leonie says she's coming at the weekend.'

'Mum—'

'I'd not be surprised if Carly doesn't come over too, after your mum spoke with her.' Dad grins.

'Oh, for goodness' sake, Mum. Can I have no privacy?' But secretly I'm pleased, if not hugely relieved that my family are rallying around when I most need them. I should have known they would but my confidence has taken some bashing. I should realise the only people I can rely on are family.

Mum picks up her mug of tea and stares at me over the rim. 'No, love, you can't.'

'Not while there's a killer on the loose,' Dad mumbles under his breath.

Under any other circumstances, I'd tell them not to

be so melodramatic, but the simple fact is, there *is* a killer on the loose. I am terrified and I can't wait until my sisters come over, but for the sake of my parents, I do need to put on a brave face or they're not going to leave and Dad really does need his own home comforts.

Also, there is another consideration. I've just discovered I'm pregnant, I've lost my husband to another woman, and I need some alone time. Just to sit and sulk.

If I wasn't pregnant, I'd have cracked open a bottle of wine last night and drowned all my sorrows.

This is going to be impossible. I'm already regretting asking Mum to come over last night, especially after she dragged poor Dad with her, claiming I need protection. Not that I believe he could possibly protect me, at the moment. He's not even comfortable sleeping here, which triggers my guilt complex. One that for the past twenty years I've tried to put to one side.

As I think about it, though, that's exactly the deep well my marriage fell into.

I snort to myself as I consider that and say it out loud. 'Marcus made me feel guilty every time he wanted his own way.'

Dad's lips compress.

'It's okay, Dad, you can say what you like. There's

no coming back from him leaving me for another woman he's knocked up.'

'I never did like the young prick.'

Shock has me almost falling off my chair as I splutter for a moment before bursting into a girly giggle. It's the kind that's totally inappropriate at a funeral, or a divorce. What shocks me though is my dad using that kind of language. I'm sure he does privately at times, but not ever in front of his three daughters.

The giggle startles me, then I'm laughing. A full-bellied, hysterical laugh, tears rolling down my face, but I can't stop. Every pent-up feeling, from burying those letters deep in my parents' house so I never had to face them, to the moment I heard Craig Lane was getting out of prison, bursts out from me.

I cover my face with my hands, aware of Mum scraping her chair back to come around and hold me.

As the room slowly falls into silence except for the occasional hiccup from me, I pull back from Mum, my hot, sweaty face drenched with tears that she mops for me with a tissue she's produced from nowhere, as mums do.

Dad is standing at the kitchen sink washing our dishes, I assume because he's completely at a loss. I've not known him like this since the day I came home from being incarcerated by Craig. Raped.

I stand and move across the kitchen to wrap my arms around him, laying my cheek in between his shoulder blades. I close my eyes.

'I don't know what to do to help you.' His deep voice, cracked with emotion, rumbles through my ear.

'This. Just exactly this, Dad.'

He turns in my arms, hands still dripping with Fairy Liquid and water and hugs me tight, pulling me into his embrace until I can barely breathe.

This is what I need. Exactly this.

39

PRESENT DAY – TUESDAY, 18 MARCH 2025, 8 P.M. – THE FOX

I thought they were never going to leave. I was about to pack up myself and go home. Then I spotted them. The tall old man came out first. He's got a heavy limp, but still insisted on putting the small suitcase in the boot of the car himself instead of letting one of the healthy-looking women do it for him.

'How times change,' as I'm told often enough. 'Women wanted equality? Give them fucking equality.' There's a certain generation still don't adhere to that though. They like to kowtow to women. Treat them like they're princesses.

I can't say I have a problem with that. I like women to be equal. I still like to be a gentleman. It was the way I was brought up. To be respectful.

I'm not feeling all that respectful as I watch them drive away. My backside is numb from sitting here for the past three hours without moving and I need a piss. Perhaps I'll treat myself to one behind the hedge before I go and pay Soriah a visit. After all, I don't think she'd be impressed if the first thing I ask her is, 'Can I use your bog?'

I reach for the car door handle and freeze.

What the actual fuck?

I almost miss the movement, it's that fast.

A dark shadow flits from the front garden next door, over the low wall and, crouching, hesitates for one moment, looking all around before it disappears down the side alley which leads to the gate into Soriah's back garden. The one I know well, as I've used it several times myself over the past few weeks.

Well, well, well. Who would have thought? Someone else was waiting for the old folk to go, too.

I reach up and press the interior light so it doesn't come on as I crack open the car door.

This could be truly interesting.

Maybe I need to wait and see what develops.

How long is it going to take, I wonder?

I never thought he had the balls. He's the note-leaving kind of man. He's left them before on those cheap bloody stupid flowers. I'm not sure what he wrote the first time, but last night, I ripped it off the bouquet just in time and stuffed it into my jacket pocket.

> *Dear Soriah,*
>
> *Please don't be frightened of me. All I want is to apologise. I've learned the error of my ways. Prison has helped me to accept that what I did was so wrong, I want nothing other than to reassure you I will never harm you, never come near you. Before I leave to start my new life, though, I want your forgiveness if you can find it in your soul.*
>
> *It's been a difficult time for me readjusting to the outside world and my mum still wants nothing to do with me. She turned her back on me the moment she found you that day.*
>
> *I'd like to make peace with her, and the only way I can do that is by finding forgiveness from you.*
>
> *I beg of you, please reply.*

He'd left a telephone number.

I'm guessing he's come around because Soriah's not called. And she's not called as I'm the one with the telephone number.

I look both ways along the street myself before I slip out of my car, quietly shutting the door behind me and ducking behind the hedge to relieve myself in peace.

It's a really quiet neighbourhood, once everyone arrives home from work and settles down to a heavy evening meal and a snooze in front of the television. I imagine it'll be a different story in a couple of weeks when the clocks change, and evenings are lighter. The place will be littered with fair-weather gardeners and kids on bikes, mums sitting outside watching them with a glass of wine in their hand and that look of perpetual exhaustion on their faces.

Most of the residents leave their cars on their drives or along the street rather than parking them in the garages every single house seems to have.

I've never quite understood that.

My parents had a double garage, admittedly with an electric opening door that made it more accessible, but they both stored their cars away safely at night. Dad said it was a matter of security, Mum thought it was because Dad couldn't be arsed to wash the bird shit off them if they parked them under the line of trees along our drive. She never actually said 'bird shit', but I knew what she meant.

Also, it meant that none of the neighbours would

be tempted to key it if you accidentally put it three inches on the kerb and some poor sod couldn't get past with their wheelchair or pushchair.

Not that we had those kind of people in our neighbourhood. It wasn't unlike this one.

At least here, you're pretty sure they all keep to themselves, no nosing around each other's business. They're mostly young couples and families. The neighbourhood is fairly new so it's not had that time to build up layers of generations yet.

I zip up my trousers and scan the place. You never know. Perhaps the guy two doors down will nip out with their beagle and let it do its business. He barely walks fifty metres before he turns around and makes his way back. Just the moment that beagle squats and he picks the shit up in a bag.

It's a bit early yet for him, though. Normally closer to ten o'clock.

I don't sneak up the pathway. I walk upright and confidently. After all, I don't think any of the neighbours know Soriah's marital predicament. If they don't look too closely, they'll assume it's her husband arriving home, parking his car further along the street as no one has the decency to leave a space outside his own house.

When I reach the front door, I take a moment to

look around. Then I slip down the side passageway in the wake of that furtive shape.

On the off chance, I try the latch and the gate creaks open.

Unlike me the last time I came around, this guy has the foresight to unlock the back gate from the inside so he can make an easy escape should he need to. Thanks, pal. It's made it easier on me too. At least I won't rip the skin from my hands this time and end up with numerous splinters in my palms.

I hold my breath, waiting for a noise.

The kitchen light isn't on, or it would be casting golden light across their pitiful little garden.

Has Soriah gone to bed already? Straight after her parents left? She's probably worn out. All those hormones. All that stress.

I give a silent chuckle. Poor Soriah.

I push away from the wall and press the handle down on the back door, slipping quietly in through the shadows. There're no lights on down here, so I assume Soriah has gone upstairs.

Which may not bode well if Craig has gone up after her. He may say he wishes her no harm, but he's a convicted rapist and she's his victim. Can he truly change his ways? I seriously doubt it.

I pause and look up the stairs between the banister rails.

This could go one of two ways and I'm not sure I really want to risk it.

I feel the soft velvet caress of a furry tail flick across my face, before I'm even aware that fucking cat is prowling down the stairs towards me. I swipe at my face, burying my nose in the elbow of my jacket as I sneeze. And sneeze and sneeze while I back away into the kitchen.

The cat follows me, and I fumble in my pocket for my Piriton, fingers trembling so hard I almost drop the small bottle.

I pop one in my mouth and hesitate to take another. I need my wits about me and Piriton makes me so drowsy, especially if I take more than one. The non-drowsy one takes longer to act and I can only take one a day of those, making it less effective.

I'll wait here. Give them some time together while I recover.

After all, timing is everything.

40

PRESENT DAY – TUESDAY, 18 MARCH 2025, 8 P.M. – CRAIG

My stomach is churning. My fingers shake as I haul myself over the back gate of Soriah's house. Jeez, I thought I'd kept myself fit when I was inside, but nothing prepares you for actual physical activity like running three miles to get here because you didn't want to catch a bus the full distance but misjudged where you were supposed to get off.

It feels like three miles, in any case. My lungs are on fire. I'm completely knackered and I realise I fooled myself when I was inside. I was never fucking fit. Fit to drop is my best description.

The last couple of times, I've hopped on a bus and it dropped me down the road a little way away, but I didn't want to ride the same route. I thought I was being clever. Just shows what being inside for twenty or so years does to your brain cells. Never mind your muscle tone.

I'm still a young man. I have time to get fit again. Maybe I should be running three miles a day, every day. For pleasure. Not for this. Still, maybe the heart attack is more my issue. I shouldn't ignore that. After all, that put paid to all my weightlifting. Walking around the exercise yard just isn't the same.

I wipe sweat from my brow and stand for a moment, gathering the strength in my limbs and the breath in my lungs, as that damaged heart of mine beats too fast and irregularly. It's okay though, I have a pacemaker fitted which keeps the arrhythmia in check.

This is not what I envisaged doing, but under the circumstances, I don't feel I have a choice.

I don't know what the hell is going on, but after the police questioned me for four hours today at the local nick, I want to know more, and I want to know now. What the hell is she accusing me of? I've done nothing but send her some letters and drop off a couple of bunches of her favourite bloody flowers. Not that I'll admit that to my parole officer. He thinks I've taken myself off to bed for the evening after I faked being worn out from the pigs questioning me. I wasn't really faking it, but I never had a choice. I reckon I have around three hours before they check on me again.

There are questions I was unable to ask officially, as they'll know I've broken the rules of my release. As soon as they do, I'm going to be banged up for the rest of my life. I'm sure they'll see it as stalking but that's not the case. I just want to see her. To see Soriah. Beg her forgiveness. Once that's done, it'll all be over. I'll move on. I promise.

I can't believe Gilly is dead, but I'm not willing to take the fall for that. It wasn't me.

I never liked the girl. She was such a user. But would I want her dead? No. Not really. I've barely given her a thought all these years inside. Although I suspect I might have got a lighter sentence if not for her blabbing her big gob all over the place, claiming it was all my idea, that I'd somehow persuaded her to convince Soriah to come along on that blind date.

It wasn't true.

It was the other way around. Gilly was such a prime schemer. No one knew that as much as I did.

I know now. Funny how maturity and the levelling out of hormones opens your eyes to the truth.

One of the things about being inside is it removes

you from the real world where you can look on things from a distance. Distance brings clarity.

It became clear Gilly was the manipulator.

She used that little body of hers with the big tits to get her own way. A young man's hormones don't stand a chance against that kind of persuasion. I mean, I loved Soriah with my entire being, but sex is sex. Right? And Gilly gave sex in a way no seventeen-year-old boy could resist. She had all the worldly experience of a much older woman, and she used it to her best ability.

More than this sexuality she used, Gilly was also a mindfuck. I mean she really messed with my head, and it was during those dark, lonely nights with only the company of some fat git or other on the top bunk – in my time, there were plenty who passed through – that the realisation came to me.

It was all about Gilly.

Gilly's small fingers walk up my naked, sweaty chest as I lie under the thick covering of rhododendron bushes that edge the sports field and hope to God she doesn't want me to go again. She's scratched the shit out of my back, layers of skin peeling away under her nails as she bounced on top of me like she was a rodeo cowgirl. She's the first girl I've been with and this is the third time we've done it in so many days. I'd thought Soriah would be my first, but somehow, Gilly thought it a good idea if she broke me in. She certainly broke me.

I puff out a breath.

Is that how all girls like it? Rough?

She's an animal.

'So, you've got it straight?' She's not even out of breath as she streaks a hand through fine blonde curls that bounce back across her forehead, and grins at me.

'Yeah.'

'She really loves you, Craig. You should have seen her face after you kissed her. It was all flushed, her eyes glowing.'

'Are you sure, because I thought—?'

'No. She loves you. She told me.' She prods me with her forefinger, insistent that she's right.

'But Mr Sharma said it was inappropriate what I did. He was going to suspend me. Or expel me, I think.'

'Well, how do you think you got off?'

I got off because I cried in front of the head of year and he took pity on me, but I'm not confessing that to Gilly. Every guy in college would know about it. She's never been able to keep her mouth shut.

Like she can't keep her best friend's secret.

Thinking Soriah has the hots for me as much as I do for her, well... that's incredible.

Gilly's finger circles my nipple and then she gives it a hard pinch and twist.

'*Fuck!*'

I shoot up, tipping her onto her backside on the soggy leaves I've been half lying on with her on top. I scramble to my knees, trying to hitch my jeans up from around my ankles while fending off the crazy harridan who's about to get us discovered with her high-pitched screeching. It was bad enough when we were having sex, but at least I was too much in the moment to bother about the noises coming from her. I just had to shove something in her mouth to keep her quiet. Worked for me.

Now all I want is to get away from her.

I've never known such a mean person. What is it with the pinching thing?

I drag my hoodie over my head and hold out a hand to help her to her feet, but she slaps it away and turns her back. She's dragging her own jeans up over her plump backside and it wobbles like one of those pink blancmange things we used to have in junior school. I almost hear the pop as she yanks her jeans up past the obstruction and her arse settles into the seat of them that squeezes so tight, her cheeks are flattened.

'Look, I'm just trying to help you get together with Soriah,' she whines at me over her shoulder.

I don't understand how that works in her mind. Why

did she have to have me first, if all of her concern lies with Soriah?

I feel used. Dirty. I don't think I'm going to do this again. Not with Gilly. It's so wrong. The girl is pure poison.

I thought I'd gain experience, so I didn't make a fool of myself with Soriah the first time. After all, Gilly reckons Soriah's had a couple of lads. Not that I've heard any rumours, but Gilly should know, she's her best friend. Don't girls tell each other everything?

I chuck my rucksack over my shoulder, peep from behind the rhododendrons and stride away.

I'm going to sit and watch Soriah run. That should make me feel better.

Mr Sharma says I'm not allowed near her, but I'm not. I'm just watching from afar.

I sit on the grass where Gilly had been not so long ago before she spotted me, and I've barely been there a few minutes before Gilly strides over again, holding out her hand.

'You owe me, dickhead.'

I glance around, panicked by her lack of subtlety. If I didn't get expelled for kissing Soriah, I sure as hell will if anyone thinks I'm drug-dealing. I'm not. They're for my own personal use. Except I had promised Gilly some for later.

'Fuck off, Gilly.'

She holds out her hand more insistently and I slip something out of my rucksack and pass it to her.

'You'll be there tonight, yeah? Soriah can't wait to see you.'

'Yeah.'

She grins. It's brief and sly as she slips her hand into the pocket of jeans so tight she can barely get her fingers back out. 'See you tonight. Don't be late. And don't let on to Soriah that I told you how she feels. You know what she's like.'

'Beautiful.'

I don't think that's what Gilly wanted to hear as she huffs out a breath and stalks away as fast as her short legs can carry her.

She's no sooner gone than I dismiss her from my mind as I turn to watch Soriah.

The love of my life.

My soulmate.

The innocence of youth. Naïveté.

If only that's where it had ended, but it hadn't and the rest is the part I have to take responsibility for. Have to own.

I do.

I know now what I did was wrong. Completely.

I've dropped Soriah's favourite flowers off now a

couple of times, together with a note, but I need to speak with her. I can't afford to have her thinking I murdered Gilly. If she believes it, the police are definitely going to believe it.

It's not true.

And I am damned if I am going back to prison.

Not because of Gilly. Not again.

41

PRESENT DAY – TUESDAY, 18 MARCH 2025, 8 P.M. – SORIAH

I am so relieved I persuaded Mum and Dad to go home.

I'm exhausted. More than that. I am soul-deep, bone-weary. I barely have the energy to climb the stairs.

I promised Mum I'd have an early night. In fact, I almost begged them to leave before, but I know they need their reassurance that I'm okay too.

The police have said they'll send a car past every so often to check on me. Even that is beyond my capabilities of giving a fuck, never mind two.

My brain refuses to concentrate. There are too many things going on for me to zero in on any one of them. Except I'm going to concentrate on getting myself back to normal. For the sake of myself and my baby bean. That tiny creature growing inside me.

That's what's important.

I turn the taps on and run the bath as I brush my teeth and cleanse my face. I feel I missed those steps this morning, but I'm not sure. It all seems so long ago.

Fenella was surprisingly great when I phoned her this morning. Shocked!

I stuttered and blubbered my way through an explanation of how I've just found out I'm pregnant and shortly thereafter discovered so is my best friend, both by *my* husband. I'm not even sure exactly what I told her. I do know I held back on telling her additional facts like I'm being stalked and a friend from college has been murdered. She knows about the murder, but not my relationship with Gilly. That may have been total overload which might sound fabricated. Because the truth is unbelievable.

I stuck to the main reason for my explanation.

It seems she's not delighted that Nola told lies to get time off. If her mother's not on her deathbed and they find Nola was in Brighton with my husband on Friday and shagging him in my bed yesterday, then that's a sackable offence. Gross misconduct. She told lies to get time off, thereby cheating the company as well as cheating with my husband.

It's not my business how they deal with Nola, but strangely, it could make an enormous difference to the way in which I'm treated there. If Nola is sacked, it means I don't have to leave. Everything I have done has been above board and truthful, which means that's one less thing I have to be concerned about.

I have the rest of the week off and Fenella hasn't put it down as holiday, but personal time, which is so kind of her given our past history. A history caused predominantly by Nola. Isn't it?

Have I fallen victim to another persuasive personality?

I need to sit down and have a firm word with myself. I am not good at choosing friends.

I pick up a length of blue silk material and do a hair wrap while I mull over what I'm going to do to turn my life around. I don't need Marcus and he's not going to share in this baby. He doesn't deserve to.

Tomorrow morning, I'm going to pack all his clothes in a couple of black plastic bin liners and dump them on Nola's doorstep.

The thought of burning them is tempting, but I

don't want to be that person. I want to rise above it, put everything behind me and get on with my life.

Nola can have them. She can have him.

I have a sour taste in my mouth and it's not through brushing my teeth, but the memory of Gilly trying to steal every boy I ever got friendly with when we were in college. If I liked them, she had to have them first.

Well, Nola can have Marcus, too. I don't want him back, even if he begs me on bended knee.

I dip my hand into the water to test the temperature and then turn off the taps, plunging myself into total silence. Oppressive, heavy silence.

Instead of stripping off my bathrobe as I was about to, I wander into the bedroom so Alexa can hear me when I ask for my playlist. If I don't make myself heard properly, she's going to play Marcus's playlist. Something I found funny until now. That's my next project tomorrow. Reset everything. Scrub him from my life.

I'll have to arrange to have the locks changed too as I'm not having him come back and take the TV I paid for, or, knowing him, the microwave and brand-new oven I'm still paying off on my credit card.

I won't be unfair. He's going to have to have some things, but I put the main deposit down on the house, and he's not walking off with half of that. Not when I'm having his baby.

Fury starts to mount. At last.

The numbness is starting to wear off.

I open my mouth to instruct Alexa and freeze.

There's a noise downstairs. Muffled movement.

I glance at my side of the bed, where Luna is curled in a tight ball.

It's not her making that noise.

My hand goes to my mouth, and I stop breathing so I can listen.

Was that the front door?

I strain to hear, my hand reaching for the bedroom door, although I'm not sure exactly what protection it's going to provide as it doesn't have a lock.

The soft shuffle of footsteps coming up the carpeted stairs has my heart hammering so hard it's almost knocking on my ribcage. I can barely hear.

My muscles quiver as my body tenses, ready to run, to hide.

That little ball of fury gathers, and I snatch up the tall, elegant figurine that stands proudly on my dressing table and clutch it in both hands like I used to clutch a rounders bat. I never missed back then. I won't now.

I soften my knees and get ready to rush at the interloper as the top of his head appears around the stairwell.

He turns his head and stares straight at me, eyes filled with surprise, and my anger boils over.

'What the fuck are you doing here?'

42

PRESENT DAY – TUESDAY, 18 MARCH 2025,
8.25 P.M. – SORIAH

'Marcus, get the fuck out of my house!'

My soon to be ex-husband hunches his shoulders and rolls his head down, mumbling under his breath. 'I need clean clothes for tomorrow. I've got an important meeting.'

'All your meetings are important, according to you.'

He nods towards the figurine. 'Were you going to hit me with that? I thought it was precious.'

I narrow my eyes, but my grasp loosens and I stand it upright on the dresser, though still within reach. I might use it yet.

'Precious as in sentimental value, so you can keep your eyes off it. It was a present from my grandma.'

'For our wedding.'

'She died four years before our wedding, you greedy beggar. It was for my twenty-first. Don't even think about it.'

He gives a sullen shrug and I swear he's looking for some kind of sympathy. Well, it's not coming from this direction.

I step to one side to let him pass. 'Make it quick. I'm tired. I want a bath and bed.'

He makes a move to go past, stops right by me and turns, mouth tight, his dark eyes boring into mine. When did he get that spiteful look? I've never noticed it before. Then again, I never noticed he was having sex with my so-called best friend. Evidently, I'm not the most observant of wives.

He grabs the soft flesh at the top of my arm and squeezes until I let out a small, distressed cry.

'It's not my fault, you know.'

I lick my lips and try to step back but come up hard against the dresser.

I can't actually believe this. How many times in my life have I heard this?

It's not my fault!

I am not prepared to listen to that shit any more.

'Then whose fault is it, Marcus? Because I don't

think men's dicks just accidentally fall into women's vaginas.'

His hand drops from my arm and he reels back, eyes flashing wide like I've slapped him. Maybe I should have.

'There's no need to be crude.'

'Crude? Marcus, you're the one who got Nola pregnant. She didn't achieve it on her own.' I feel a ball of despair rise in my chest and my voice turns husky and tear-filled. 'We were the ones supposed to be trying for a baby.'

I sniff.

'That's what I mean.' His eyes are hard. Defiant. 'If you hadn't forced me into starting a family when I wasn't ready, put all that pressure on me, made me have sex like an automaton at the right time of the month for you, in the right position, and not at all when I was in the mood, when I had needs and desires, this would never have happened.' His anger boils, flushing his face a mottled puce. 'You brought it upon yourself, you stupid bitch. It's your fault. Not mine. I was happy the way we were and you changed it. *You* changed.' He stabs his finger into my breastbone and pushes his face into mine, his hot breath puffing out in a combination of spice and alcohol.

'*You* put the pressure on our marriage, our relationship.'

My mouth drops open and I cover it with my hand.

I cannot believe this man.

Where does all this spite and vitriol come from? This is not the man I married. Is it? Dad seemed to think this was the real Marcus. He said he never liked him, that he was selfish and egotistical. Well, it looks like my eyes have been opened at last.

I drop my hand to my side. 'No.' I'm not answering a question, I'm stopping him mid-stream.

His brow creases in a quick spasm and then clears. 'No?'

'No. You're not getting away with that. You agreed to start a family. We discussed it. In detail. You said you wanted a little girl just like me, with my green eyes.' The memory of his words floods back to spark my anger, which is stronger than any upset. 'Just because you couldn't keep your dick in your pants doesn't mean to say you can hang the blame on me. I'm not having it.'

He's not finished yet, though. There's more blame to attribute. He just can't help himself as he sighs, shaking his head. 'It's not like that and you know it,

Soriah. You're okay having sex if you can lie on your back with your legs open, but anytime I suggest something more adventurous you clam up. I'm not a monk. I want more than pedestrian sex.'

I suck breath in through my teeth.

He's not wrong. He had made suggestions. I had nixed them.

Because his sexual fantasies involved bondage and under no circumstances could I possibly do that.

I press my lips together, my whole body going still.

I look him in the eye, raising my chin just slightly.

He doesn't deserve this, but he's getting it in any case.

My voice is flat. Even. This could destroy him. 'When I was eighteen, I was kidnapped. I was tied up and locked in a wardrobe and brought out at intervals to be raped, time after time, for days on end.' I take pity on him and save him the details. 'I don't do bondage for a reason.'

He can't disguise the revulsion that flickers across a face completely devoid of compassion.

I puff out a laugh. I'm surprised Nola never told him, but then again perhaps she thought he would pity me, return to his poor, miserable wife and stop seeing her. I'm sure she had her reasons. She wasn't to know how my husband would react to the news his wife was raped.

'I bet you think that was my fault, too.'

He says nothing. I wonder what I ever saw in him.

'Get out!' I push him on the shoulder, needing the space to breathe, to escape the claustrophobia and the panic setting in. 'Get out of here and never come back. I don't ever want to see you again.' I give him another push, this time harder and he takes a step back onto the landing.

Anger replaces his disgust, and he dares to push back, a palm on my shoulder, but he's not quick enough. I raise my arm, block him and then slap his face so hard the sound ricochets around the small landing.

He lets out a surprised yelp as I gasp at my own actions, raising his hand to his injured cheek.

I'm too angry to feel any kind of regret. It will come. But not yet.

Marcus's face flushes red and fury dashes across it. He takes another step back to give him room to swing and I see the fist coming.

'Don't you fucking touch her!'

Shock freezes me to the spot and Marcus blinks, his fist mid-air, eyes filled with confusion.

The man who steps up the last stair behind him is distinctive, even in the shadows. Even after all these years.

He's unmistakable.

It's Craig Lane.

The man who kidnapped and raped me.

43

PRESENT DAY – TUESDAY, 18 MARCH 2025, 8.45 P.M. – SORIAH

Every expression drops from Marcus's features to be replaced with shock as he does a slow swivel to face Craig, who towers over him like a prize boxer. Taller by several inches, broader than the skinny boy I knew in a life long ago, he's grown so much since I last saw him. But everything else about him is familiar. His sandy hair, his sharply astute blue eyes now edged with a feathering of fine lines.

Horror claws at my insides.

I stumble back several steps until I'm in the doorway to my bedroom. I have nowhere to run.

'Who the fuck are you?' Marcus's voice barely grates out, but he stands square to the stranger, ready to take this interloper on.

Craig's gaze flickers with disdain past him to me, and my bladder chooses that moment to weaken so I almost pee myself.

'Did he touch you? Did he hurt you?' His voice is gravel rough.

I can't speak. This is surreal beyond words. *Craig* wants to know if another man has hurt me?

I shake my head once.

Marcus makes a half turn so he's sideways on, a dawning light crossing his features as his jaw slackens. 'You filthy bitch. After all you've just said to make me the guilty one and it's you all this time, fucking around with someone else.'

'No! No, that's not it at all.' My lips have turned numb, and I can barely get the words out to explain. How do I explain? Maybe I should have told him the truth long ago.

He sneers at me. 'Un-fucking-believable.'

He turns to Craig. 'Did she give you the all-clear to come on up? Did you think I was gone? Good luck, mate. Just wait until you find out how frigid she really is, you won't want to hang around for long.'

He looks back at me, a bitter smile plastered on his flushed, furious face, even though he has no right. 'Well, I'll have half the house that you tried to guilt me out of.' He steps into the bedroom and points at

Luna. 'I'll have her, too.' I know he's saying that just to hurt me. He won't want her, and Nola isn't a cat person.

His gaze flicks past me and he reaches out for the figurine, snatching it off the dresser. 'And this!'

He shakes it in my face and I snatch at it at the same time as a huge hand lands on Marcus's shoulder. His fist loosens and I grab my granny's precious gift and hug it to me like it's the most important thing in the world. A piece of sanity to hold on to.

'No!' I shout in his face just as Craig spins him around.

'Get the fuck off me, man.' Marcus throws a punch and Craig dodges so Marcus's fist glances off his chin.

When Craig punches him back, it's no competition. Marcus staggers back into me and I almost drop my figurine, clinging on to it as I steady him. I've always thought Marcus was fit and strong, but it seemed he wasn't getting the exercise he'd told me about. Not in the gym, in any case.

There's a natural instinct to protect him. To protect me, because the man behind him is our mutual enemy.

Marcus may have been about to hit me, but he is, after all, my husband and has every right to be here.

Craig does not. I have no idea how he's been getting in my house, but it's evident now who has been lurking around.

'Get out!' My cry is high pitched and I don't care. I want them both out of my house, now. I shove Marcus, just to get him out of the way. 'Get out!'

Marcus stumbles forward into Craig. They grab hold of each other, bear hugging, bouncing off the walls as they scramble to get purchase on each other through bulky hoodies and coats.

My scream echoes through the small hallway, bouncing from the walls in the same manner as these two hulking men, only their thumps are muted, accompanied by grunts of pain as each of them lands punches on the other.

'Marcus!' I shriek because I love him. I don't care if he's a cheating bastard in this moment, I want him out of my life, but I don't want him to die. He's still my husband, the father of my unborn baby, and this madman is attacking him. My rapist. Who has broken into my house, believing I was alone.

If only I'd been able to explain to Marcus. To make him understand. The time for that has gone.

What were Craig's intentions?

Why has he been breaking into my house? Stalking me again.

If I'd been in the bath... defenceless... naked?

I shudder with horror.

The two men circle each other and I step into the hallway behind them, still shrieking for them to stop, grabbing at their clothes with my free hand, tugging them apart.

I've not even got my phone. It's on the windowsill in the bathroom. I can't call the police. Even if I did, they would never get here on time. They'd be too late.

I knew Craig was stalking me. I recognised those flowers. It was never a figment of my imagination, my paranoia.

Why didn't they believe me?

Why didn't they arrest him when I told them it was him who had to have murdered Gilly, instead of checking to see if he'd reported in twice a day to his social worker?

The pair of them stumble back into me, and I screech as they pin me against the wall, Craig's back against my chest, a small bald patch visible as Marcus lands a punch and Craig's head snaps back.

Craig throws his own punch and follows through as Marcus staggers backwards along the landing, my husband's lip split and bleeding, blood spraying up the wall.

I scream again. Racing forward, I lift the figurine

high above my head, two-handed, and bring it down with all my weight onto that bull's eye of a bald spot.

Craig's knees crumple from under him and he is felled like an oak tree, crashing into Marcus, his arms instinctively wrapping around him to save himself so they hug in a macabre lovers' embrace. Marcus is trapped. His eyes go wide and I scream his name.

Down the stairs they go, both bodies bulldozing down to make it feel like the house is shuddering on its foundations, taking out several balusters on their way, the sharp smash and crack of them filling my head with noise.

When they reach the bottom, the world goes still.

Not even the sound of breathing fills the air.

I sink to my knees at the top of the stairs, melting against the wall. I still hold the jagged remains of the figurine in my hands. My throat is raw from screaming, my chest burns and I have no energy to descend the stairs and check on the two men at the bottom.

I can see, however, that Craig is face down, partially on top of my husband. They are still for a long moment before he struggles to get to his feet, but instead flops back down again. I close my eyes briefly against the scene, unwilling to look.

I wipe my cheek with the back of my hand, and it comes away wet.

I notice a movement and turn to look through the broken balusters at the young police officer from last night peering up at me from the hall below, his pale eyes glowing. In the moment, I've forgotten his name. But he's probably the one they sent to do a drive by and check on me tonight too.

'Soriah, are you all right?'

Laughter hiccups out of me. I'm not all right. I never will be again.

He places a hand over his uniformed chest where his radio is, his movements calm, his voice controlled as he speaks into it before looking up at me again.

'Police and ambulance are on their way.'

He steps over to the two bodies and crouches beside them. There's a buzzing in my ears and I can't actually hear what he's saying, but he's cuffed Craig with thin cable ties and I idly wonder if they would hold him if he decided to make a break for it.

I don't think it's an issue. The man looks too weak to do anything.

The police officer glances up every few seconds, concern etched across his young face. I can't do anything to help. I can't move. My body is lax. If I attempt to get up, I'm likely to land in a heap at the bottom of the stairs with the rest of them.

A quiet sob slips from my lips.

I know, just from the position of Marcus's immobile body once the police officer moves Craig to one side. One of Marcus's legs is at a peculiar angle, his head twisted abnormally to one side. His eyes are wide and vacant. I don't need the police officer to press fingers against his throat and shake his head. But he does it anyway before he speaks into his radio once more.

My stomach lurches and I close my eyes against the wave of sickness that threatens, but even that seems too much.

I just want to lay my head down and sleep.

My husband is dead.

The man who raped me twenty-one years ago has killed him.

44

PRESENT DAY – THURSDAY, 20 MARCH 2025, 11.25 A.M. – SORIAH

When I open my eyes, the first thing I see is Mum's face. She's leaning over me, almost nose to nose.

'I'm alive,' I mumble with as much dryness as I can muster in my voice.

She gives a little jump which tells me she's been leaning over me for some time and she never expected my eyes to open at all.

I blink against the strong lighting on the hospital ward as she stands upright and turns to my dad. 'She says she's alive!'

I look past her and he gives me a watery smile. His eyes are red-rimmed and my heart squeezes that once more he's had to witness his daughter in a situation beyond his control. I want to reach out and hold his hand but he's too far away and I don't have the energy to move.

'The doctor says you can go home whenever you're ready, love.' Mum rubs the cold arm I have draped over the top of my sheets.

'Good.'

She's very quiet for a moment, then murmurs, 'The baby is fine.'

I nod, tears filling my eyes. 'I'm not sure how.'

'It's strong, that's how. It's hanging on. The doctor says all the vitals are fine for both of you. Beyond belief, if you ask me. I hope they're not just trying to get rid of you to free up a bed.'

'Mum, don't fuss. I'm okay.'

'You couldn't open your eyes when we came to visit yesterday, love. Carly and Leonie were here, and you didn't even know.'

That does surprise me, although I have no recollection of yesterday, only vague shadows and muffled voices.

Guilt pulls at me that I've caused them so much worry.

'The doctor said your body had closed down because you were in shock. They had to put you on a drip and everything.' She digs in her pocket and pulls out a tissue, giving her nose a hard blow. Always a dead giveaway when Mum is truly upset.

'I'm okay, though. The baby is okay.' My voice is husky from a raw throat.

I turn my hand over to offer her the comfort of my touch.

'It's a miracle.' The heat of her skin feels good against the chill of mine and we sit quietly for an age before I sigh.

'I should get up, Mum. Get dressed.'

She chews the inside of her cheek, I guess to stop herself from crying as she gets up and takes a bag from my dad.

'We called in at your house on our way this morning. We took Luna back as we'd kept her at ours, so she wasn't stressed by all the activity. I fed her and picked up some clothes for you to come home in. I figured you'd want something warm and cosy.'

The dressing gown I'd been wearing had been warm and cosy, but I see her point. It's not going to look good arriving back home in my dressing gown with all the neighbours to see. Doubtless they all know by now with all the activity from the emergency services the night before last. I wouldn't be surprised if it was splashed all over the news. I wonder what they will say.

'Knickers would be good,' I reply and she gives me a bright smile as she hands over the small bag. There's a definite sense of déjà vu.

I swing my legs off the bed and my dad gets up, discreetly pulling the curtains around my bed with him on the outside. I imagine him standing like a sentry on guard duty.

'Are you hungry?' Mum asks, delving into a carrier bag she's brought with her.

I let her fuss. It's good for her. It keeps her mind occupied with looking after me instead of thinking of other, darker thoughts. Like the death of my husband.

The mere thought of him lying broken at the bottom of those stairs almost brings me to my knees and I steady myself by leaning on the bed for a long moment before replying. No point in Mum suffering as well. Not every time I get a flashback.

'They brought breakfast around before you arrived.' I don't mention that I hardly ate any of the thick grey sludge they declared was porridge and something dark and rubbery which was supposed to be wholemeal toast. 'You didn't need to come so early, Mum.'

She pushes the bought sandwich back into the

bag. 'When I phoned, they said we could pick you up whenever we liked.'

'I think I have to get my discharge papers.'

'Your dad got them while you were sleeping.'

I sigh as I pull on knickers, socks, thick jogging pants, my bra, a T-shirt and a soft teddy zip-up fleece. I know it's cold outside, but in here, I might just expire from the heat.

'Let's go.'

I rip back the curtain and Dad jumps as though I caught him doing something he shouldn't. It's so incongruous, I almost laugh. If I had the strength.

By the time we reach the car, I'm already exhausted again. Trauma will do that to a person.

I try and cast my mind back to how I felt when I was raped all those years ago. Was I this tired then? Did I want to sleep until the world righted itself without my presence in it?

This time, it's not me who is injured, though.

I am conflicted.

My husband is dead, and I have absolutely no recourse to the truth now. I will not ever know the reason why he left me, why he truly felt our marriage was so awful that he needed to betray me. Except for what he said last night, most of which was designed to hurt me. Anger burns inside, so strong I wonder if it can be seen from the outside. There is nothing to put out those flames. No resolution. I have to live with that.

The tiny flicker of hope under all those flames is that I have wanted a baby for years. It's a sweet consolation.

'Your dad's got his date through for his operation.'

Mum sounds a little edgy, nervous as Dad drives the car. She leans forward from her place on the back seat. She'd insisted I sit in the front of the car as my legs are so much longer than hers. I suspect it's because she could watch me more easily from the back.

I can barely move my head, I'm so exhausted, but I manage to muster up a smile. 'That's good news. When?'

There's a long silence until I roll my head and look at her face which is almost between the two front seats. 'When?'

'Tomorrow. They phoned today. They've had a cancellation and as your dad's had his pre-op questionnaire within the last three months, they chose him.'

'I'm not going.' His voice rumbles out darkly.

'Why not?' I'm confused, he's been waiting so long.

Again, silence. The penny drops. 'Because of me?'

They say nothing.

'Look, I'm going to be fine. Physically, I am. We've just had that confirmed. Mentally might take a little time, but to be honest, the threat is over. Just knowing Craig is behind bars again makes all the difference in the world to how safe I feel in my own house.'

Mum reaches over and places her hand on my shoulder as we pull into my driveway.

'It was a mess when the emergency services left, love. The police finished all their crime scene stuff last night. Leonie's husband is coming at the weekend to fix the banister for you, but Carly's been helping me tidy all the broken bits up this morning. She's had to go to work but she's coming to stay tomorrow night. She's got some time off work.'

'We might drive each other mad.'

Mum purses her mouth and gives me that stare. A silent rebuke.

'I'm going to be fine. I need to be here on my own for a while. Sort my life out. Come to terms with Marcus's death.' I turn and stare out of the side window, tears blurring my vision. 'His betrayal.'

Mum starts to protest, but I hold up a hand. My voice when it comes is thick and low. 'Dad needs his rest too before his operation. It's no good him going in worn out to start with. I have a phone and I promise to use it.' I turn my head to look at my dad. 'You need your operation. If you miss this date, who knows when you might get another chance?'

Mum nods. 'I agree. Except we'll stay with you until tomorrow morning when I take your dad into hospital. He's got to be there by seven, so we won't be hanging around too much.'

There's no point in arguing and, truth be told, Mum is insistent and from the set of his jaw, Dad is too. He's a man of few words, but I know neither of them is going to be moved.

Besides, I'm not sure I really want to be alone.

45

PRESENT DAY – FRIDAY, 21 MARCH 2025, 6.15 A.M. – THE FOX

I wipe condensation from the small shaving mirror with the corner of the dull brown hand towel, and stare back at myself.

Well, that didn't go as planned.

My cheeks crease into brackets and I pause with my hand halfway to my face, lightly holding the razor in my fingers as my smile spreads.

The outcome, though. That was supreme. Craig back in the slammer where he belongs. Justice served. And that husband. Heh, well, he was just collateral damage. Nasty shit. He absolutely got what he deserved.

I'm surprised Soriah was so rocked by it all. What did she expect? She surely can't still love a man who was about to run off with her best friend. Her pregnant best friend.

The smile drops from my face, and I lean in to scrape the whiskers from my cheeks, humming tunelessly to myself.

Someone takes that moment to bang on the door and I jump so hard, my razor nicks my top lip.

'Bugger!'

Never a moment's peace in this house. I can't wait to find a place of my own. A small flat would be preferable to this cattle market. There are only supposed to be the four of us, but there's always an extra two or three, especially at weekends. They think it's okay to doss on the floor or the settee when they've had a few drinks.

Blood oozes from the cut in a thin stream, in the way only a razor blade cut can cause.

'Are you going to be all day, mate? I need a shit.'

I sigh as Sean hammers on the door with the side of his fist. He always needs a shit when any of us chooses to spend more than five minutes in the sacred bathroom.

'Use the downstairs bog,' I reply as I run the razor over my jawline.

'Jem is in there. He's going to be hours.'

My irritation hovers just below the surface, and

just like the blood that's trickling down my chin, once it starts it's difficult to staunch the flow.

I sigh. 'It's only a toilet, for God's sake. What's he doing in there? Decorating?' There's no doubt it could do with a lick of paint.

'He's constipated again. Says he needs some alone time. He took a book in there.'

'Jem doesn't read.'

'He does now.'

A thought occurs to me. 'I hope that's not my book.'

There's a long silence and then a snicker. 'It won't be his, he doesn't have one. Will you be long, then?'

I close my eyes, tempted to fling open the door and jab my razor into his jugular so he bleeds out on the floor in front of me. But it's a safety razor, and I have better things to do with my time.

This is the main bathroom we all share. It's my turn in here.

'I'm having a shave, you'll have to wait.'

There's a pause before Sean speaks again, his voice lowered from a shout as though the desperation of the moment has passed. 'You off to work? I thought it was your rest day.'

'It was,' I reply, unperturbed. 'Tim asked me to swap shifts, he's got his kids this weekend.'

'Ah.'

The silence lasts so long this time, I think he may have moved away as I keep swiping the razor through the thick shaving foam and then dipping it into the hot water in the sink. I prefer a wet shave. The way my dad taught me.

A wave of sadness passes over me and I stop what I'm doing, watching as my slowly evolving reflection clears in the main mirror. None of this would ever have happened if only my mum had taken more care. If she'd not died.

'So, are you going to be long?'

I blink away tears forming in my eyes. 'Fuck off, Sean!'

I hear the quiet shuffle as he takes himself away from the door, knowing he's pushed as hard as he dares. He'll have to hang on. I need to finish up and get to work.

After all, I have a job to finish.

46

PRESENT DAY – FRIDAY, 21 MARCH 2025, 6.15 A.M. – SORIAH

I close the door behind Mum and Dad and breathe out a sigh of relief.

We're all exhausted and I've struggled to sleep. I've not dared to come down in the middle of the night to make hot chocolate because I know the moment I do, Mum will be there beside me wanting to fuss, wanting to help.

I lean forward to press my forehead against that little square pane of glass in my front door.

There's a time to fall apart and let people help you. Then there's a time to pick yourself up and pull yourself together.

If I wallow in self-pity, I know it will destroy me

and I have a life to live, one that I will do my best with for the sake of this baby.

I push away from the door and race upstairs, stripping off as I go. I need exercise, fresh air.

I yank on my running gear and trot back downstairs as Luna comes along the hallway to cry at me for more food.

'Grandma just fed you. You can wait until I come back.'

I snatch up my phone and slide it into my new armband that arrived yesterday. I swipe the house key from the hall table and dash out of the front door.

The key safe is stiff and I promise myself I'll order a new one when I get back. There are jobs I'm going to have to do myself now. Ones I should have done in the first place. I'm quite capable and I'm never going to be reliant on anyone again. My family are the only ones who have ever stood beside me. They always will.

Tonight, Carly is coming to stay with me and Leonie will be with Mum. We'll all meet up tomorrow for breakfast. There are bridges to be built between us so my sisters understand the full story. The time for the whole truth is here.

I set off on a gentle jog, already appreciating the

fresh air as weak sunshine breaks through clouds that scud across the sky.

I need something to distract me from every single thought racing through my mind currently like those clouds. Foremost is my dad and his operation. I can't wait to hear that he's through it and out the other side. My mind refuses to dwell on any more darkness.

There's something so cleansing about running and I shake off the fear I no longer need to accompany me. There is a certain relief that the dark shadow has stopped following me. It's all the surrounding stuff I now need to deal with.

As I round the corner of the park, Nola is waiting there. I'm not sure how long she's been there, or how often since I caught her with my husband, she's visited this little park where she knows I run, but I don't need to see her. Anger boosts my system and I go to run past her but she calls out.

'Soriah.' Her cry is plaintive. Pitiful. 'Soriah, please...'

I stop.

'I thought you'd want to know, I lost the baby. The shock killed it.'

I'm breathing harder than I should from such an easy run, so I curl my body down and rest my hands on my knees, my face turned away from hers as I stare at the ground. 'I'm sorry.' I'm not sure I am truly, but there's no need. The woman has already suffered without me making it worse.

She shrugs. 'Apparently, it's really common to have a miscarriage early on. I was barely four weeks. I didn't want a baby in the first place. Not with Marcus. He didn't love me, you know, he loved you.'

I straighten and look her in the eye, seeing all the regret there. 'He had a funny way of showing it.'

I've heard it all before. When Gilly and Craig had sex when he professed to love me. Funny that way people have of showing how much they love you.

She nodded. 'He was going to come back to you. He certainly wasn't enamoured when he discovered I was pregnant. I think he was about to dump me when you caught us.' She gives me a sideways glance before staring off into the distance. 'You know, that was the first time I'd ever been to your house.' Her face flushes like she feels this is important. To her, it may be. To me, it's not. 'I only came around because he tried to call the whole thing off while we were away.'

'In Brighton?'

She nods.

I let out a soft snort. Maybe he would have tried harder if he'd known I was also pregnant with his baby. What a choice that would have given him. We'll never know. 'He would have found it hard. No one lets me down more than once.' I hope that message is loud and clear to her, too.

I turn to go.

'I've lost my job, you know. That bitch Fenella said I was going to be dismissed for gross misconduct, so we came to an agreement, and I resigned before she could fire me. It means she can't give me a poor reference.'

I nod. It's good to know. I feel nothing though, no sympathy, no joy. No guilt. I've lost someone I considered a good friend. I'm not good with friends. I don't think I'll bother with them in the future. I don't mind getting along with people, but I know deep inside my trust issues will never let go.

I can't hold out a hand of friendship, but I can wish her well.

'You'll not have any difficulties finding somewhere new.'

She sucks in a breath through her teeth. She's ready to go now, too. I can tell from the way she makes a slight turn away from me.

'Yeah, I think it might be beneficial for me. I was too good for that place.'

Modesty has never been an issue with Nola. Maybe that's what swayed her into having an affair with my husband. Perhaps she thought I wasn't good enough for him, but she was.

'Good luck,' I say.

'You know, Soriah...'

I pause, waiting for her next words.

'You never deserved any of this. I am so sorry. For everything. I never meant to hurt you.'

I lower my head in a nod, then let the smile that wants to come through spread and dissolve my anger as I raise it again. 'I know, but you did.' That feels good. Speaking the truth. Letting her know it isn't alright.

We won't see each other again. We don't need to. We're no longer friends, but I wish her no harm.

'Have a good life.'

I turn and slowly jog in the opposite direction and a part of me is set free. Is that what it feels like to forgive?

Sweat beads my forehead as I let myself in the front door and place the key on the hall table again, knowing there is no one else around to misplace it.

I dash up the stairs and strip, glancing at the messages on my phone as the water heats up, and then step into the shower. My mind dwells for a moment on my dad, but there is nothing I can do. Mum texted to say he's waiting outside theatre and he's third on the list which means we won't hear back for several hours now.

I step from the shower, wrapping a large towel around me and pad along the landing into my bedroom to gather some clean clothes. I'm going to sit on the sofa now with a cup of mint tea and snuggle my cat while I watch some mindless film just so my own mind can stop playing its reels. Carly will be here before nightfall to chase away the shadows for me. I'm looking forward to that.

Arms full of clothes, I pause.

Luna isn't on the bed where I expected to find her when she didn't greet me at the front door begging for food. I thought I'd won myself a little time.

There's a slight shuffle behind me and I turn, expecting to see my British Blue Shorthair coming along the landing.

Not the tall, young police officer called Kelvin.

My heart stops as I meet his familiar eyes. His handsome face twists as he breaks into a bitter smile.

'Hello, Mum.'

47

PRESENT DAY – FRIDAY, 21 MARCH 2025, 8.55 A.M. – SORIAH

'Do you know, I actually thought you were more intelligent than that.'

I'm staring at him, but I can't comprehend what I'm seeing.

'Kelvin,' I whisper. The child I gave birth to twenty years ago. His name is Kelvin.

'That's right, *Mum*.' His voice has the smooth eloquence of someone who has been well-educated.

His eyes narrow at me and I suddenly feel vulnerable in just a towel. He may have come from me, but I don't know him. I have no idea what he's capable of.

I tug at the ends of the towel and tuck it in more securely between my breasts.

'Do you want to give me a minute to get dressed?'

I hope he'll agree. It might just give me the edge to find a weapon, throw something through the window to attract attention.

There's something familiar about his smile. It's his father's smile. Ugly and cruel in his beautiful young face.

'I don't think you'll be needing to. I think it's better this way.'

He pulls a blue silk wrap from his pocket and lets the material waterfall through his fingers. My blue silk hair wrap, that I use to keep my hair from getting wet, and when I go to bed. I last had it when I was at the top of the stairs after the fight. When Kelvin came up to check on me.

Did he take it off me then? My mind is hazy, but I have a vague recollection of him cradling me in his arms.

My blood runs cold.

'What is it you want from me?' But I'm pretty sure I know.

'I want to know why you gave me up. Abandoned me.'

He's been writing to me for the past year, begging to see me, begging for details of why I didn't want him.

Why would I burden him with that knowledge?

That his father was a psychopath. That the man who got me pregnant had kidnapped and raped me. What child wants that knowledge in their life?

'Because I had no control over my life at that time.'

'Liar!' His reply is savage as spittle flies from his lips.

It's a half-truth.

'My real dad told me.' He moves closer and I back away, trying to look around the room for something that might help me. There is no figurine any longer. Nothing I can use as a weapon to defend myself.

'I'm sure whatever he said, it was skewed so he didn't look so bad.'

'You and that fat Gilly set him up.'

I stutter. 'You know Gilly?'

'I knew Gilly. Of course I knew her. She was the whiniest person alive.' He snorts. 'She's dead now though.' There seems no remorse in his dead eyes.

'But you never declared it to the police? When Craig killed her?'

'I am the police! Silly woman.' He says it with mock affection. 'And for your information, Craig never killed her.'

A chill runs over my skin.

He takes another step closer, a superior look

spreading over his features, and I move back again, putting my hand on the wardrobe door to steady myself, but it rattles like it does when I've not locked it properly and gives, swinging open just a fraction.

I hold on to my towel with one hand and tilt my head to the side, trying to keep my expression neutral.

'How do you know?' I don't really want to know the answer. I think I know. That realisation has already come to me.

He chuckles. 'Oh, come on, Mummy dear, don't be naïve. Craig couldn't kill her because he wasn't even there. He was staking out your house while you were staying at your parents'. I'm glad I got your brains, because I'm not sure he's too bright. I gathered that from the letters he wrote back to me, explaining every conniving, deceitful step you took in tempting him. Every evil thing you and your best friend Gilly did.'

'It's not true. Let me explain.' I hold a hand out to placate him, a plea for him to listen.

He slashes his own hand, the blue silk waving like a flag in the wind. 'No! You had your chance. I asked you time and again in my letters and you ignored me. Treated me like I never existed. Like you were punishing me for something I had nothing to do with.'

I control my voice, stopping it from rising to an hysterical wail. 'I can't deny that. I thought it was best for you to live your life without the knowledge of what your dad did.' Where he came from.

But he now knows, and the question rises in my mind, is he like his father? Is psychopathy hereditary? Can this young man have inherited the same tendencies as Craig? Nature versus nurture, when nature wins with the most disturbing of consequences.

'Don't you think I looked it up? I've had a damned good education and I've been in the police force since I was eighteen.'

I do a quick calculation, but it's hard to focus. He can only have been in the force little more than eighteen months, then. I knew when I looked at him that he was young.

'So you have to know the truth. The details of what your dad did to me.' What exactly had Craig told him?

'He said it was a miscarriage of justice. That he was sorry for what he'd done. That they never believed him.'

'If it was a miscarriage, he would have had that sentence overturned.'

'He really believed you loved him, you know. I read it in the court transcript. He was adamant you and Gilly set him up. He told them, time and again, he said there was no evidence that he'd raped you.'

'The evidence was me falling out of his wardrobe, tied up, beaten and repeatedly raped. What more evidence did they need?'

'You could have been playing sex games. People's tendencies no longer surprise me.'

'It was no game.' My voice is strong, I'm not going to justify myself to him. He must have read past newspapers, too. 'Craig almost killed me.' I spread my hands. 'I would never have survived if it wasn't for his mum. Your grandmother.'

I take a quick glance at my own wardrobe as the door edges open further, my heart hammering at both my present situation and my past memories.

'Then it was Gilly who set him up?'

'She set both of us up. Yes.'

That seems to ease his tension, knowing that truth. His face relaxes and the fist curled around my silk wrap eases.

My voice has calmed now. I settle. Speak to him as if he is a young boy, because emotionally that's what I'm feeling. He's not my son. I may have given birth to him, but ironically, he has become the product of my biggest fear. A psychopath like his father.

I never had the opportunity to deal with Craig

properly back then. Now I am an adult and I have more control over my emotions, more understanding of his.

Our eyes meet.

'It doesn't make your dad an innocent man, you know. There was a point at which he could have put a stop to all of it back then. He didn't take responsibility, though. That's not a good thing. It's not healthy. People need to acknowledge their wrongs before they can even attempt to right them. But he's going back to prison for the death of my husband and Gilly's murder.'

'He never murdered Gilly, and you know that.'

My breath shudders in. 'I do now.'

He continues talking as though I never spoke. 'He hasn't got the balls for it. What he did to your husband was more by accident than design. I was at the bottom of the stairs the whole time, waiting for something exciting to happen. I couldn't have asked for anything more perfect. Unless both of them had died. *That* would have been perfect.'

'I never knew. Never realised you were there the whole time.' Shock is running through me. He could have helped. Could have put a stop to the fight.

'You would have, once you had time to put the

facts together. Then you'd start to wonder. To delve. I know you handed in all those letters as evidence.'

My heart stutters. 'What have you done with them?'

He laughs, long and bitter. 'Me? Nothing yet. But I will. I'll find a way to dispose of them when I get the chance.'

'Because someone is going to identify your handwriting forensically.' I realise and almost laugh.

He gives a slow nod and then takes hold of the loose end of my blue silk and snaps it between his hands. 'Sadly, even without that, you are the biggest common denominator in this whole sorry tale. You know about me now. You know Craig wouldn't have killed Gilly.'

'I didn't.' I edge closer to the wardrobe, my legs freezing now as air cools the beads of water still on them from the shower.

'Of course he wouldn't. That's the whole issue. He's found God, don't you know? While he was in prison. He wanted to redeem himself. That's the whole pitiful thing. The reason he sent the flowers. The notes…'

He laughs and slaps a hand on his forehead in an exaggerated motion. 'Of course. You never read his letters, his notes. He wanted forgiveness. He was asking permission to visit so he could apologise face-to-face. The only reason he sent those particular flowers was so you would know they were from him and maybe take notice.'

'I hate gerberas.'

He snorts. 'I knew you did. Gilly told me. You know, I visited her regularly. Made friends with her. It was our little secret. I thought it was hysterical. That's why I told him he should send them. Encouraged him. The thick shit.'

My stomach gives a little hitch. What a revolting human being. The man is worse than his father. Craig may have been obsessed with me, but it was only me. This man's hate runs deep.

'Then you killed her.'

He shrugs. 'Again, it was more of an accident. Clumsy woman ran right into the knife.'

'That you just happened to be holding?'

'Ha!' He throws back his head. 'I wish we had more time, I really do like your sense of humour. I can see now where I get mine from.'

I narrow my eyes and tap the wardrobe door so it rattles again while he's laughing.

The smile drops from his face and he tilts his head as I freeze. 'Do you want to do this the easy way, or the hard?'

I raise an eyebrow. 'There is no easy way.'

He laughs again. 'Fuck, but you're right. You are going to have to die. In a fit of grief for your dead old friend and your dead husband who left you for your other best friend who is pregnant with his child.'

I don't correct him about Nola's baby, just allow him to continue his rant.

'What a mess, Soriah. Your life is not worth living, so you can go now.'

I quiver as he confuses me. Is he letting me go?

'Say your goodbyes.' The glint in his eye holds no kindness. 'Oh, hold on. You don't have anyone worth saying goodbye to. I'm sure your parents – my grandparents – are going to be happy to see the back of you. You've caused them so much stress. They'd probably like to get on with their lives instead of babying you all the time.'

His mouth curls up at the edges. 'Maybe I'll call in and give them my condolences. Maybe I'll let them know who I am. Introduce myself as the police officer who helped you in your hour of need, never realising you would take your own life. I will be grief-stricken, of course. All the time they won't have a clue. Not until I decide they should know.'

Rage bubbles up inside my chest and I clamp my

teeth together to stop from saying anything. It's too late now in any case.

Kelvin steps forward and snaps the blue material again, just as Luna chooses that moment to poke her head from the top of the wardrobe where she's been sleeping. Where I knew she must be when I rattled that door to wake her. She's taken her own sweet time.

She sees me and takes a leap to the top of the dresser where I normally feed her.

With lightning reflexes, Kelvin whips around at the perceived threat, his hands bunching into fists to defend himself as my blue wrap flutters to the carpet in slow motion and he steps directly into Luna's path.

Luna twists mid-air to avoid him, but it's too late. She lets out a screech of indignation as her body crashes into him, her claws digging deep into his face as she tries to break her own fall, scrabbling for a moment as he bats his hands at her in vain. She hisses like a wildcat scrambling over the top of his head, her powerful back legs kicking free of him and shredding his skin. She lands with a loud thud on her feet and races downstairs away from the monster.

Kelvin's screams are deep and guttural but before he has the chance to recover from the long, vicious scratches down his face and across his eye, I step forward and knee him in the groin while he's incapacitated, almost losing my towel in the process.

As he hits the floor, curling over in agony, I dash full pelt down the stairs, my bare feet barely touching them. I throw open the front door and race down my path, clutching desperately at the towel. Bare feet or not, unless that man is a long-distance runner, there is no way he's about to catch me. As I reach the road I hesitate, checking both ways for traffic just as a police car pulls up.

Sergeant O'Dwyer leaps out, closely followed by another police officer.

'Where is he? Where is he?' she screams, but all I can do is wave a hand towards my open front door as I sag to my knees, every ounce of energy draining from me.

She catches me and sinks down to the ground with me, cradling me in her arms as another car with sirens blazing pulls up, disgorging uniformed officers from it who race past us to my house.

'It's okay, everything is going to be okay.'

'How did you know?' I sob.

'It was Craig. Craig told me while we were questioning him. He was worried about you.'

48

PRESENT DAY – SUNDAY, 28 SEPTEMBER 2025, 11.55 A.M. – SORIAH

I spoon cat food into Luna's bowl and run my hand the length of her back, so she arches with pure pleasure.

Mum smiles as she steps inside the open double doors from the late summer sun-soaked garden where Dad plays with my nephews and nieces.

'He'll be needing another hip replacement the way he's going. I've not seen him as active in years. I think he's having his second childhood.'

I smile as I take the lid off one of the casserole dishes Carly has brought and inhale the spicy tang of her signature barbecue pork. She'll have brought my favourite pilau chicken too. But I think I might not get chance to eat it. Dad might have to eat my share.

'He's made an amazing recovery. Who knew he'd be back on his feet so quickly?'

'He was determined to be there for you, love.'

I grin as I watch him kick a football with ease and the kids race the full length of the garden after it. 'He loves having his grandchildren all together.'

She wraps an arm around my back and places a hand on my rounded stomach where his next grandchild resides for the time being.

'Not long now. She's a feisty one, this one.'

I press my own hand against my side and hum a little to myself as my stomach muscles tighten and harden. Sooner than she thinks. Sooner than we all thought by a few weeks. She'll be early, but not too much. My baby is keen to come into this world. I hope I can keep her safe from the monsters without smothering her with my anxieties.

I shake off that thought.

'What do you think of the house?' It's a good job I moved when I did. Or maybe it's the move and the security I feel that makes this the right time.

It's the first time we've all been together since I moved in on Friday. The garden is huge and makes it so easy to have everyone.

'I love it. I love that you've moved closer to us, and it's such a beautiful home.'

Just around the corner, in fact. Into a house Marcus and I would never have been able to afford, but with the Death in Service pay-out from his work and the money from Marcus's life insurance, together with the huge increase in value of our own home over the past few years, I bought this without requiring a mortgage.

Which means that once I've had my baby, taken my full maternity leave and pay, I will be free to search for my dream job coaching children in athletics. I never wanted this job. I never wanted to work in an office. I just let myself drift there, like I let myself drift into a marriage with Marcus. My heart gives a painful squeeze.

I did love him and that will never change, but I find it hard to mourn his loss after what he did. He was never my hero. It turned out I was my own hero in the end.

I'll be able to work part time around my commitments to my baby and when she gets older, I can do more. Mum will help out and both my sisters are keen to be there for me too. I need to let them into my life more. Let them take care of me and my baby. They're the only ones I will truly trust. Family is everything.

I have my life all mapped out now. I can see my

way forward, clearer than ever before.

'Sergeant O'Dwyer visited earlier. Came around for a coffee. She even brought her own biscuits.' Gorgeous chocolate biscuits for us to share. I have some left for later.

'Oh?' Mum's not bothered about the biscuits, she just wants to hear what happened. We've not attended court this time, only when we were required on the witness stand. I wasn't going to put any of us through that pain again.

'Kelvin got twelve years.'

She gasps and clasps her hands to her heart. 'No!'

I smile at her; she loves a little drama but not too much. 'That was for breaking and entering and attacking me. He got life for murdering Gilly. He'll never get out. The judge apparently said he had never come across anyone from such a good background, with no reason for anger, who has acted in such an evil, manipulative manner.' I try to remember the words Sergeant O'Dwyer used. 'That there was no excuse, particularly from someone who had chosen to uphold the law, to protect and serve. Instead, he chose to use that law to his own advantage.'

'Wow!'

'Yeah. The judge was harder on him than he would have been with a member of the public, especially as he used his uniform to commit those crimes. Sergeant O'Dwyer said apparently his face is still a mess. His allergies set up a terrible reaction to the scratches and he contracted sepsis. He's had to have plastic surgery to remove the dead skin around his eye and across his nose.'

Mum covers her face with both her hands, her eyes squeezing closed. 'That's a terrible thing.'

'It is. I wouldn't wish it on him.' But nor can I find it in my heart to feel sympathy either. He may have come from me, but in the end, he was no child of mine. He had every advantage possible. A loving, beautiful family. The possibilities of a wonderful life. There was no excuse.

We both fall silent.

We watch my sisters and their husbands as they lounge outside. I'm not sure I could have done it without all their help. Survived. Moved on. Moved house. They've barely left me alone for more than a few days at a time. Just when they sense I need it. Carly and Leonie have both attended all my check-ups with me, taking it in turns to come along, and I was right, my pregnancy was further along than I'd realised just purely because I'd stopped trying so hard and never noticed immediately.

I put my hand on Mum's arm. 'Mum. It's time.' I

tell her as calmly as I can, so she doesn't panic. I've known for the past two hours that my contractions have been getting stronger and closer together, but I didn't want to spoil the day if it was just those Braxton Hicks they warn you about. But the last fifteen minutes seems to have moved the process on rapidly and given how quickly my first came, I think it's time to move.

She gives me a blank look and then shock chases it away.

'Oh my God, Soriah!'

She dashes in one direction, then another and then comes back to me, skidding to a halt as if she'd forgotten to take me with her. I start to laugh as she grabs me by my arm, yelling as she drags me through the house to the front door. 'Quick, everyone, our baby is coming. Soriah is in labour!'

* * *

MORE FROM DIANE SAXON

Another edge-of-your-seat psychological thriller from Diane Saxon, *My Mother's Lies*, is available to order now here:

www.mybook.to/MotherLieBackAd

ACKNOWLEDGEMENTS

As always, I have a list of people I'd like to thank. There are so many these days to whom I am so grateful, for their support in all manner of ways. If I've missed anyone, I apologise.

For some time now, I have gathered names of real people who attend my talks, and my book release parties, both on Zoom and in person. I hold competitions for them and pick out a name or two on the understanding that the character I create can be anything from murderer to murdered, dog-walker to police officer. Good, or bad.

It's never easy to choose names, so, to these wonderful people who throw themselves at my mercy, I am exceedingly grateful.

This time it's the lovely Nola Jacobs – I did ask if it mattered whether she was one of the good guys or bad, and she said she didn't care, she just wanted to be featured. Just as well, really.

Soriah Howell kindly allowed me to use her name

even though I indicated I may put her through very gruelling and traumatic times. I appreciate your trust in me.

Thank you to Chantel Leigh Hughes-Johnson, not only for her unending support of my books by reviewing them, writing blog posts and promoting them, but also for the loan of her gorgeous British Blue Shorthair cat, Luna. Without her, the story may not have panned out the way it did. Also to Chantel for graciously reading through my almost final version and giving me a reality check on box braids and the length of time they take to dry.

One of my other fun facts is introducing 'items' that are picked by my audiences. Technically, Luna was an item.

Others included were:

A Ferris wheel – Janet Kempson.

A rolling pin – Meena Kumali.

I write these items down on my whiteboard and give them very little thought until my subconscious drags them out of my mind and plants them appropriately inside my manuscript.

For the wonderful support of Andi Miller and her Facebook group, Books with Friends.

Thank you to Telford and Wrekin Libraries, specifically Wellington who are so supportive allowing me to bring along a whole host of people each time one of my books is released. And to those who come along to the book releases to make it a celebration.

To my amazing family, Andy, Laura and Meghan.

To my sister Margaret, as always, for reading through my manuscripts and loving every story I write.

Thank you also to Francesca Best, my editor at Boldwood Books, who loved this book and is always tasked with helping me unravel my timelines.

And lastly, thank you to all my readers. Without you, I would be writing solely for myself.

ABOUT THE AUTHOR

Diane Saxon previously wrote romantic fiction for the US market but has now turned to writing psychological crime. *Find Her Alive* was her first novel in this genre and introduced series character DS Jemma Morgan. She is married to a retired policeman and lives in Shropshire.

Sign up to Diane Saxon's mailing list for news, competitions and updates on future books.

Visit Diane's website: www.dianesaxon.com

Follow Diane on social media:

- facebook.com/dianesaxonauthor
- x.com/Diane_Saxon
- instagram.com/DianeSaxonAuthor

ALSO BY DIANE SAXON

DS Jenna Morgan Series

Find Her Alive

Someone's There

What She Saw

The Ex

Standalone Novels

My Little Brother

My Sister's Secret

The Stepson

The Good Twin

My Mother's Lies

The Quiet Wife

THE Murder LIST

THE MURDER LIST IS A NEWSLETTER DEDICATED TO SPINE-CHILLING FICTION AND GRIPPING PAGE-TURNERS!

SIGN UP TO MAKE SURE YOU'RE ON OUR HIT LIST FOR EXCLUSIVE DEALS, AUTHOR CONTENT, AND COMPETITIONS.

SIGN UP TO OUR NEWSLETTER

BIT.LY/THEMURDERLISTNEWS

Boldwood

Boldwood Books is an award-winning fiction publishing company seeking out the best stories from around the world.

Find out more at www.boldwoodbooks.com

Join our reader community for brilliant books, competitions and offers!

Follow us
@BoldwoodBooks
@TheBoldBookClub

Sign up to our weekly deals newsletter

https://bit.ly/BoldwoodBNewsletter